'I meant it wher⋯⋯⋯⋯⋯⋯⋯⋯⋯⋯⋯mured. 'Rebecca, ⋯⋯⋯⋯⋯⋯⋯here alive.'

'I know.'

'And the only thi⋯⋯⋯we have is each other.'

She felt suddenly breathless. 'I know that, too.'

'We like one another and we're both consenting adults.' Guy paused and Rebecca waited in a delicious, trembling anticipation. She wondered how he would make his proposal to her. Would it be light-hearted and humorous? That would be typically Guy. Or would he take a more serious tack? She had never had a man ask her to sleep with him, and she relished the moment for all it was worth, her eyes on Guy's face, on the stillness she saw there. But when he spoke, it was with such a bitter grimness that she was taken aback and shocked out of the sweet web that his words had spun.

'Will you sleep with me, Rebecca,' he asked, 'before we die in this godforsaken place?'

Claire Harrison was born in Brooklyn, New York and spent her first nineteen years in a small town which had once been a whaling village on the north shore of Long Island. She is happily married to a tall, dark and handsome man she met while at university in Binghamton and they have two daughters. Always a compulsive 'scribbler of short stories and poems', her first romance novel appeared in 1979. Six years and seventeen romance publications later sees Claire Harrison and her family living in Ottawa where, along with her novel writing, she prepares book reviews and articles for *The Washington Post*. Her documentary on 'The Romantic Fantasy' won her a Best Radio Program award. ARCTIC ROSE is her first novel for Worldwide.

ARCTIC ROSE

BY
CLAIRE HARRISON

W🌐RLDWIDE ROMANCE
London • Sydney • Toronto

First published in Hardback in 1985
by Worldwide Romance,
15–16 Brook's Mews, London W1A 1DR

This Paperback edition published in 1986
by Worldwide Romance

Extract from HAIR on page 231 by kind permission of Belwyn-Mills Music Limited

Australian copyright 1985
Philippine copyright 1985

© Claire Harrison 1985

ISBN 0 373 50300 8

09/0286–77,100

Set in 10 on 12 pt Linotron Palatino

Photoset by Rowland Phototypesetting Limited
Bury St Edmunds, Suffolk
Printed and bound in Great Britain by
Cox & Wyman Ltd, Reading

PROLOGUE

IT was the shuddering of the plane that woke her, a deep shuddering that made Rebecca sit up in alarm and stare wildly around her. It was dark in the Twin Otter even though it was the afternoon, and rain was beating against the small, oval windows, the drops streaming against the glass in trails that looked like skeletal fingers. A flash of lightning cut through the black, roiling clouds like a gigantic spear and was followed by the heavy rumble of thunder. The plane shook with it, and she could feel the vibrations in her hands, her feet, even in the pulsing of her heart. She clenched her hands on the armrests of her seat as the plane was tossed first to the left and then to the right, its substance delicate and fragile against the fury of the elements.

There were only two other passengers, a man and a woman, in the plane's six seats, and she could see the tops of their heads in front of her, across the narrow aisle from one another. When she leaned sideways, she could look directly into the cockpit where the pilot sat, large earphones placed on his head. Although she could barely hear anything over the sounds of the storm, she thought he was trying to make some sort of contact for the radio above his head crackled occasionally as if a distant voice was trying to reach them through all the electrical interference. She tried to see how close the plane was to land, but there was no view out of the windows except for the opaque clouds whose form could barely be discerned even when the sky was lit by the strobe-like flashes of lightning. And when the cabin lights flickered on, the view reflected back to her was that of her own face, pale and round, haloed by the waves of her auburn hair.

There was a sudden, ear-shattering crack of thunder, and Rebecca's heart leaped as if in response and her fingers dug into the fabric of the armrest with such intensity that two nails cracked off. The pilot turned his head and yelled something to the passenger sitting right behind him. Rebecca leaned forward into the aisle, the strap of the seat-belt cutting into her stomach, and tapped him on the shoulder. 'What did he say?' she asked.

The man twisted around to her, his mouth set in a tense line. Although he had barely noticed her when he had got on the plane, Rebecca had been quite taken aback by his good looks. He could have been a movie star with the deep-set dark eyes, aquiline nose and square jaw, and he had the air of a man who is used to being outdoors, his skin bronzed and crinkled around the eyes as if he spent a lot of time looking into the sun. 'He says that he's off course and he's going to try for a landing.'

'But . . . can he?'

The grim expression on his face yielded to something self-mocking and ironic. 'Pray, lady,' he said. 'If you believe in God, that is.'

'Oh.' All her nervousness about flying coalesced inside her into one terrifying lump of fear. Rebecca could literally feel the blood draining from her face as she sat back in her seat, and her heart began to drum in heavy, chest-shaking beats. She could hear it in her ears and feel it in her throat where the breath came in short gasps. She wondered if they were near civilisation and tried desperately to remember what lay between Inuvik and Fort Good Hope. It seemed to her that the maps she had looked at back in the safety of her apartment in Fairfax had shown nothing more than a vast territory of boreal forest and innumerable lakes. That vastness had seemed thrilling then as if she were a pioneer in a land of new opportunity, and she had boasted to several friends about the life she planned to lead in Canada's north. But now, it seemed neither so wonderful nor so exciting. The land was open and forbidding, an area of jutting Canadian granite cut through by the Mackenzie River with only a few outposts of human habitation dotting the wilderness like tiny, insignificant specks.

There was no sound in the plane except the roar of the engines as they slowly descended, and Rebecca pressed her face against the window and stared into the greyness outside, wondering what lay below the clouds. The heavy throbbing of her heart had now intensified until she felt as if she were in the middle of a race. Beads of perspiration began to dot her forehead and she felt dampness run down her sides and sweat drip between her breasts. She could barely breathe now and wished desperately for the warm comfort of a human hand or even the companionship of a stranger. Not that the two other passengers were talking despite the flirtation that had sprung up between them before the flight started. Their mutual spark of interest seemed to have disappeared for each sat staring out of a window, no doubt wondering, as she did, whether they would all die within the next few minutes.

Suddenly there was a scream. 'My God!'

It was the other woman, and Rebecca saw her trying to rise in her seat as the plane suddenly seemed to rush into the tops of trees; crashing through them and tilting as it did so, the branches making a horrible scraping sound against its sides and windows. Panic made her instinctively lean forward and bury her face as close as possible to her knees, her arms bent protectively over her head. She felt the nose of the plane rise slightly as the pilot revved the engines in a desperate attempt to bring it up out of the trees, but it was too late. There was a sudden explosion, and Rebecca's whole weight was thrown against her seat-belt as her head hit the wall. Pain burst inside of her, great golden globes of pain exploding behind her eyes like fire-crackers. She heard a scream just before losing consciousness and wondered vaguely where it came from. It wasn't until much later that she realised that she had been screaming, the thin screech rising and warbling high above the horrible rending sound as the plane cracked in two.

PART ONE

CHAPTER ONE

IT was quiet when she opened her eyes except for the sound of raindrops falling off the leaves of trees on to the top of the plane. The air was grey and misty, and all she could see from her vantage point were clusters of birch leaves moving in response to a chill breeze. It was a while before Rebecca realised that she was sitting sideways, still strapped into her seat, her body pressed against the window of the plane, her head thrown back so that she was looking upwards into the dense foliage and beyond that into a heavy fog that obscured the sun. Water, she thought, was trickling slowly down the side of her face and into the collar of her blouse, but when she reached up to brush the drops away, she discovered that it was blood from a small gash near her hairline and stared at her hand with an almost dumbfounded incomprehension. It was moments before she remembered that the plane had crashed.

Her head ached intolerably, and it was only with the greatest effort that she could lift it enough to see the area around her. Her eyes took in the thick expanse of trees to her sides and back, the spread of rock below, the lake not a hundred yards away and the body of a man in a suede jacket lying on the platform of stone at its edge, one hand hanging over the lapping waves. Beyond him was a jagged island, or so Rebecca thought until she realised it was the front of the plane, turned upside down with only the edges of torn metal left exposed by water. The rocky ground around her was covered with the branches of trees broken by the plane's fall, and she herself was hanging a couple of feet above the surface. If she twisted her head far enough, enduring the excruciating pain as she did so, Rebecca could see the tail of the plane angled above her, the rudder caught in the trees.

She suddenly discovered that she was cold and began to shiver. At first only a slight amount and then almost uncontrollably, her teeth chattering against each other, the clicking audible in the silence. She recognised the trembling as the after-effect of fear and shock, but the knowledge couldn't stop it. She rattled and shook, every limb quivering even though she pressed her legs together and wrapped her arms around her chest. There was nothing she could do but let the storm in her body pass and, when it finally did so, she closed her eyes in utter and complete exhaustion, every muscle feeling limp and drained.

It was a while before the full horror of what had happened came home to her. The plane had split in two, she realised, just inches in front of her seat, and the front half of the fuselage must have bounced off the rock and into the lake, carrying with it the pilot and the woman passenger. They were buried in the grey water and probably . . . Rebecca took a shuddering breath as she opened her eyes . . . probably they were dead. And just by chance, by the mere fact that she liked to sit in the back of a plane, she had been saved with nothing more than a cut on her forehead and a bad headache to show for the experience.

A bird whistled up in the high branches of a pine; there was a skittering in the underbrush as if a small animal were busy foraging. It came to Rebecca how alone she was then. There wasn't the sound of humanity within miles; not a voice, the roar of a machine or the sound of traffic. There was nothing around her but forest, rock, water and sky. She had left Fairfax two days ago, flown to Toronto, then to Edmonton and on to Inuvik, each a bustling city where she had been surrounded by people. Here there was nothing but the elements and the animals. Here she was isolated beyond anything she had ever experienced before. Of course, she would be rescued; she didn't doubt that, but for the moment the awful loneliness of it hit her hard and her pulse began to race as panic set in.

There was the stranger lying on the rock, but he was so still that she was afraid that he, too, was dead. How would she survive all by herself in an alien environment with only the whisper of the trees to speak to her? Rebecca's heart thudded heavily in her chest at the thought of storms and snakes and grizzlies, of having no shelter and no way of reaching civilisation. Suddenly she was desperate to find out if the stranger were alive, and her headache receded as she struggled to get out of a seat that had been bent inwards during the crash, the armrests pressing against her thighs. It was the tightness of the seat that had probably saved her, holding her in so that she wasn't flung out of the plane to land on the hard rock, but now she fought wildly to be free of it, pushing against its edges and

trying to slither out sideways. Her efforts made the
blood run faster out of the cut on her forehead and drip
into her eyes. In frustration, she reached upwards,
grabbed a leaf and stuck it on the wound.

Finally, Rebecca was free, although she had torn her
slacks against a jagged piece of metal and scraped her
legs in several places. She slipped out of the plane,
trying to avoid the sharp edges where it had broken in
half, and dropped to the ground below. A small moan
reached her ears just as she landed, and she realised,
with an immense feeling of relief, that the stranger
was alive. She ran as best she could, on legs that
wobbled and trembled, towards the narrow promontory of rock where he was lying on his back with his
head to one side, his dark hair falling over his forehead. As she drew close, she could see that his skin
was greyish and his face was twisted in a grimace, his
eyes clenched tight as if he were fighting pain.

Rebecca knelt down beside his head and touched his
cheek. He was icy cold and she wished that she could
cover him with a blanket. He moaned again and his
eyelids flickered. 'Take it easy,' she whispered.
'You're going to be fine.'

She pressed a hand to his neck and, feeling a strong
pulse, gave a sigh of relief. At least his heart was
beating well and his blood pressure was normal; that
reduced the risk of internal haemorrhaging. She un-
zipped his jacket and unbuttoned his shirt, running
her fingers over his chest and abdomen to feel for
broken ribs or protrusions. Although she suspected
that he was bruised from his fall, she felt nothing but
smooth muscle and crisp hair beneath her palms. One

part of her mind registered the facts; that he was a male of strong musculature and no fat, while the other part took in the sleekness of his skin, the hard flat stomach and the pattern and colour of his chest hair: triangular and lighter than the hair on his head—almost a chestnut.

Rebecca buttoned up his shirt, zipped up his jacket, and ran her hands clinically down his legs and over the thick denim of his jeans to his ankles. His right foot appeared to be fine but his left was bent at an angle that didn't seem possible. Tentatively, she slipped a hand up the leg of his jeans to a spot above his ankle where a lump had formed and pressed one finger slightly against it. He groaned more loudly then, and Rebecca guessed that he had a broken tibia, one of the two leg bones that extended between the knee and the ankle. It felt like a bad break, but at least the bone hadn't cut the surface of the skin. That eliminated the risk of infection.

'Sorry about that,' she said and, as she moved back to a kneeling position by his head, she noticed that his eyes were open and that he was looking straight up.

'Can you hear me?' she asked.

No response, and Rebecca's heart sank. There was always the possibility of spinal and head injuries that could cause crippling or, even worse, total disability. She had seen even the strongest of men reduced to pitiful infantile states and, in some cases, the tragedy was underlined by the fact that a body could be so helpless while the mind was as sharp as ever.

Still, she tried again. 'See anything exciting?' she asked.

For a second there was silence and then he cleared his throat. She noticed that it was done with effort but she never would have known that from his words. 'Only the goddamned sky.'

Rebecca allowed herself a cautiously optimistic, 'How do you feel?'

He took a deep breath and then winced. 'Great —just how you'd feel if you'd been run over by ten bulldozers and half a dozen rickshaws.'

'Rickshaws?'

He turned and looked at her then. 'It isn't the wheels that hurt, it's the coolies' feet.'

She liked his sense of humour, but even more she liked the fact that he was lucid and could move his neck. 'Can you move your fingers?'

His eyebrows pulled together as he frowned. 'You sound like a doctor.'

'Actually—I'm a nurse.'

'How convenient.'

She had met patients of this ilk before. They laughed and joked; they kept up the appearance of non-chalance; they made light of their pain to the point that a doctor or nurse couldn't be precisely sure just how serious an illness or injury was. 'Fingers, please.'

He lifted an arm and waggled his five fingers. 'Satisfied?'

'Lift your right leg.'

He cocked an eyebrow at her. 'Only the right?'

'I think you may have a broken bone in the left one.'

'God,' he breathed. 'That's why it hurts so much.' Slowly and very painfully, he raised himself up on his elbows and stared down at his twisted left foot. 'Doesn't look good, does it?'

Rebecca shook her head. 'No.'

For the first time he looked around him; at the forest and the half of the plane dangling in the trees. 'Where is everyone else?'

'I . . . I think they're dead.'

He glanced back at her. 'Think?'

'The front of the plane landed nose down into the lake. I assumed . . . well, it seemed impossible that there was any chance—' Rebecca's voice trailed off as she stared towards the lake at the broken edges of the fuselage and his eyes followed the direction of hers. Although the sun was obscured by an overcast sky, the white metal was reflected in the water of the lake as it rippled around the broken plane. The small waves seemed almost playful as they lapped up against it, hiding the tragedy which lay below.

'They're dead,' he said flatly.

There was a long moment of silence as both contemplated the fragility of human life and their own mortality. Rebecca knew that the stranger was also wondering, as she had done earlier, why he had been spared while others had not been, why a quirk of fate had determined that he would be flung free while the woman across the aisle had remained in her seat and plunged to her death. It was a sobering and frightening thought, and Rebecca could see a range of emotions cross his face; shock, sadness, and finally resignation.

'So be it,' he finally said. The words were simple, but they seemed fitting to the occasion and there was a

tone of elegy to them that comforted Rebecca. It was as
if she had been waiting for some sign, some gesture, to
mark the end of those unknown human lives. He
turned back to her. 'You're bleeding,' he remarked.

Rebecca touched the forgotten leaf on her forehead
and felt the sticky trails of blood on her face. 'It's
stopped, I think.'

'Are you okay?'

'It's just a cut.' She leaned over the edge of the rock,
wet her hand in the lake and rubbed the water over her
face. 'There. Is that better?'

He grinned at her. 'You've smudged your make-up,
nurse, and your fig leaf needs adjustment.'

For a second, Rebecca was taken in by the grin, the
lightness of his tone, the jaunty look in his eyes, but
then she noticed the white look of the skin under the
darkness of his close-shaven beard and the deep lines
etched around his mouth. 'We're going to have to do
something about your leg,' she said.

He had pulled himself upright now and frowned
down at the offending leg. 'We're going to have to
do a lot of things. Think you can get back into the
plane?'

Rebecca glanced back at the broken remnant of
plane hanging in the low branches of the trees. 'I . . .
suppose so.'

'Maybe the first-aid kit is in the baggage compartment. I'd get it myself, but unfortunately I'm slightly
indisposed at the moment.'

She gave him a tight smile as she started to stand up.
'I'll go.'

He too tried to rise and, immediately, she was

kneeling beside him, her hand on his shoulder. 'What are you trying to do?'

'I'll sit near the plane and you can throw whatever's in the baggage compartment down to me.'

'You can't walk,' she insisted firmly.

'I'll hop.'

'The jolting will make the fracture worse.'

'I'll crawl then.'

'It's going to hurt,' she warned.

'Damn it!' he said, grinding his teeth together. 'It hurts already. What the hell is the difference? And I'm useless lying out here on this godforsaken rock.'

'Look,' she said softly, 'maybe we should wait for the others to come. After all . . .'

'What others?'

Rebecca glanced at him in surprise. 'They'll send a rescue plane out for us.' During the moment of silence, a squirrel chattered in the trees. 'Won't they?'

'If they can find us,' he replied grimly.

'But they knew where we were going,' she protested.

'The storm blew us off course.'

'But surely . . .'

'You've never been in the Northwest Territories before, have you?'

Rebecca shook her head.

'We could be anywhere in miles of uncharted forest. Finding us might be like looking for a needle in a haystack.'

'But there's the lake.'

'One of thousands and not a particularly big one.' His dark eyes took in the stunned look on her face and his voice softened. 'Look, it might not be as bad as all that. It's just that the mist is covering everything, and I can't get a bearing right now. Who knows? Maybe we're only yards away from the Mackenzie River.'

Rebecca's mind refused to take in what he was saying. She was well aware that they might not be rescued on the day they crashed, but she was positive that help would come within a few days. After all, the pilot had been trying to make contact with ground control during the storm and, surely, there was a good chance that he had. That meant that a rescue team would have a fair idea of their location and would make every effort to find them. And the thunderstorm had been one of the summer variety; ferocious but short-lived. The plane couldn't have been blown that far off course. She tried to make an estimation. One mile? Ten? She discounted the stranger's pessimism as a result of his pain and firmly shut her mind to any other possibility than rescue. 'I'll try to get into the baggage compartment,' she declared, standing up. 'Please, stay here.'

'I'm coming,' he insisted and, seeing the muscles clench in his jaw, she knew he wasn't going to stay put.

'I'll help . . .'

His voice was curt. 'I don't need any help.'

Rebecca looked down at his dark head and sighed. He was stubborn and recalcitrant; fighting him would be like beating her head against an implacable stone wall. 'All right,' she said, and then gave a silent prayer that he wouldn't pass out from the pain.

Getting back into the plane was far harder than

getting out of it. It was off the ground and tilted at an angle so that the very tail end was at the highest elevation. It was only with the greatest effort that Rebecca could pull herself up to her seat and she had to crawl on her hands and knees beyond it to reach the baggage compartment at the tail. She slid backwards a couple of times on the rug-covered floor and broke three more manicured nails as she tried to keep herself from falling. Once she slid all the way back to her seat and ended up wedged against it, clenching her fists in frustration, beads of perspiration dotting her forehead. She felt clumsy and awkward and totally inadequate. She knew that if the stranger had changed places with her, he would have been at the door of the baggage compartment in minutes.

But he couldn't change places with her. He had numerous bruises and a broken leg. He was slowly inching his way across the expanse of rock, his progress minute and agonisingly slow. It was taking all his strength, Rebecca knew, to pull the dead weight of his hurt leg, and every bit of concentration he could muster to ignore the pain. Even from where she was sitting in the plane, she could see and hear how difficult it was for him. His breath rasped in his chest and, whenever he lifted his head, the lines of strain were apparent.

Rebecca suddenly felt ashamed of herself and once again tried to reach the baggage compartment. This time she was successful, although when she got there she was panting from the exertion and could feel the fabric of her blouse sticking to her skin. Now that the storm had passed, the temperature was rising. The chill breeze that she had felt after the crash had abated, leaving the air feeling heavy and moist. As she rested against the door to the baggage compartment, her breath coming in heavy gasps, Rebecca wiped her face with the back of her hand, leaving it streaked with blood and sweat. For the first time she wondered what she looked like and winced at the thought.

Since the door to the baggage compartment opened towards the back of the plane and, therefore, in an uphill direction, it was moments before Rebecca could even open it and when she did, she had to lean her body against it to keep it that way. The baggage was, ironically, neatly arranged as if it hadn't suffered through a crash at all. There were several suitcases and some equipment that belonged to the pilot, but she couldn't see a first-aid kit and, with a sinking feeling, realised that it must have been in the cockpit.

'What's in there?'

She couldn't see the stranger, but his voice came from below the plane. 'Suitcases. No first-aid kit.'

There was silence and then, 'Can you get them down?'

'I'll have to let them slide.'

'Okay.'

The first piece of baggage was made of a brown tweed and strapped together with leather buckles. It made it down safely; she could hear it thud on to the rock and then there was a scraping sound as if the stranger were pulling it to one side.

'Next!'

The next was her own and when it went she heard it crack open against the rock. 'Oh, no,' she groaned.

'You *are* a nurse,' she heard him say. 'Uniforms and everything.'

'Did you think I was lying?' Rebecca yelled down to him in sudden outrage as her muscles protested painfully against the effort she was making.

'It had occurred to me that you were trying to make me feel better,' he yelled back. 'If so, you were a great actress.'

'Damn him,' she muttered under her breath and then let out, 'Timber!'

The other woman's suitcase hit and also opened. A low whistle came from beneath the plane.

'What are you whistling at?' she demanded.

'Sequins, froth and a see-through nightie. V-e-r-y cute.'

He sounded amused but Rebecca was sure that he was also regretful. Given a choice of either the other woman or herself, he would have chosen the former, she was sure. After all, they had struck up a flirtation as soon as he had entered the plane and, even two seats back, Rebecca had been able to sense the undercurrent of sexual interest between the two of them. The other woman had been tall, slender and blonde with long hair she had tossed to one side with every vivacious glance. What man in his right mind wouldn't prefer to be stranded in a desolate wilderness with a woman whose sex appeal smouldered and sparked? Rebecca wouldn't blame the stranger if right now he was fingering that see-through nightgown and wishing . . .

'Did you fall asleep up there?'

Rebecca shook herself slightly. 'Sorry,' she said and

heaved out a duffel bag that had belonged to the pilot. As it thudded to the ground she noticed a narrow box beneath it. 'I think I've found the first-aid kit,' she announced with excitement as the duffel bag fell to the earth. 'We can really use the bandages and medication and . . .' Her voice died away suddenly.

'What's the matter?'

Rebecca glanced down at her lap where the tangle of hooks, sinkers and flies winked up at her. 'It's . . . it's a tackle box.'

'A what!'

'A fishing box!' The pilot, she realised, must have planned a fishing expedition from Fort Good Hope. She had noticed one more piece of baggage in the compartment as she lifted the tackle box out—a long cylindrical canvas bag that probably held a rod and reel.

'We may need that more than bandages. And don't throw it down; I don't want it to break. Can you manage to carry it down with you?'

'I'll try.'

She held the fishing-rod bag in one arm and tackle box on her lap as she slid on her bottom down to the seat and then eased herself out of the plane. When she got to her feet on the rock she found that the stranger was sitting nearby, leaning up against the bole of a tree. All round him were spread the articles that had come out of the suitcases; trousers, tops, underwear, a hair-drier, several nightgowns. Rebecca couldn't help smiling as she handed the tackle box to him.

'What's so funny?' he demanded, looking up at her.

'It looks like you're having a garage sale,' she said,

running her hands through the tangled mass of her hair.

He smiled a little. 'I guess it does—at that.' He looked exhausted with dark circles now apparent under his eyes, and Rebecca thought that she saw his hands tremble as they took the box.

'I may have some aspirin in my overnight case,' she offered. 'Let me see if I can find it.' She rummaged through her belongings which were strewn over the moss-covered rock. Her overnight case had broken apart along with her suitcase, sending her cosmetics in every direction. The sun was now trying to break through the clouds, and the gold and silver decorations on the lipsticks, compacts and eye-shadow containers glinted among the leaves and pebbles. 'There,' she said when she found the bottle of aspirin in a small crevice. 'This should help the p—'

His head was thrown back against the tree trunk and his eyes were shut, his dark lashes making deep crescents against the pallor of his skin. For a second, Rebecca was frightened that he had passed out again, but slowly his eyes opened. 'I think I'll drink instead,' he said.

'But water won't . . .'

'I'm not talking about water. I've got a flask of the hard stuff in my suitcase.'

'Hard stuff? Whisky?'

'Good Canadian born and bred whisky. The most medicinal you can get and one of the best painkillers around.'

Rebecca supposed that he was right. The aspirin would help a bit, but an alcohol-induced stupor would be even better—he wouldn't feel a thing. Still, she didn't much like the idea of being stranded in the wilderness with a drunken man. 'Could we set up some sort of camp first before you begin . . . drinking?' she asked delicately.

He grinned at her then. 'I'll save it for when you set my leg.'

Her eyes widened in shock. 'Me? Set your leg?'

'Well, you're a nurse, aren't you?'

'Yes, but . . . well, I've never set a broken leg before. The doctors did it.'

'Well, you know what they say—there's a first time for everything.'

'But when the rescue plane comes,' she protested, 'I'm sure there will be a doctor on it.'

He shrugged. 'I'm not the kind who depends on wishes and miracles. The leg needs setting, doesn't it?'

'Yes, but if I don't do it properly then . . .'

'Then I'll break yours in return. Come on, nurse, didn't you take the Hippocratic oath? Aren't you obliged to heal me?'

'Doctors take the Hippocratic oath,' she said as she began to pick up the strewn items of clothes. 'Not nurses.'

'Hell, you must have taken some sort of vow to heal the sick. I'll have you drummed out of the nurses' corp. Can't you see it now in the headlines? "Nurse Refuses Plea of Broken Man."' He grinned mockingly. 'It has a scandalous ring to it, don't you think?'

'Do you have any idea,' she said, 'just how painful it would be? I'd have to pull your leg straight to get the bone back in position.'

He gave her a jaunty grin. 'Blessed are the benefits of whisky.'

Rebecca sighed and saw that there was no convincing him that he should wait to have his leg set by someone more qualified than she was. She could see his point in a way. If help didn't arrive—although she didn't believe that for a minute—then his leg wouldn't heal well and the doctors would be forced to break it again for proper setting. It was not a prospect that anyone would face with pleasure and, although she was sympathetic, Rebecca still found the idea of inflicting such pain and taking on the responsibility of a physician unnerving. 'I'd really prefer . . .' she began.

'Coward. And it isn't even going to hurt *you*.'

It was true; she would inflict the pain and he would bear it. If he was courageous enough to go through with it, who was she to refuse him? 'All right,' she said reluctantly. 'I'll do it, but you'd better get stinking drunk.'

He smiled at the look of distaste on her face. 'I love your bedside manner.'

'It comes with the patient,' she replied tartly.

Rebecca set up a make-shift camp as the stranger drank from the flask in his suitcase and gave instructions. She organised the clothing into piles and climbed into the plane once more where she removed the cushions from the two plane seats and discovered a blanket jammed into a cabinet above the baggage compartment. Using cord and the tarpaulin they found in the pilot's duffel bag, she set up a clumsy sort of a lean-to between two trees about five yards from the plane. She hadn't a clue how to knot the rope so it took several tries and some terse commands before the rope remained taut enough to support the tarp and, when she was done, she found that she had scraped both her palms raw. The resulting tent was barely big enough to house two people, but Rebecca supposed it would protect them from rain if it were necessary. She kept looking at the sky as she worked in expectation of a rescue plane, but the only things to be seen were the occasional hawk circling lazily over the lake or the tiny V made by a high-flying flock of Canadian geese heading north to breed.

If the stranger noticed her expectant looks, he ignored them. His main interest was in items that would aid in survival, and he bestowed a blessing on the dead pilot's head for his love of camping and fishing. In addition to the fishing gear and tarpaulin, they found two wool plaid shirts, a set of overalls, one sleeping-bag made of down, a small axe, some boxes of matches and a metal mess kit for one; a compactly packed unit that included a frying-pan, pot, plate, knife, fork and spoon. The sight of the latter reminded Rebecca that she hadn't eaten for hours and that there was a gnawing emptiness at the pit of her stomach, but she didn't mention it. What was the use? There was nothing to eat for miles.

The stranger slumped lower and lower against the tree trunk as the whisky began to have its effect. His speech was slightly slurred and a tinge of red coloured his high cheek-bones. Rebecca was secretly praying that he would pass out before she had to set his leg, but he seemed to be in high spirits as the alcohol numbed his nerve endings and reduced his pain. He began to sing as she ripped strips of denim from a voluminous skirt that she had found in the other woman's suitcase and wrapped them around the most slender and straightest branches she could find. She needed splints to hold his leg firm as it healed, and branches were all she had, but she didn't want their rough edges to press and scrape against his skin.

'There once was a man who had twenty-four lives,' the stranger sang in a strong baritone that stopped the squirrel from chattering overhead. 'Twenty-four lives and twenty-four wives. And on every night when he took them to bed . . .' Rebecca glanced at him suddenly and the stranger, giving her a sheepish look, admitted, 'It's a bit on the dirty side. In fact, it gets downright obscene.' He cleared his throat. 'Something more, uh, convivial?'

Rebecca nodded and he started again, this time switching to a well-known drinking song.

Ninety-nine bottles of beer on the wall,
Ninety-nine bottles of beer.
If one of those bottles happened to fall,
There'd be ninety-eight bottles of beer on the wall.

Ninety-eight bottles of beer on the wall
Ninety-eight bottles of beer.
If one of those bottles . . .

He was down to sixty-six bottles of beer, each round seemingly louder and more raucous than the last, when Rebecca finished making her splints and was prepared to set his leg. She washed her hands and face as best she could in the lake water, dried them with the edge of the blanket and then, taking a deep breath, walked over to him.

'I'm ready,' she said, breaking into the refrain of his song.

He winked at her. 'Sweet Nurse . . . what is your name anyway?'

'Rebecca Clark. And yours?' She knelt down before him and wondered if her knees would last out the day. They were already bruised and scraped from kneeling on the rock before, and they hurt merely when she put pressure on them.

'Guy McLaren,' and then in a burst of drunken generosity, 'but just call me Guy.'

'Okay, Guy, you're going to have to lie flat and I'm going to tie you to the tree.'

He winked again—this time lasciviously. 'Kinky. Do you tell all your patients that?'

Rebecca had been around hundreds of male patients. There were some who were polite and others who complained. And then there were the flirtatious variety who positively blossomed in a hospital setting, thinking every nurse was a nymphomaniac in disguise. This type tended to ignore Rebecca except when they were frightened and in pain; then they bucked up their bravado with the most outrageous statements they could imagine. Her response was to smile and ignore the comments as if they had never been uttered.

'And I'm going to have to cut the leg of your jeans up to the knee.'

Guy whistled. 'Anything that turns you on, Nurse Clark.' But he obediently shifted to one side of the tree and, pulling a cushion over for his head, lay flat.

She looped a belt that she had found in his suitcase to the belt he wore at his waist and then buckled it around the tree, asking him to move down so that the belt was as taut as possible. That would anchor him to the tree when she pulled; she knew she would need the leverage. Then she slit his pants with the razor and then pulled off his loafer. The break was above the top of his white sock; she could see the discoloured bruise where the bone had broken and was pressing against the skin. The leg had swollen considerably, and she winced inwardly when she thought how painful it was going to be when she forcibly pulled his leg straight. If only the lake's edge hadn't begun below a sheer drop of rock—he would have been able to soak the leg in the chill of the water and keep the swelling to a minimum. Now the tissues were hot and tight, and she could imagine how they must throb and burn.

'How many bottles of beer were left?' she asked.

'Sixty-six,' he said. 'You a heavy drinker?'

'Sixty-six bottles of beer on the wall,' she sang softly, and he joined in with her. 'Sixty-six bottles of beer. If one of those bottles happened to fall, sixty-five bottles of beer on the wall.'

Rebecca grasped his ankle as she sang and, with all the force she could muster, she pulled the leg towards her, suddenly thankful for her weight and strength as she felt the bone move into place.

'Sixty-five bottles . . .' his voice choked, wavered and then went on, 'of beer on the wall.'

His body strained against the belt and, when she glanced at him, she saw that his eyes were shut tight, a slow trickle of tears making their way down the sides of his face to his ears where the dark hair made wings at his temples. His jaw was clenched so tight that the veins stood out on his throat and his hands were tightened into fists with knuckles as white as a sheet. He was neither as drunk as he had pretended, she realised, nor as impervious to pain. A lesser man might have fainted; another with less fortitude would have at least let a groan escape his lips, but Guy was neither. He expelled a deep breath and then, with eyes still shut and a voice that had lost most of its earlier resonance, he sang.

'Sixty-five bottles of beer.' He gained a bit of strength then and went on. 'If one of those bottles had happened to fall, sixty-four bottles of beer on the wall. Sixty-four bottles of beer on the . . .'

His courage touched Rebecca deeply and tears pricked her eyes as his voice filled and soared. She was gentle as she strapped the splints to his leg, winding the strips of fabric around his foot, up the ankle and beyond the break towards his knee. He winced occasionally, but she could feel his body relaxing. It was a while before he opened his eyes again, but when he did, he propped himself up on an elbow to watch her.

'You're very competent, Nurse Clark.'

She saw that he had regained his earlier cool persona. 'I've been doing this for a few years.'

'How long?'

'Five.'

'You're twenty-five or twenty-six?'

'Twenty-six.'

'You're pretty, Nurse Clark.' Startled, she glanced up at him. 'Beautiful blue eyes.'

The compliment came as such a shock to her that colour flared in her cheeks, and she glanced quickly down at the improvised splint, her hands suddenly trembling.

'Hey,' Guy said, 'I'm sorry if I said anything—'

'No, it's just that . . . I'm not used to . . .' A compliment like that would never have flustered her before. She was used to the crazy things that patients said when they came out from under anaesthetics or when they were wildly grateful because she alleviated their pain. She had always known how to mask her emotions behind a façade of cool professionalism, but now she couldn't seem to pull on the mask, her nursing face. Perhaps it was the trauma of the crash, the fact that she was exhausted and hungry, the emotional aftermath of setting Guy's leg, all combining together to make her vulnerable, her defences down, her emotions raw and visible.

'Because you're . . .'

'Because I'm fat,' she cut in bitterly. 'Obese is the precise medical term, I believe.'

CHAPTER TWO

Guy hadn't meant to hurt her. It was just that he was so thankful that she had helped him, and he didn't think he would ever forget the cool, gentle feel of her hands on his bruised chest when he had been lying on the promontory or the intense blue of her eyes as she had knelt over him then. They were the colour that the sky should have been, clear and light, their length framed by long, dark lashes that quivered slightly when she had looked down at him. And she was pretty if you discounted the double chin, the thickness of her neck and the shapeless, lumpy body beneath the tunic top and slacks. She had masses of auburn hair that fell to her shoulders in waves, a small straight nose and, beneath the grime on her face, a smooth skin tone that would have made most redheads grind their teeth in envy.

But he was truly sorry that his words had so unnerved her; he could see how rigid she had gone, kneeling there at his feet, her hands motionless on the bandage she was wrapping around his leg. Guy supposed that, being so fat, she simply wasn't used to having a man compliment her and he cursed himself for having hurt her.

'Forget I said anything, and I take it back anyway.' He tried to joke. 'Worst pair of eyes this side of the Arctic Circle.'

'It's all right,' Rebecca said grimly, starting to wind the bandages again. 'I know I'm not attractive to men. I'm used to that.'

There was silence then as Guy lay back down again and stared up into the interlaced mesh of branches and leaves. He didn't know what to say to her and he didn't want to make the situation any worse than it already was. He was the kind of man who gave compliments to women easily. He liked women; he liked their faces, their shapes and the crazy ways their minds worked. He didn't pretend to understand what they were thinking, but he relished the fact that they were different, mysterious and often elusive. He liked to be kept guessing.

Take the other woman on the plane. What was her name? Sandy, Sandra, something like that. There had been that click of understanding between them, not spoken but registered, accepted and eventually to be acted upon. She had been really lovely; blonde, slender and shapely. He hadn't been in a big hurry to make a pitch to her, and she had seemed experienced enough to keep the pace at a lazy, sensual level. Her presence on the plane had added a bit of spice to what otherwise promised to be another humdrum job. He had anticipated the evening to come, thinking that he would take her to dinner in the watering-hole that passed for a restaurant in Fort Good Hope and then possibly to bed, although he hadn't been certain of that. There had been something mischievous about her, and he had wondered if she was going to make it easy for him or not. He had sensed her need for a chase, a hint of pursuit, and he liked the idea of a challenge and then the ultimate and mutually pleasurable conclusion. Although he didn't put it to himself in such terms, Guy liked to hunt when he knew there was a quarry to be snared at the end.

It was ironic, he thought, that, but for a twist of fate, he could have been marooned with Sandra what's-her-name in the middle of the Mackenzie Valley without a sign of rescue for weeks. If he didn't bother to think about the difficulties of survival, he could easily drift off into a warm and delicious dream of orgies under the stars and hours of lovemaking from morning to night. No newspapers, no telephones, no interruptions—just one long holiday where nothing mattered but the two of them. He felt a stirring in his groin at an image of his body and Sandra's wound together, a cocoon of limbs, damp with a sensual sweat and smelling of the musky odours of love. He could imagine her head thrown back, the blonde hair rippling over his arm, her mouth parted slightly as he touched the softness of her. Despite the pain that throbbed heavily in his leg, Guy grinned to himself. It was satisfying to know that it would take a hell of a lot more than a plane crash and a broken leg to keep him down. As long as the idea of a woman could still turn him on, he knew he wasn't six foot under yet.

Guy wondered if any woman could really understand what sex meant to a man. It was an affirmation of life, of virility, of existence. When he felt great; when his business was going well and the world seemed to understand that it owed him a living, he wanted sex as the icing on the cake. When he was low and things looked bleak, he wanted sex as an antidote, a remedy to take away the pain. Even when he was feeling just middling and maybe the sun was shining and maybe it wasn't, the thought of a woman would buoy him and put a special patina on to the day. And he wasn't any different from the next guy. He had spent enough time on isolated rigs with a group of men to know that. Sex was always the main subject of conversation; the men would joke about it, tell anecdotes about it and savour their moments of triumph.

But women weren't like that and Guy had had enough to know. It wasn't that they didn't like sex, most of them did. It just didn't seem to be a preoccupation with them; it didn't hover in their brains and come to the surface at such frequent and regular intervals. Take Maureen, his wife, his *ex-wife*. She had been as passionate as he had been in the beginning, but during the seven-year span of marriage, her interest had waxed and waned, her moods had become unpredictable, her urges seemingly controlled by such vagaries as the temperature, the barometric pressure and the time of sunset. He hadn't been able to make head or tail of her near the end and, when she had become so frantic over her inability to conceive—that had been at about the five-year mark—sex with her had become as contrived as artificial insemination. Then the moon had ruled their lives and a thermometer. He had hated it, but he had been sympathetic to her misery. He hadn't really wanted a child at all, but he had tried to understand her feelings. He realised now that the marriage had been dead for him at that point and probably for her as well. The sudden driving force to have a child had been her last-ditch effort to keep their relationship alive.

A pang in his leg and a soft murmur of apology from Rebecca brought Guy back from his thoughts, and he wondered how those pleasant dreams of sex had drifted into the sour memories of his marriage. It wasn't a time that he enjoyed remembering and, besides, he wasn't the type who dwelt on the past with morbid fascination or deep analysis. He preferred action to contemplation; he liked to look ahead. Which was just as well considering that he would be spending the next week or month merely thinking about surviving from day to day. Sex wouldn't be an issue and, even if he yearned for it, the sweet torment of being in close proximity with a desirable woman wouldn't exist. The nurse was nice enough, but her body turned him off. Just the thought of making love to all that flesh caused his earlier surge of manhood to wilt.

No, he would have to count on Rebecca for survival not for sexual games, and he supposed he was lucky that she wasn't the lovely, blonde Sandra. Sandra wouldn't have known how to set his leg, and she had looked too fastidious and fragile to lift logs, clean fish, clear underbrush and carry supplies. Within five minutes of meeting her, Guy had had Sandra's number. She was a rich man's daughter who was playing at being a photographer. She had come to the Arctic to take nice pictures, knowing that Daddy's connections would get them published. She hadn't had a clue what the Arctic was really about. Look at the ridiculous clothes she had brought with her; diaphanous nightgowns, high-heeled sandals and a sequined gold evening gown. The closest she had come to the reality of travelling in a country that was rough, harsh and primitive were the clothes she had been wearing on the plane; designer jeans and a spanking new corduroy jacket with fancy puffed sleeves.

Rebecca, on the other hand, struck him as being stubborn, pragmatic and resourceful. The splints she had designed were clever, and he had watched the way she had set her chin at a determined angle when putting up the tarp. She hadn't mentioned the raw spots on her palms, the cut on her forehead or the amount of strength it had taken for her to set his leg. Guy didn't think he had known any woman who could have matched the same accomplishments without complaining or letting him know just how much she was suffering. Rebecca's silence earned his admiration, and he was thankful for her presence. Guy wasn't a pessimist by nature, but he had spent enough time in the Arctic to have a very good idea of what the future held for them. Both of them were going to need every bit of determination, strength and guts that she had.

Contrary to his comforting words to her earlier, Guy had no real belief that rescue would come either in two days or even within two weeks. As far as he had been able to ascertain, the pilot had been unable to make ground contact during the storm, and they had been blown deep into uninhabited wilderness. Searching for them would be like trying to find a needle in the proverbial haystack and, despite his own knowledge of the Mackenzie Valley, he had no real idea where they were. Guy thought he could see the outlines of the Richardson Mountains in the misty distance above the trees. That would put their location somewhere west of the Mackenzie River, but he would have given his right arm to know if they were north or south of the Dempster Highway. Given that co-ordinate, he would have been able to know the general direction of civilisation. Without it, he was as hopelessly lost as any newcomer to the Northwest Territories.

And he was hampered by his leg. He had forced Rebecca to set it, knowing that if help didn't come, their only salvation would lay in his ability to lead them out. The flares and the radio had gone down with the plane, and Guy believed that rescue, if it came, would be purely luck. The pain involved in the setting of his leg was nothing compared to the tortures they would suffer if days stretched into weeks and then into months. Guy unfortunately knew enough about the Arctic to understand just what survival entailed. It meant living through cold even in the summer, hunger and the danger posed by accidents and animal life. The Arctic was a hard taskmaster; it destroyed those who weren't able to adapt.

He knew that the pilot's fishing gear was going to be a godsend. Fate hadn't dealt them a particularly favourable hand; they had no first-aid equipment, no emergency ration pack, and barely enough material to set up a decent shelter. Guy supposed that he should be thankful that he wasn't stranded in the Arctic during the winter or caught in a lifeboat in the ocean. Although the nights would get cold, they were in the land of the 'midnight sun', and darkness only lasted a few hours. And they would never die of thirst. The lake looked to be several miles wide, and he prayed that it would be well-stocked with fish. Their chances of catching any other food was unlikely; they had no gun, no traps and no way of snaring anything that moved on land. Berries, leaves and fish were going to be the staples of their diet. There wasn't much that was poisonous in the Arctic, but he also suspected that there wasn't much that tasted good either, not when the only food source to tantalise the taste buds were plants like dandelions and cattails.

'Done,' Rebecca said, and Guy pulled himself upright to survey the way she had bandaged his leg. It was an odd arrangement with strips of denim stretched this way and that, and the tops of the branches poking up at his knee.

'It doesn't look good,' she added, 'but it'll keep. And I left your sock on for warmth.'

'You're all heart, Nurse,' Guy said, and from the look she gave him, he knew that she preferred him this way—flirtatious, ironical and slightly mocking. In that respect, she wasn't much different from other women.

He grew more serious then and, ignoring the steady throbbing in his leg and the way his bruised ribs protested his breathing, Guy launched into a discussion of their plus and minus points in terms of food and shelter. He listed the available plant-life which made an expression of distaste pass over her face, the possibility of catching fish and the necessity of obtaining bait.

'You mean me, don't you?' Rebecca asked. 'I'm the one who's going to have to find grubs and frogs.'

'Are you hungry?'

'Starving,' she admitted.

Guy suggested that they spend the rest of their daylight time building a fire and gathering whatever food they could find. He didn't think a tarp stretched over a rope would provide them with much shelter and suggested that they spend the next day constructing a viable lean-to out of branches. Rebecca sat through his recital with those intense blue eyes on his face, her hands resting on the thickness of her knees. She had, he noticed, an air of peacefulness about her that he had never come across in a woman before. When she was still, her whole being seemed to be in a state of arrest; when she was in motion, she did everything with great economy and a surprising amount of grace for a woman of her size. It was as if she had inner resources, a well of personal strengths to draw upon, and he wondered if she had been forced to develop those because of her weight. She had already admitted that men didn't find her attractive, and he suspected that her life was one of isolation and loneliness.

'Have you done this before?' she asked when he had finished speaking.

'I've spent a lot of time in the bush.'

'Do you work in the Arctic?'

'I run seismic surveys for companies who are exploring for gas and oil. I've got a crew of men working just south of Fort Good Hope.'

'I see.' She looked down at her hands with their

broken nails and dirt caught in the pores. 'I . . . don't know the first thing about living in the wild.'

Guy gave her an encouraging grin. 'Consider this your initiation.'

Rebecca's return smile was only half-hearted. 'I don't even like camping,' she admitted.

'I guarantee you'll love it by the time we're done.'

'Do you think . . . is there a chance . . . that we'll starve to death?' And then she amended that, 'If no one comes, that is?'

He didn't want to admit that there was always that possibility. 'You *are* hungry, aren't you?'

'Seriously,' she insisted.

'All right,' Guy said flatly, 'we could starve to death but not if we're energetic, ingenious and co-operative. I can't do much but fish, and you're going to have to scrounge for plants, chop and gather wood, build the lean-to and manage all the other dirty work. I've got the know-how and you've got the mobility. You're going to have to be damned careful where you step and what you do. If you trip over a log and break your leg or burn yourself in the fire, then we'll really be in trouble.'

Guy could see that it was a while before the full responsibility of her burden became obvious to her. She seemed strong enough to bear it, but he hoped that his blunt words didn't frighten her too much. The truth of the matter was, without her, *he* would starve to death. With his game leg, he wouldn't have a chance in hell of survival. He would either slowly fade away from lack of food or develop pneumonia from exposure. She was his ace in the hole, the lucky card dealt to him by the fates. What good was all his technical know-how when he was so damned helpless?

'Do you really think we can live on the occasional fish and plants?'

'Occasional fish?' he demanded in mock-anger. 'You don't think much of my angling abilities, do you?'

'It's me,' Rebecca replied with a grimace as she stood up. 'I don't think I can catch any frogs.'

'You're smarter than they are,' he reminded her. 'And take that jar from the tackle box to put them in after you've caught them.'

'Optimist,' she said.

But she was game, Guy saw, and that lifted his spirits. He smiled a bit as he watched her set her shoulders and then set off to circle the promontory. She was going to have to find a way down to the shore, to the rocky, shallow part of the lake where frogs tended to live. He didn't think he had set her an easy task, but he trusted in her ability to see it through. A scrabbling sound of pebbles falling and slate cracking made him call out, 'You okay? Anything broken?'

'Just my dignity,' he heard over the rippling sound of the lake. 'Nothing serious.'

Guy set himself the task of putting together the rod and reel as the thought of a dressed filet cooking on an open fire whet even an appetite dulled by pain. He had taken some of the aspirin that Rebecca had offered him earlier, and the throbbing in his leg had eased as long as he didn't try to move. One small motion, however, would set it off again with a jolting start, making him bite his lip in an effort not to cry out. He had shown Rebecca his most courageous face; he had hidden his own weaknesses from himself, but they were getting the better of him. The pain had taken its toll of his energy and strength, and his hands trembled as they tried to unwind the fishing line, his eyes blurring when he looked at the hooks in his lap. Despite a valiant attempt to stay awake and do his bit for their survival, Guy finally succumbed to sleep and a desperately-needed oblivion, leaning back against the tree, his chin slumping towards his chest, his eyes closing as if leaden weights were pulling them down.

What was there to say about frogs except that she had developed an instant hatred for them? They could jump quicker than she could; they could disappear in the water at a second's notice; and they seemed to mock her with their unblinking eyes. They were tiny things with brains the size of peas, but Rebecca had the frustrated feeling that they were laughing at her, and it made her furious. She had already slipped half a dozen times on the wet, shiny stones at the edge of the lake and her feet were soaking and cold. She also had the uncomfortable feeling that she was part of some gargantuan and unreal farce. Surely cameras were rolling behind her back, and some film director who had a sense of the absurd was immortalising her frog-hunt as comedy.

She could just imagine how ridiculous she looked. A large, obese woman hopping on stones at the lake's edge, imitating the leaps of elusive little frogs, and tearing her hair out in desperation. She was glad that Guy was immobile and hundreds of feet away; she would have been humiliated beyond all belief if he could have seen her performance. Yet, she had to catch one of the damn things. Their dinner depended on it, and Rebecca was famished. Not with the superficial hunger that drove her to compulsive eating, but the real McCoy, a deep-down aching sensation in her stomach that demanded satisfaction. She had gone for hours already without sustenance, and she was amazed to think how long it had taken before she had noticed. Rebecca was used to being obsessive about food. She was usually in one of two states; thinking about it or eating.

She hadn't always been that way. Once she had been a slender, little girl with big blue eyes and thick auburn braids that she could sit on. She had been so pretty at that stage that a local photographer had used her as a model for his studio advertising and her face had graced the pages of the *Fairfax Gazette*. She had been active and busy, going to school, fighting with her sisters, playing hopscotch and jumping rope. She had eaten her meals with no great interest in them, only marking time until she could play again. She had been normal then, just like everyone else.

But adolescence had arrived at the same time as her parents' marriage had come violently apart at the seams, and Rebecca had discovered that there was sweet solace in candy, cake and ice-cream. She had started gorging at thirteen and, by the time she was fifteen, she no longer even remotely resembled that small girl in the photographs, except for her eyes. The rest of her was submerged in rolls of fat. At that point, it hadn't taken much to trigger her appetite. A small rebuff, an angry look, a bad grade, and a vast and overwhelming hunger would beset her. It didn't seem to matter if she had just eaten, the hunger was vicious and seemingly insatiable. It controlled and mastered her with a domination she couldn't break no matter how hard she tried. Like a helpless puppet, she danced to its manipulation of the strings.

A small movement caught her eyes, but once again Rebecca was too late to catch the elusive frog. She swore and, pulling off her blouse, folded it in half. Roll the cameras, she thought wryly. Catch the fat lady in her bra looking for frogs. But this time when she saw a gleaming eye under a leaf, she threw the blouse over it and caught the frog just as it was leaping in the air. 'Gotcha!' she cried with triumphant glee and dropped it into the jar. 'You're a condemned frog.'

Although it wasn't as easy as it appeared the first time, Rebecca managed to catch five frogs that way. When she was done, she put her blouse back on, shivering at its dampness, and deposited her jar of frogs on the promontory. She would have pointed out her success to Guy, but she saw that he had fallen asleep, his long legs stretched out before him, his hands resting on his lap, their palms upwards as if in a mute and helpless gesture. She knew how badly he needed rest. The tension of the last two hours had been extraordinary, and his pain alone would have worn out a weaker man. She was tired too, but her hunger was paramount. With the bait caught, she now had visions of fish broiling over an open fire, and just imagining the smell was enough to make her mouth water in eager anticipation.

She searched for firewood on the ground below the area of the plane where so many branches had fallen, and behind it in the brush where there would be twigs for kindling. She had been a Girl Scout once, and she did remember the sequence of setting a proper fire; first digging a hole in the ground circled by stones, then building a teepee of brush and twigs that would immediately spark and catch, and gradully adding larger and larger logs. The wood had to be piled in such a manner that the fire could breathe and grow. It was while she was mentally arranging and re-arranging logs that Rebecca caught a glimpse of blue beneath the sloping branches of a spruce tree.

With a cry of happiness, she sank down on her knees and pulled her purse towards her. Since she had come to the dismal conclusion that it had ended up in the front half of the plane buried in water, she had resolutely put it out of her mind. Now, she turned it over and over in her hands in utter delight. The canvas had torn in several places and one corner was completely bashed in, but the catch had held and she knew its contents were intact. Rebecca's fingers shook slightly as she opened it, and she sat back on her heels when the treasures inside were revealed. What she had carried on to the plane was more precious, she realised, than diamonds, infinitely more valuable than gold. It wasn't as if she had thought about them that way when she had filled her purse; she had never considered that they might be the answer to her prayers or help to save her life. She had simply bought them the way she usually did, in large quantities to carry with her wherever she went, just in case she needed them, just in case hunger sank its claws into her.

Her purse was full of candy bars; made of sweetened peanut butter, caramel or chocolate and filled with coconut, nougat, almonds and deep red cherry interiors. She swallowed convulsively as she looked down at them. They smelled wonderful and brought back to her long afternoons she had spent in cinemas, the scent of buttered popcorn and chocolate wafting all around her, or the times she had sneaked candy into her bedroom and eaten it under the covers when the lights were out and her mother thought she was asleep. The memories were so pleasurable and her hunger, legitimate this time, so pervasive that Rebecca knew she couldn't wait another minute. She scooped out three candy bars and, rigid with a lovely suspense, tried to decide which one she would eat first. The caramel? The bar of bitter chocolate? The peanut butter cup whose taste she could already imagine, its rich thickness melting on her tongue?

Her fingers fumbled as they ripped open the wrapping and tore apart the metallic, rippled paper that held the peanut butter cup in its shape. The smell of it made her stomach lurch, and she opened her mouth, closing her eyes in heady anticipation as she did so. Then she lifted the candy up to her lips and . . .

. . . And thought of Guy whose hunger must equal her own. And the fact that they had no actual food at all besides her horde of candy. Rebecca opened her eyes and looked down at her hand where the peanut butter cup stood in enticing splendour. Couldn't she take just one bite? One small bite that would ease the gnawing hunger in her stomach? Everything within her screamed for that bite, screamed for satiation and fulfilment. Her mouth watered even more; her hand trembled against the invisible force that wanted to lift it again up to her mouth.

Rebecca knew that if she yielded, if she allowed herself even one small nibble of that peanut cup, she would be lost. She would gobble the rest of it down and then systematically go through the entire contents of her purse. It was like standing at the edge of a crevice and knowing that one step would plunge her to doom. Her pattern of convulsive eating was all too familiar. Once she started, she literally could not stop. She could remember one afternoon when she had brought back to her apartment two quarts of coffee ice-cream, a box of Oreos and a mocha cake. She had eaten everything, even licking the crumbs off her fingers and mopping up the melting ice-cream with bits of cake. She had felt sick when she was done and hated herself venomously for having eaten that way, but the frenzy of cramming her mouth full had made her forget an awful day. Some people drank, some took drugs and Rebecca was addicted to food; that was the way she consoled herself.

But if she ate the peanut butter cup and all the rest of the candy in her purse, there would be nothing left for Guy, or for the next day when her hunger would return just as if it had never been abated or appeased. There were valuable calories in the nuts and chocolate and sugar, and if they didn't get rescued, the candy would provide sustenance that they badly needed. Guy had talked about fish and plants, but suppose he couldn't catch any and they were reduced to a diet of roots and lichens. The protein in the nuts alone would give them badly needed energy. Rebecca's hand slowly dropped to her knees as she realised that she had no right to consume in one selfish sitting what should be rationed out to each of them day by day.

Her stomach tightened and twisted with pain as she rewrapped the peanut butter cup and put it, and the other two bars, back into her purse. It took every bit of resolve that she had to pull the catch closed, shutting away the glorious sight of all that candy. When it was done, Rebecca took a deep breath and put the purse down by the small pile of twigs she had accumulated. She hadn't yet collected enough wood for a decent fire, and she knew that Guy would not only want to have enough logs tonight but also for the next morning. She might have been a novice when it came to camping and the Arctic, but she realised how important a fire would be when night descended and there was nothing to ward off animals and fear except that heat and crackle of flames.

Guy was still sleeping when she returned with her purse strung over one shoulder and her arms full of wood. She made several trips back to get more of the bigger logs and then finally slumped down by the tree in exhaustion, wondering how he could sleep when she had made so much noise. But sleep he did, as if he were a baby, his breathing smooth and regular, his face relaxed and open. Rebecca didn't want to wake him so she sat there instead, appraising him and wondering about him, where he came from and who he was.

She didn't think he was married or had a family; he hadn't mentioned a wife, children or parents at all, and the way he had struck up a flirtation with the other woman on the plane suggested that he was a footloose and fancy-free bachelor who was accustomed to picking up women easily. Surely, it couldn't have been difficult for him; he was far too good-looking with those high cheekbones, dark eyes and sculpted jaw. Rebecca thought that he must be in his early or mid-thirties; there was a hint of grey in the thick, brown hair at his temples and he had the casual, sophisticated charm of a man who has seen the world, judged it and found it amusing.

If she had been another woman, his looks would have thrilled her and she just might have looked on their isolation as a godsent opportunity to be with a man who was clearly sexy and desirable. But being who she was, Rebecca didn't think along those lines. She knew very well that Guy found her unattractive and would probably end up considering her as a buddy and helper rather than as a woman who had normal wishes and desires. She was used to that type of treatment. Men were usually repulsed by her and, rather than show it, took on a friendly, asexual demeanour. Which was all right with her. Rebecca liked men but only in the abstract. Every once in a while a sexual warmth might come over her at the thought of making love or meeting someone who might want her, but she was used to dismissing such feelings since they led nowhere. And she hated her own body so viciously that she could well understand why men would hate it, too. She had grown quite adept at avoiding full-length mirrors and, if she was forced to stand before a window or plate of glass that reflected her whole image, she had learned only to focus her face and her head. She was much happier that way.

'How long did I sleep?' Guy was awake and stretching, wincing as he moved and rubbing the back of his neck as if he had a crick there.

'About an hour.'

'Hell, I didn't mean to. I wanted to start fishing.'

'You needed it,' she said. 'Now you won't doze off while the fish are biting.'

He ran his fingers through his hair with a weary gesture as if the hour's rest hadn't even begun to satisfy his need for sleep. 'Did you catch any frogs?'

'Five,' she replied proudly.

'I told you that you were smarter than they were.'

'Not by much,' she said, 'and they're a lot faster than I am.'

'Trout like their frogs fast and sassy.'

'Is that what there is in the lake?'

He shrugged and yawned. 'Or pike. I don't much care at this point, do you? I'm too hungry.'

She held out her purse to him. 'I found some food.'

His dark eyes were quizzical as he took the purse from her, and Rebecca held her breath as he opened it. She had always been secretive about her eating habits, and it was excruciating to watch him pore over her cache of food. She knew how it looked for a woman of her weight to be carrying around huge quantities of candy; it looked as if she didn't have control, as if she were a slave to her fat. Her mother had thought she was utterly disgusting and told her so at frequent intervals. Rebecca didn't suppose that Guy would think any differently and, steeling herself for humiliation, she waited for him to come out with the appropriate sarcastic and cutting remark. She clenched her hands in her lap and felt a flush of anticipatory embarrassment rise in her cheeks.

Guy's eyes met hers when he looked up, but he didn't miss a beat. 'God, she must have been starving,' he said.

Rebecca blinked at him in confusion. 'She . . . ?'

'Sandra. The blonde with the see-through nighties. She must have had a thing for chocolate.'

Guy had been perceptive enough to see her pain and kind enough to spare her from exposure. A lump formed in her throat making her cough slightly. 'I . . . I guess so.'

'We'll each have one a day,' he went on with a hearty enthusiasm as if he hadn't heard the catch in her throat, 'starting with tonight after supper. Just think of the menu; filets of bass broiled to perfection over an open grill and served with squares of luscious milk chocolate.'

'Stop it!' she cried. 'I don't think I can wait.'

'Me either,' he grinned. 'So let's go catch the main course.'

Guy couldn't walk, of course, or even lean against her and hop so it was a matter of his sliding and inching his way over the rock while she carried the tackle box and fishing rod. She could just imagine how each movement and bump caused his leg to flare with pain, but he never made any sound other than a quick intake of breath when the going got especially rough. She would have liked to touch his shoulder or arm just to indicate her sympathy, but she knew that he wouldn't have wanted that. He was too independent, too determined to share his half of the burden. But he had to rest when he reached a place where the rock jutted out over the grey-green water of the lake, and Rebecca could see how white he had gone beneath the bronzed tone of his skin. Nothing in his words, however, indicated that he was suffering.

'Okay, fish,' he called out jauntily so that his voice rang out over the lake. 'Here we come.'

Rebecca felt unaccountably happy as she sat beside Guy watching the white ripples on the water and the mist hover over the lake like a blanket, keeping the rays of the sun at bay. She had pulled a sweater over her blouse, but the air wasn't that chilly. And it looked as if the sun wouldn't be setting for hours even though it was almost seven o'clock. She no longer even noticed the wreck of the plane in the water and her indifference didn't stem from callousness, but from the feeling that the plane ride had been months ago instead of just that afternoon. So much had happened since the crash that the memory of it was already fading like an old snapshot. She was far more interested in the possibility of dinner and Guy's baiting of the hook. They sat in a comfortable silence after he made his first cast, the frog and line curving in a huge arc in the air before hitting the water.

'Poor thing,' she finally said.

He glanced at her questioningly. 'Me, the fish or the frog?'

'The frog.'

'Consider it a sacrifice for the greater good of mankind.'

'I was thinking of the frog's mother,' she replied. 'Think of the pride she took in him.'

Guy slid into the spirit of the thing. 'He was planning to be a doctor, wasn't he? Specialising in froggy disorders.'

'He had only two years left in medical school,' she confirmed with a sigh.

'And now he's bait. That's life, Nurse Clark. Up one moment and down the next.' Guy tugged experimentally on the line and they both stiffened when it went suddenly taut. Guy tried to reel it in and then gave a grunt of irritation. 'Damn frog just crawled under a stone.' He yanked hard this time and the line went suddenly slack. When he pulled it in, they discovered that not only was there no frog on the line, but that they had also lost a hook.

'Oh, no,' cried Rebecca with disbelief, 'he got away.'

'Don't worry,' Guy vowed, 'the next one isn't going to be so lucky.'

Another hook was attached to the line, another frog was baited and another cast was made. They were both silent this time, their bantering camaraderie completely wiped away by the loss of the frog. Rebecca didn't know what Guy was thinking but she was praying. There were only three frogs to go, and she dreaded the thought of having to get more in case all of them were smart enough to disappear under rocks.

And hunger was making her feel faint inside. All the strength and resolve that she had called on earlier to set Guy's leg and put up the tarp and catch the frogs seemed to have dissolved. Even the moment of happiness that she had had when he started fishing had dissipated before that overwhelming hunger.

Guy suddenly gave a low hiss, and Rebecca's eyes widened as she saw his line start unreeling out over the water. 'What is it?' she asked.

'A fish this time,' he said. 'He's got hold of the frog and he's running with it.'

'Won't he eat it?' she asked. They were both whispering now as if they were conspirators and the fish might overhear their plan.

'He'll go with it for a while before stopping to swallow it. Watch.'

Nothing could have induced her to look anywhere else. The line kept playing out, the reel making a clicking sound as it turned. Guy's hands had gone white at the knuckles as he gripped the rod, and when she flicked a glance at his face, she saw that a muscle was leaping in his jaw as he ground his teeth in concentration. She swallowed hard and her mouth seemed as dry as the desert.

Suddenly, the line went slack and sagged towards the water. It was then that Guy jerked hard on it, pulling the rod up and backwards with all his strength.

'What are you doing?' Rebecca asked.

'Hooking him,' Guy replied grimly. 'I hope.'

Then the line started to run again and, when Guy tried to wind it in, the tip of the rod curved into a tight arch. 'Got him,' he said with intense triumph. 'We've got him.'

Rebecca suddenly discovered that her heart had risen to her throat and her breath was short. She gripped her hands together as Guy continued to reel the fish in while it fought to be free of the hook. The rod bent and swayed in his hands as the fish swam first to one side and then the other against the inexorable pulling in of the line.

'Is it a big one?' she asked.

'Hard to tell. They're all fighters. We're going to have to tire him out.'

Suddenly, there was a splash, a spray of water and a gleam of silver as the fish leaped high in the air. Rebecca gasped. 'Don't lose him!'

'Not on my life,' he promised. 'I plan to eat this one.'

The fish leaped again and again, but each jump brought him closer to the shore, and it was clear, even to a novice like Rebecca, that he was losing the battle. By the time Guy was content to reel him in, the fish could no longer jump but swam back and forth in a futile effort to release himself from the hook. With one smooth gesture, Guy lifted and swung the rod so that the fish was pulled out of the water and dropped to the rock a safe distance from the edge of the promontory.

'Three pounds, I bet,' Guy said. He was panting from the exertion and grinning with satisfaction.

Rebecca grinned right back at him. 'Poor thing,' she said.

'His mother misses him already?'

'His father—he wanted to bring him into the family business.'

'And now he's dinner.'

'That's life,' she commiserated. 'Up one moment and down the next.'

CHAPTER THREE

IT was some time during their third day that Rebecca remembered that she had a notebook and pen in her purse. It was a loose-leaf book with ruled pages that she used to jot down grocery lists, appointments and phone numbers. Although she had never once considered herself a writer or had ever attempted to keep a diary, something drew her to the notebook. It was as if she were compelled to keep a record of what was happening, if not for posterity, at least for her own satisfaction. Although their days had taken on an odd sort of regularity, Rebecca was not blind to the fact that she and Guy were living an extraordinary existence, and she was afraid that if she didn't somehow make it permanent, it would disappear the way childhood memories do—remaining only as wisps of remembered events and places.

She kept the journal only for the first three weeks of their encampment and, in later years whenever she went back and read what she had written, Rebecca was always struck by what she had chosen to say and what was left unspoken. The journal showed an optimism that she didn't always recall feeling and it tended to minimise the real hardships; the cold nights, the discomfort of sleeping with only a cushion between her hips and the ground, the ever-present dirt, the primitive latrine system, and the constant awareness that one accident or one mistake might jeopardise their lives. In the journal, she had faithfully recorded events as she had seen them; the triumphs and the failures, the fears and the satisfactions. What she had not recorded were her deeper emotions, but anyone reading between the lines would guess them easily. The only mystery for the casual reader might be the journal's abrupt termination. There seemed no rhyme or reason for its ending, yet she had been unable to continue, her pen stilled, the subtle outpouring of her heart stopped as if by accident.

Tuesday, July 1

Guy tells me that today is Canada Day, a national holiday, and we plan to celebrate at breakfast by each having a chocolate bar instead of sharing one. I'm looking forward to that extra mouthful with the sort of anticipation I used to bring to one of my binges. I know what an aura it will bring to the morning; it will make the day special. Guy has taken to fishing early in the morning and later in the afternoon when the fish are biting. We keep the ones we don't eat right away hooked to a chain in a shallow part of the lake and pray that nothing else eats them. When Guy isn't fishing he works on our campsite. I think he's very ingenious; using the knife we found in the tackle box, he's whittled extra spoons for us and is working on a bowl. The pilot only had one place setting of everything so we've been forced to share utensils. Guy has also built a twig broom and a washing stand between two trees where we hung the mirror from my compact. This is where he shaves and I brush my teeth. I told him that I expect a house before he's finished; he tells me I'm lucky just to have a roof over my head. I'm proud of it, of course. It took me a whole day to cut down the branches for our lean-to.

Thursday, July 3

I decided to wash this morning and now understand why man invented the bath-tub and plumbing. Rather than use up wood and wait hours while water boiled, I washed in the lake and it was absolutely freezing cold. I shivered and shook for an hour afterwards, even though Guy rubbed my hair down with a blanket to dry it more quickly. The answer would seem to be less baths, but I can't stand to be dirty. Guy and I have made an inventory of toilet articles and we have three toothbrushes, several tubes of toothpaste, shaving materials, nail-scissors, emery-boards (which Guy uses in place of sandpaper for his whittling), face-cream, a couple of bars of soap and assorted and useless bits of make-up. Guy decided to give himself a scrubbing with a washcloth and ordered me to leave the campsite and not come back for an hour. I told him that I knew how to give bed-baths but he refused my services. When I got back, he was clean but out cold. The effort of washing had done him in for the afternoon. The pain in his leg is slowly subsiding which is good since we have only a few aspirin left.

Saturday, July 5

A plane went over today but it was too high and too far north to spot us. We both went a bit crazy even though we realised it was too far away. Guy kept piling wood on the fire, hoping to attract the pilot's attention with the smoke, and I, like some crazy fool, ran up and down the promontory waving my arms in the air and screaming as if I thought he could hear us. Of course, when it flew off, I was devastated and began to cry, and even Guy looked grim when he put his arm around me. He's usually quite cheerful and I'm not sure we'd survive without his sense of humour. He tends to see the funny side of things; lately, he's taken to giving our hunger names, his is Lucifer, mine is Jezebel. It's so much easier to scold Jezebel, I find, than my stomach when its rumblings go beyond the bounds of good taste. We can't ever seem to catch enough fish to fill us, and Jezebel and Lucifer go to bed with us at night and get up with us in the morning while we pray that the fish will bite that day. Thank God, I've become quite adept at catching frogs.

Sunday, July 6

I'm beginning to understand why primitive man didn't have time to become civilised—coping with food and shelter is taking every moment of our day. We are either thinking about a meal, trying to catch a meal or cooking it. Everything takes so much time and effort. Today, for example, we decided that we had to add to our diet, if not only for taste, at least for vitamins and roughage. Since Guy can't forage, I headed out into the brush, pulling up any interesting plants that I could see. He warned me about poisonous berries that are red and white so I avoided those. I'm determined to brew a tea out of leaves so that we can have a hot drink in the morning. I miss my coffee dreadfully. Guy discarded everything I'd brought back except a fern that he called a 'fiddlehead'. He said he thought we could eat it raw but I voted to have it boiled. The fiddleheads didn't taste badly, but cooking them took all the wood I'd gathered so I was forced to cut some more. If we hadn't crashed, I never would have known what a terrific axe-woman I am. My arms and shoulders hurt every night, but I can cut down a small tree now in five or six strokes.

Wednesday, July 9

It's amazing how one's perspectives can change. Yesterday, I would have given anything for a decent meal when the sun was shining. Today, I would gladly sacrifice a steak dinner if only it would stop raining. When I woke up the sky was almost black, and it started to thunder after that. The raindrops are enormous and drum on the tarp over our lean-to. We have a leak in one corner and had to move the clothes to the other side where we usually pile the cushions from the plane and the sleeping-bag. It's dark and grim and everything seems cold and mouldy. I'm thankful for all the clothes that we have, damp as they are. Guy has a sheepskin jacket and I am wearing four layers of blouses and sweaters. I thought we'd have a breakfast only of chocolate, but Guy told me it would be fish again. I assumed that he had some clever way of building a fire in the lean-to, but I was soon disabused of that notion. We ate the fish raw and I was so hungry I

didn't really care! And to think that, in my past life, I
didn't even like . . .

Guy leaned back again, watching Rebecca as she sat
hunched over her notebook, scribbling away. The
rain outside the front opening of the lean-to made an
incessant pattering sound on the leaves, and the drops
were coming down so heavily that the view outside
was of a lake scene shimmering behind a curtain of
glass. It was dismal and cold and, despite the warmth
of his jacket, he had pulled its collar up around his ears
and covered his legs with the blanket they had sal-
vaged from the plane. Rebecca looked as round as a
snowman dressed in layer upon layer of clothes. She
had pulled her hair back with a rubber band to keep it
out of her face, but tendrils kept escaping and falling
forward. So great was her concentration on her writing that she didn't seem to notice except to absent-
mindedly push them backwards so they could fall
again.

Although he looked relaxed enough, leaning
against the cushions and sleeping-bag, Guy was re-
hashing for the umpteenth time problems he hadn't
yet been able to solve. His biggest worry was food. The
chocolate wasn't going to last much longer, and
although the fish were running well, he didn't suppose their luck would hold out for ever. And they
needed protein badly; it was the nutrient that kept up
their energy level, allowing them to build and forage.
His dark eyebrows almost met in the middle as he
frowned and stared out at the pelting rain. What they
needed was a snare to catch squirrels and other small

animals, and he wondered if he might not be able to devise something out of the wires which were laid bare in the frame of the plane. Loops attached to a large stick? Some sort of primitive trap? The trouble was that it was Rebecca who was going to have to climb up to the plane and try to pull the wires loose. He knew how difficult it was for her to get up there and was well aware that she didn't have one-fifth the strength in her hands that he did. Guy glanced at her bent head. She would do it if he asked, but he dreaded doing so. Damn his leg! Damn, damn, damn.

Well, at least the lean-to was holding up; that was one consolation. It had taken him hours of lying on his side and hacking away at the ground with the axe to create a narrow gully all around the lean-to and down the slight incline so that they wouldn't find themselves swimming at night if it rained. As far as he could tell, his engineering was working. Water was flowing around both sides of the opening, into the main trench and then down on to the promontory. Except for the leak in the roof they were relatively dry. Not bad considering their shortage of tools, the single tarp and a length of rope that wasn't adequate to the job.

And the inside was sufficiently dry even if it was too small for the two of them and their belongings. It was about the size of a king-size bed and designed so that they slept from one side to the other, Guy insisting on taking the spot closest to the opening. The floor was earth covered with grass and leaves, and the roof was made of logs under the tarp. It had taken Rebecca a full day to cut down enough trees the right size, but she hadn't complained, only rubbed her shoulders that night as if they ached badly. He would have offered to massage them for her, but Guy had noticed that she didn't like being touched. She shied away whenever their hands met.

Now Guy studied her, his eyes narrowing in speculation as he watched her write. She was an odd sort, he thought, not like any other woman he had ever met. First of all she was quiet; she didn't chatter to fill up the empty space around her or yammer to get his attention. She went about her tasks with a minimum of conversation and an abundance of concentration that impressed him. She also had a good sense of humour and she didn't complain: not about the hard labour, the endless diet of fish, their lack of sufficient food or their isolation. He knew that she was as hungry as he was and that her hands were raw from chopping wood, carrying logs, scrubbing clothes and foraging in the brush. The other thing that struck him was that Rebecca wasn't vain. He couldn't think of another woman who wouldn't be trying desperately to look like a Vogue model in the middle of the wilderness, bemoaning her chipped nails and lack of a decent mirror.

She was a good sort to be stranded with, he decided, a terrific and reliable worker who wasn't as abrasive as another man might have been. She accepted his superior knowledge about camping and rarely questioned his decisions. Guy could think of half a dozen pals and buddies who would have driven him up the wall within twenty-four hours of their constant companionship. Rebecca had the opposite effect on his psyche; her presence soothed him. For the first time since the crash, he wondered about her. Who she really was, where she had come from, why she was so heavy. Oh, he knew the basic facts; that she came from a small upstate New York town, that she was twenty-six years old, that she had two sisters, that she had left a sheltered environment to take a well-paying but arduous post at a nursing station in Fort Good Hope. But suddenly the facts weren't enough.

'What are you writing in there?' he asked. 'Poetic passages about raindrops on leaves?'

Rebecca turned to him, and he noticed, not for the first time, that she had a pretty smile which revealed straight white teeth and put a dimple in one cheek. 'Hardly poetic,' she said. 'I'm writing about fish.'

Guy grimaced. 'Broiled, baked, or roasted?'

'Raw actually. You know, it wasn't as bad as I'd thought it would be. It tasted like . . . like . . .' She put her head to one side as she debated finding the right word.

'Like raw fish,' he said, supplying the answer for her. 'It's inescapable. Raw fish is never going to taste like chicken wings or steak or hamburgers.'

A dreamy look came over her face. 'Think of a hamburger,' she said, 'slathered in onions, bacon, relish and . . .'

'French fries,' he enjoined. 'Crisp and golden.'

'And a milkshake, vanilla-flavoured.'

Guy gave a half-laugh, half-groan, as he imagined it. 'We sound like an ad for McDonald's.'

'My sister, Tamara, did an ad for McDonald's once. She had to dress as a clown with a red wig and a red bulb for a nose.'

'Your sister's an actress?'

'She's trying to be. She's got herself into a few ads and was a walk-on in a soap, but she'll make it eventually. Tamara's like that.'

'Like what?'

'Oh—ambitious and energetic and strong. She's one of those people who always gets what they want because they go out and fight for it.'

Guy didn't really want to talk about Tamara. 'And what about you? Didn't you leave a nice, cosy job for a risky proposition?'

Rebecca shrugged as if taking a nursing post near the Arctic Circle was an everyday occurrence. 'I'd gone as far as I could in the hospital in Fairfax. It wasn't big, only a hundred beds, and the head nurse had fifteen more years until retirement. I'd thought about moving to a bigger city where there might be more opportunities, but that would have been expensive. Then I saw an ad in the *Times* asking for nurses in the Arctic and thought it might suit me. It's more challenging, you see. Nurses up here almost have the responsibility of a doctor; they deliver babies and . . .'

'Set legs?'

She had the grace to look rueful. 'I hadn't actually taken the job yet,' she said as a sort of defence.

'You sound just as courageous to me as your sister.'

Rebecca forcibly shook her head. 'Tamara's the brave one in the family; she'll talk to anyone; she's not afraid of any situation.'

Guy wondered what made Rebecca so self-effacing.

It was as if she wielded a large eraser and was determined to wipe herself out of existence. Every time the subject of the conversation veered in her direction, she switched it on to another track as if she couldn't bear to talk or think about herself. Guy was perceptive enough to realise that Rebecca probably used her own shape as a form of evasion, and he speculated on whom and what she was hiding beneath her humility and fat. He didn't for a minute believe that humour, forbearance and serenity were her only characteristics; she would have to be a saint. Beneath those façades; the competent nurse, the stalwart helper, was someone else. Someone who had emotions; anger, impatience, and irritation, who laughed, screamed, cried and loved. Guy tried to probe a little deeper. 'You don't think working in the Arctic takes bravery? It's hard to exist here even with the help of the government. We suffer from boredom, food shortages and a climate that discourages even the Eskimos.'

Rebecca looked uncomfortable. 'I needed a challenge; I was stagnating at my other job.'

His voice was soft. 'Maybe you wanted to get away from your family—or someone.'

Guy could see that he had reached pay dirt, because her face immediately turned away from him as if he had slapped her across the cheek. 'What do you mean?' she asked cautiously.

He shrugged. 'A lot of people come to the Arctic in the aftermath of a rotten love affair or a family crisis. Most of the men who work for me are either divorced or separated. It's isolated up here,' he added by way of explanation, 'and any happily married man would be crazy to leave his wife and family to spend two or three months of the year in the bush.'

It was a second or two before Rebecca spoke. 'And are you one of those divorced or separated men?' she asked.

Guy shouldn't have been surprised that another woman lay below the façade, but he was. He hadn't guessed that her peacefulness could conceal the ability to attack and that her serenity hid an uncanny talent for being right on target. He shifted uneasily and rearranged the blanket over his legs. 'I'm separated,' he said.

'I see.'

Did she? He doubted that Rebecca knew the first thing about the hideous battling and intense acrimony that had taken place before the separation. 'The divorce is supposed to come through some time this fall.'

But then, once again, she proved that she was different from other women. She didn't ask the typical hard-to-answer questions that Guy had finally learned to fend off with slick answers. She didn't want to know how long he had been married or what his ex-wife was like or why they were getting a divorce. She wasn't curious, it seemed, about the juicy details that other women thrived on knowing.

She asked only one thing. 'Did you have any children?'

Guy was surprised enough to offer more information than he usually did. 'No—my wife . . . well, she couldn't have any.'

'Did you want them?'

'No,' he said, and he couldn't prevent the coldness from coming into his voice. 'No, I didn't.'

Saturday, July 12

Triumph at last! I've finally discovered a plant that makes a decent tea. We've been experimenting with eating and boiling the leaves and roots of half a dozen plants. Guy operates on the principle that we taste a bit and see if it kills us. So far nothing has, although sometimes the taste is awful. Guy thinks I found a plant called Labrador Tea—so named by early settlers who found that it was perfect for making tea. At first I tried boiling the leaves in water, but now I've discovered that it's much more effective if I dry the leaves out over the fire, crumble them into bits and then pour boiling water over them. When it's hot and strong, we both feel better and I suspect that the leaves are high in vitamins. I'd once read that nettles are edible and tried to collect some. Unfortunately, I made the mistake of touching them and got a rash on one hand and up my left arm. I've been using the face-cream on it, but nothing really helps.

Sunday, July 13

Guy insists that he's ready for real walking since I took off the splints and re-wrapped his leg in stiff bandages. The leg is every shade of the rainbow, but it seems to be healing. So far Guy has either been crawling around when I'm out foraging or leaning on me and hopping, so today I cut down two trees for him that had crooks at the tops which he can use as crutches. When he doesn't shave and hops around on his crooked sticks, he reminds me of Long John Silver, evil and villainous-looking. He says he can't decide whether to grow a beard or not so he compromises by shaving every third day. My suspicion is that he'll quit when the shaving-cream is gone. Our soap is too precious to be used for personal appearances. I used to take such pride in my hair and nails, but now I tie my hair back to keep it out of the way, and my nails look as if they've been through a masher. It's odd how a person can adapt so easily. The day we crashed, I never thought we'd survive. Today, I feel as if we've been here for ever and are going to stay for the rest of our lives. I guess I've picked up a bit of Guy's philosophy. He's not a procrastinator and he doesn't just think of the short-term. He told me from the very beginning that we mustn't wait for rescue, but must consider what long-term survival entails. That meant building better shelter and carefully rationing our food supplies. He's taught me to think about conserving my energy and my resources and using them only when necessary. I've never met anyone like Guy, I admire him immensely.

Monday, July 14

A truly wonderful thing happened today! I was out on my usual foraging expedition and was following an old trail of mine, marked by bits of Sandra's gold sequinned evening gown, when I heard a rustling in the bush and then saw a fox streaking away. At first, I thought nothing of it, but then I wondered if he'd caught something, so I beat through the bushes and found a dead snowshoe rabbit with only the marks of the fox's teeth in his neck. I've always liked animals and I suppose that I felt sorry for the rabbit, but not for long. I came rushing back into the camp, yelling at the top of my lungs and waving the rabbit in the air like a flag of victory. I'll never forget that smile that came across Guy's face at the sight of that rabbit. He hasn't complained once about our constant diet of fish but, like me, I'm sure he was desperate for a change of menu. He hugged me, kissed me and then asked me if I wanted to skin it, but I preferred to rest in the lean-to while he played butcher. I'd heard that rabbit tastes like chicken but really, truly, it tastes far better than that. I hadn't realised how sick I was of fish and chocolate and roots. I sincerely hope that our lunch went to bunny heaven for he deserved it more than any other rabbit I've ever known.

Wednesday, July 16

Another plane went overhead and didn't see us. This one was far closer than the first and it seemed impossible that the pilot couldn't spot us. Guy went madly to work on the fire and I did my customary frenzied dance on the promontory, but it was no use. I felt so hopeless, and even Guy shook one of his crutches at the departing plane. It was one of the first times I've ever seen him get really angry; he has quite a colourful vocabulary. I tried to convince him that we should keep the fire going constantly and I offered to cut wood from here until doomsday, but Guy said it was unrealistic and a waste of my much-needed energies. The only saving grace to the plane's arrival and departure was a theoretical one. Guy is beginning to think that the planes are following flight routes along the Dempster Highway and, if so, it means that he can pinpoint our location as east of the Richardson Mountains, west of the Mackenzie River and south of the Highway. He spent quite a bit of the afternoon analysing this information as to latitudes and longitudes and distances, but I have a small confession. I discovered that I don't quite share his eagerness to leave here. Of course, I want to get back to civilisation, and I know that my mother and Tamara and Celia are probably going crazy worrying about me, and I am always hungry, but I'm not unhappy here. I don't know why, but I'm not.

Thursday, July 17

Guy and I have decided to start a restaurant when we're rescued. The location really doesn't matter, only the menu. This morning while Guy fished and I sewed a hole up in the sleeping-bag, we argued over whether to serve good home-grown American fare or Italian and finally compromised by deciding to split the menu in half. Guy is for thick, juicy and medium rare Porterhouse steaks served with baked potatoes piled high with sour cream and chives, sautéed mushrooms, acorn squash with maple syrup and fresh-baked apple pie made with MacIntosh apples topped with Hagan Daz vanilla ice-cream. I suggested fettucine in a white clam sauce served with toasted garlic bread, red wine and an antipasto salad with olives, lettuce, squares of cheese, and anchovies. Dessert would be Italian almond cookies rolled in sugar and cinnamon. Our mouths watered up until the point that Guy pulled in a catfish with its whiskers waggling in the air and reality set back in. Actually, catfish isn't as bad as it sounds, only there isn't enough of it.

Saturday, July 19

I met my first bear today while I was out gathering food in the afternoon. He (or she) was big and brown and collecting the same berries that I was. I froze when I realised that we were sharing the same berry patch, and my heart was beating so loudly, I thought the bear could hear it. It ambled back and forth for what seemed like hours while I debated in panic whether to stay or make a dash back to the camp. Then I thought of Guy who still couldn't walk very well and the fish he'd caught and fileted lying right on the promontory and the dwindling pile of chocolates and knew that I mustn't budge and lead the bear into our camp. Guy now tells me that bears have terrible eyesight so I guess it didn't see me and the wind was in my favour for it eventually wandered off, leaving me in such a terrible state that I collapsed to the ground and shook for minutes. I have never seen such claws; they were inches long and capable of destroying me in a second. We've decided that I'm not to travel so far out in search of new plants, and Guy is making me a billy club. I don't think I'd have a chance against an animal like that even with a weapon, but it's better than nothing. Still, I dreamt about the bear last night and woke up in a complete sweat. I realise now that I've been thinking of our stay here as idyllic despite the lack of food. I hadn't wanted to believe that it was truly dangerous.

Sunday, July 20

We've been here for three weeks now on a diet that Guy says is so effective that we could write a bestseller if we ever get back to civilisation again. I'm losing weight, and Guy is beginning to look gaunt. It isn't as noticeable on me because I have such a long way to go, but my pants are so loose I need a belt, and my bra doesn't fit any more and I had to discard it. Well, not discard it actually— merely alter its function; we never throw anything away. I took the straps off because we always need ties, sewed the cups together into a small bag and have cut the back into strips to make elastic bands. That's one of the things that Guy has taught me about surviving, to make use of every item, every idea and every bit of strength that I possess. I used to squander everything; time, energy and food. Now, I've learned to conserve and I've lost the desire to eat the way I used to. I'm hungry, but the feverish intensity that I used to feel is gone. Maybe it's because we have only a small pile of chocolates, and I'm not tempted by grocery stores packed to the rafters with temptations, but I really think that civilisation wasn't healthy for me. There were too many pressures, disappointments, arguments and tensions. Here, we've nothing but sky, water, land and fire.

Guy had intended to take a cat-nap in the sun, but he ended up sleeping for two hours. He hadn't meant to;

it was just that his leg had been acting up the night
before and he hadn't slept enough. When he awoke he
saw the sun had moved closer to the mountains and
cursed himself for wasting so much good time. He had
planned on building a picket-type fence around the
front of the lean-to. Rebecca's meeting with the bear
had convinced him that they should have more protection from predators, and he had racked his brain for
days to come up with a wall that would be easy to build
and erect. Small trees with sharpened points at the top
could be dug into the ground, he had decided, and
would support one another if properly positioned.
Rebecca had already cut down some trees for him, and
he had intended to start building after lunch.

Now, there was barely enough time to prepare for
dinner. Guy pulled himself upright on his crutches
and tentatively put his injured leg down first. Pain
shot upwards; he winced and then cursed. God, but
he was tired of hopping, tired of crutches and tired of
pain. For a brief second, he allowed himself the
indulgence of self-pity and then, shrugging his
shoulders as if he could rid himself of it like an
unwanted cloak, he made his way to the shallow edge
of the lake to get some water. His way was marred by
the usual difficulties; uneven ground that made his
crutches lean at an uncomfortable angle, stones that
hurt the bottom of his good foot and twigs that wanted
to trip him up. His need to be mobile was urgent, but
his ability to get around was limited and torturous. It
took him twenty minutes to travel the distance that a
whole person could have done in five.

He didn't notice Rebecca until he had almost

reached the shore of the lake and was still standing in a thicket of trees. She had been washing and was stepping out of the lake, her auburn hair hanging down her back like a dark, gleaming river. She hadn't heard him coming, Guy realised. Because she had been swimming, she hadn't heard his noisy progression over leaves and twigs. And she had probably thought he was still sleeping because, if there was one thing he had noticed about Rebecca, it was her modesty. She always went deep into the bush to change and had always warned him when she wanted to bathe.

He couldn't help the sudden dryness of his mouth, and he couldn't bring himself to turn away or even let her know that he was in the vicinity. Because she had been so fat when they crashed and she kept herself so covered up with baggy clothes, he hadn't really been aware of how much weight she had lost. Of course, he had noticed the slimming contours of her face; it was no longer quite so round and her cheekbones were becoming evident, but he hadn't really speculated about the rest of her. In his mind, Rebecca had remained what she said she was—obese.

But even if she didn't come close to qualifying as willowy, she was no longer obese and she was tall enough, only four inches shorter than his six feet, to carry her weight well. She was voluptuous, he saw, as she bent forward to towel her legs, and fair except for the dark triangle between her thighs. Water coursed in rivulets down a body that was formed of the kind of curves and smooth indentations that made a man's breath quicken, and she possessed full breasts tipped in dark pink that arched forward as she put the towel to her head, their nipples standing out from the coldness of the lake. Her ignorance of his watchful presence allowed her to be natural and she had, quite unknowing to herself, an enticing air of innocence and abandon. She reminded him of the Arctic rose that blooms so unexpectedly in the wilderness, its flower defiantly opening its petals to the chill winds and the thin heat of the sun, its beauty unafraid and exposed.

Heat moved through him as he watched her vigorously rubbing her hair, and he felt the familiar swelling and ache in his groin. The sensation was both highly pleasurable and painfully agonising, yet he couldn't bring himself to do the decent thing and avert his eyes from Rebecca's nude shape. Guy wondered if the isolation was getting to him or if he was going a little bit crazy from abstinence. It had been so long since he had slept with a woman, and he had put sex out of his mind ever since the plane had crashed. He had followed a strict course of mental celibacy, made all the easier because he had never really considered Rebecca as a bona fide woman and worthy of his attention. He had, therefore, failed to see the transformation that had taken place before his very own eyes.

Guilt at his voyeurism made Guy finally come to his senses; guilt and the knowledge that he had an overwhelming urge to yield to the hot flame of desire that threatened to consume him. His imagination followed the heavy, thudding beat of his heart. If he let her know that he was there, she would pause long enough for him to reach her. Then he could take her in his arms, taste the dampness of the lake on her skin and feel the softness of her breasts against his chest. He could sink with her to the ground and . . .

It was a mad dream, Guy knew, yet he didn't dare move, knowing that if he made one sound, Rebecca would realise what he had seen and would be mortified by her exposure. Their easy camaraderie, the co-operative spirit that made them work so well as a team, would vanish as if it had never existed. It was going to be difficult enough for him to treat her as he had before, as a buddy and with the same sort of careless affection that he would bestow on a male friend. But if she were aware of what he had seen, her attitude towards him would never be the same. She would become awkward and embarrassed; it was possible that a deteriorating relationship between them would hurt their chances of survival. He had no choice but to stand there like a statue and suffer in silence from an acute and advanced state of arousal.

The situation had its amusing points, Guy acknowledged ruefully to himself, but he didn't even dare smile. He merely moved his eyes one inch to the right in an attempt to remove Rebecca from his view. He thought that staring at the lake would be far easier to bear than watching a naked Rebecca towel her hair, but he was wrong. Her image was reflected back to him in the water's glass-like surface; an image that shimmered and gleamed, breaking into dancing diamonds when she moved and coalescing when she stood still. Ethereal as the image was, it did not release him. It was very lovely and very, very female.

CHAPTER FOUR

REBECCA was splitting wood for the fire by placing a log on a tree stump, holding it upright and cutting it in half with the axe. Despite the fact that it was only eleven in the morning, the sun was hot and its rays were beating down on her head. She had already stripped off the clothes she had worn that morning when it had been cool and changed into lighter apparel. She was wearing a halter top, a striped blue and white bandeau that she had found in Sandra's suitcase, and a rolled-up pair of Guy's jeans. She estimated that she had lost forty pounds, roughly a pound a day, since the crash, and nothing she owned fitted her any more. Her blouses were like tents, her slacks wouldn't stay up and even her shoes were loose. She had been forced to borrow from Guy and squeeze into Sandra's clothes. The other woman had been shorter and more fine-boned so her things were generally too short and too snug for Rebecca. The stretchy fabric of the bandeau, for example, barely held in the round fullness of her breasts.

Her body had changed so drastically, and in such a short time, that Rebecca could hardly grasp the reality of her thinness. She had no full-length mirror to gauge the changes, only the surface of the lake reflecting her outline in a wavering, shifting image. Sometimes, in the night, she would run her hands down the length of her sides and wonder at what she felt; the emergence of a hip bone, the structure of her rib-cage. Seeing her feet when she looked towards the ground was a novelty and, whenever she was chopping wood, she would find herself marvelling at the fine detail of bone in her wrists. Had she been living back in Fairfax, Rebecca would have been in a state of ecstasy at her weight loss. She could just envision the way she would have acted; every penny of her salary would have gone on new clothes. Tight slacks, clingy knits, slender dresses. No more gathered skirts, elasticised waistbands and blouses that looked like maternity tops; no more shopping in stores where the sizes began with 20 and went up in gradations of halves.

But she wasn't back in Fairfax. She was nowhere from nowhere with a man whose personality seemed to have changed overnight, and Rebecca was far too concerned with Guy's behaviour to find much satisfaction with her ever-increasing thinness. Even now, as she picked up another log, she couldn't help glancing unhappily towards the promontory where he was fishing, his bare back to her, the skin of his shoulders bronzed from long hours of sitting in the sun. As she wiped the sweat from her forehead and retied the string that held the heavy hair off her face and neck, Rebecca wished desperately that she could know what was going on in his head. He had changed so dramatically, frowning often now, his mouth set in a grim line, the lips pressed tightly together as if there was a fountain of anger within him that threatened to gush out. He was curt to her, abstracted and even irritable. He had stopped his light-hearted banter, he had given up cracking jokes, and there were longer silences between them. No matter what Rebecca said or did, she couldn't seem to make a dint in the blackness of his mood.

At first, she had blamed his change of behaviour on the day they had caught sight of three planes flying to the north of them. Each time they had heard the roar of an engine, she had seen his eyes light up in anticipation, his hand shading his face as he stared into the sky, only to watch the small shapes shrink into dots and then vanish beyond the horizon. He had shown a rare display of temper at the disappearance of the third plane, throwing the fishing rod down on to the ground, cursing as he did so and then hobbling off into the woods. He had emerged an hour later, picked up the rod and started fishing again, all without uttering a single word. She could understand his anger and frustration then, she thought. It had been an exceedingly discouraging day.

But his usual optimism hadn't returned, and she wondered if it were due to the way the days were shortening. When they had first crashed, the days had been more than twenty hours long with sunrise at about three o'clock in the morning and sunset at eleven at night. Now, dawn didn't come until an hour later and the sun went down at ten o'clock. It was a visible reminder that time was passing by and that, although they were still in the middle of the summer, fall was approaching with a fearsome rapidity. Fall meant cold weather; winter meant snow and blizzards. They both knew that they weren't going to be able to survive much past the end of August when the days would be only fifteen hours long and the nights would be freezing. If they weren't rescued by then, they would have to find their own way back to civilisation. For a while, Rebecca assumed that this was the burden on Guy's mind. His leg was not healing as well as it should, and he had developed a slight limp. She knew that he was worried about his ability to walk out of their camp and hike the miles necessary to reach the Dempster Highway.

Then, there was the shortage of food, a subject which concerned Rebecca as well. They were, for all intents and purposes, slowly starving. Their diet lacked carbohydrates and fats now that the candy was gone, and they faced a constant struggle to have a decent supply of protein. Both of them fished for long hours at a time, but it required ten or more fish on a daily basis to give them even a minimum number of calories for survival. Rebecca foraged every day for plants, but the roots, leaves and stalks never seemed to provide enough sustenance. She knew that they wouldn't die from actual starvation, but they would suffer from various kinds of mineral deprivation and the lack of a balanced diet. Already Guy was showing evidence of malnutrition. He had never been heavy, but he had had a strong, muscular physique. Now, he seemed to grow leaner by the day. Rebecca could see every bone in his spine and his shoulders were no longer so broad. It was ironic, she thought, that although she was presumably of the weaker sex, it was apparent that she would survive far better than Guy. Her fat had saved her and was still supplying her with endurance and energy. Ultimately, her condition would equal his but, for the moment, she was stronger and healthier, and she wondered if that galled him.

Even given the fact that their situation would have sent anyone into a dizzying depression, Rebecca worried that she was the burr that had worked its way underneath Guy's skin. She analysed their conversations, sifted through her words and wondered if she had offended him. He seemed at his blackest when they were together and that hurt her far more than she would have expected. She tried hard to smile and be pleasing, but nothing softened him. The Guy whose leg she had set, who had sung forty bars of a raucous drinking song through severe pain and joked even at the bleakest moments seemed to have disappeared altogether. In his place was a man with a constant grimness around his mouth and a look of disapproval in his dark eyes whenever he glanced at her. Not that his head turned to her very often. Rebecca had noticed that he rarely looked at her, that he deliberately seemed to avoid her eyes. She was beginning to think that Guy hated her, and this upset her so much that old feelings returned with an intensity she hadn't felt since the crash; despair, depression, a desire to withdraw, and severe hunger pangs that made her grit her teeth and break out in a sweat. She began to dream of candy again, of cartons of ice-cream, of pies and cakes sitting on a bakery shelf.

Although she wasn't a crier, Rebecca couldn't prevent sudden tears from welling in her eyes. She tried to blame them on hunger, on fatigue, on the burning rays of the sun, but she knew that they originated out of Guy's rejection of her. She hadn't realised how important their camaraderie had been to her until it no longer existed. For the first time in her life, a man had treated her as an equal, as a person worthy of respect, and Rebecca had thrived on the attention. She had thought that he accepted her for who she was and unfortunately had come to believe, with all the gullibility of one who has been frequently hurt and disappointed, that Guy actually liked her and, perhaps, even cared for her a bit.

The tears threatened to spill over as she lifted the axe and brought it down over and over again in a repetitive motion. Why, she wondered, had she thought that Guy would be any different from the other men she had known? She knew how men felt about fat women; they didn't like them, they were threatened by them, they were *disgusted* by them. Rebecca had seen herself reflected in too many male eyes over the years. Even the fact that she had shed so many pounds didn't allow Rebecca to think of herself as a slender woman. The memory of her former self was too recent; the outline of her fat clung to her like a constant shadow. She knew that Guy wouldn't be able to forget what she had been; shapeless and round, ugly and grotesque. She had had no neck, a belly that had merged with her breasts into one gargantuan lump, thighs like tree stumps, calves so big that she hadn't ever been able to buy boots.

The axe went up and down as Rebecca mentally chanted the litany of her sins and blinked back the tears that swam in her eyes. She refused to cry. Hadn't she survived all those years, those horrible adolescent years, without crying? She wasn't going to start now because another man didn't like her. Guy was just one of a number of men, an insignificant link in a long chain of rejections. Rebecca had always been too proud to cry; she had turned to her refrigerator, the grocery shelves, the candy counter in the corner store rather than let a tear drop. Not even her father had caused her to cry, or her mother. The axe slammed down into the log she held in her hand and was raised again high in the air. And Guy wasn't going to prove the exception to the rule. She wasn't going to give him a glimpse at the misery he had caused; she would be damned if she would ever let him see her cry.

It happened so fast that Rebecca almost didn't have a chance to save her hand. The log slipped, the axe fell and missed her fingers by a hair's breadth, its blade slamming down into the stump, its handle quivering with the impact. Inadvertently, she screamed as if the axe had truly sliced through her hand, had actually severed off her fingers instead of sliding so close to them that she could still feel the sensation of metal against skin. As the scream echoed through the stillness of the trees, she stood stock-still and stared down with horror at the fallen log, the now innocent axe and her own trembling hand. She had been so involved with her thoughts and so confident of her chopping abilities that she had grown careless. She had done just what Guy had warned her not to do and had come one centimetre short of losing her fingers. The shaking in her hand spread up her arm to her shoulder and she clasped her hands to her chest and clenched her eyes shut as if she could erase the bloody image of what might have happened from her mind's eye.

'Rebecca! Are you all right? Rebecca!'

She hadn't heard Guy's voice or the sound of his footsteps against the rock. Now, she turned towards him and saw the look of concern on his face and the occasional grimace of pain. He was trying to run to her with the support of only one crutch, forcing his injured leg to bear his weight.

'I . . . almost had an accident with the axe.' She lifted her left hand as a demonstration and then hugged it back to her chest. 'I almost cut myself.'

'Are you hurt?' He grabbed her hand, the back of his wrists brushing roughly against her breasts.

'No.'

But it seemed as if Guy hadn't heard her. He was examining her hand, his head bent before her, the dark hair glinting black-brown in the sun. He was wearing jeans that were supposed to be held up by his belt but, because of his lost weight, now hung around his hips. Sweat glinted in the chestnut hairs on his chest and ran in runnels over the well-defined muscles in his abdomen. Rebecca had the insane urge to pull him to her, to told him against her own body, as if she could stop him from getting any leaner, as if she could give him some of her fat for sustenance. She was afraid for him, she discovered, afraid that he would become fragile and lose the essence of masculinity that she had come to admire in him. He was a handsome man who had grown too thin. His cheekbones were so high in his face that the dark eyes were now too deep-set. Lines of strain cut along his mouth and down the ridges from his nose. He seemed to be held together by a flame that burned too intensely for his frame. When he looked up at her again, his hands still clenching her fingers, the flame had split in two and flickered angrily in the depths of his eyes.

'How could you?' he demanded.

'Could I what?' she asked, taken aback by the sudden change of tone.

'Take such a damn risk.'

'But I always chop . . .'

'I told you to watch what you were doing.'

His attack caught her unawares and she stared at him. 'I was,' she protested, 'but the log slipped and . . .'

A muscle moved in his jaw. 'Logs don't slip by themselves.'

Rebecca took a shaky breath. 'I was thinking . . . about something,' she confessed, 'and I forgot what I was doing.'

'You could kill yourself, did you know that?' he said accusingly. 'That axe is a weapon, not a toy.'

He was still holding her hand and clenching it so tightly between his fingers that she felt as if the bones would break. 'I'm usually so careful.'

'Usually,' he said, mimicking her tone. 'Usually isn't enough, Rebecca. I've told you that.'

'I know,' she replied miserably. 'I promise that I'll . . .'

'It only takes once. One slip and you could have lost your hand. Then, where would we be?'

So that was it, Rebecca realised. Guy wasn't concerned about her or her hand or her pain, but of their survival. It was his motto, wasn't it? All for one, and one for all. 'I'm sorry,' she said tonelessly, pulling her hand away from his. 'I'll never do it again.'

'I'll split the logs from now on.'

'But I . . .'

'No.'

'It was only one small mistake,' she pleaded. 'There's no reason . . .'

'I said that I'll do it from now on.' He ran his fingers wearily through his hair as he leaned against the crutch.

'Guy, please.' The tears had come back in full force and shimmered in her blue eyes. *Please,* she wanted to say, *I can't handle you when you're like this, when your approval of me has slipped away and your hatred assaults me like a physical blow.* But she said nothing, only lifting her hand to her breast in a motion of entreaty.

He glanced at the shadow that her fingers cast on the creamy swell of her breasts and then looked away as if the sight of her body was distasteful to him. 'Start up the fire,' he said flatly. 'I've caught a couple of catfish.'

Rebecca watched him hobble away, watched the play of muscles in his back and along his upper arms and willed herself not to cry. But, for once, her will-power failed her. She had lived through a lot worse, she thought in despair, as the tears began. There had been her parents' divorce, the war that had raged through their house, and the way she and Tamara had been dragged through every battle, their love used as if it were a pawn in a vicious chess game. There had been the long years living with her mother in a house that seemed to tremble with tension and anger and

resentment. There had been the high-school years
when her school-mates had treated her like an outcast,
and her lonely sojourn in nursing school.

No, she hadn't even cried over that. It was Guy who
had broken down the high wall of her stoicism and her
resolve, leaving her emotions open, raw and vulnerable. She cared; that was the problem. She cared that
Guy found her an object of disgust, that his dislike of
her had so obviously deepened into hatred. She had
let him down; she had grown careless and her irres-
ponsibility threatened their very survival. In a way she
couldn't blame him for his anger, but the force of it
hurt more than anything had ever hurt before. It cut
into the fragile shell of her self-esteem, through her
newly-found confidence and deep into her heart. As
Guy walked towards the promontory, Rebecca stood
there and cried silently, the tears rolling down her
cheeks, gaining speed as they went and falling like a
light rain on to the hands she held out before her, their
palms turned up in a gesture of mute pleading.

As the relationship between Rebecca and Guy took a
nosedive, their surroundings grew ever more idyllic.
The sun shone every day, and there was hardly a
cloud in the sky. The forest seemed to teem with life. A
small herd of caribou came down to drink at the lake
one morning several hundred feet away from their
camp and its presence made Guy groan with frustration. Geese, heron and duck flew overhead and the
underbrush hummed with small animals; rabbit,
squirrels, martens, otter and beaver. Guy devised a
trap that involved stakes and a noose of wire that

Rebecca managed to pull out from the frame of the plane. They captured two squirrels and a porcupine before a fox was caught in it. They heard the thrashing at night but in the morning found the trap empty, two of the stakes broken and the noose presumably still around the animal's neck. The only way they knew it was a fox was because of the chunks of reddish fur that had been caught in the wood.

Guy and Rebecca rarely talked to one another now about anything other than food, shelter and escape. Guy plotted escape routes and decided that they would leave within two or three days. He was now able to put his full weight on his injured leg and, although Rebecca worried that he would grow fatigued from too much walking, he brushed off her concern, saying that anything was better than sitting around and waiting for winter to descend on them. He spent hours calculating food and shelter supplies and set Rebecca to sewing packs out of clothes and canvas. She sat cross-legged in the lean-to, stitching for hours like an old-fashioned tailor.

Their personal conversations were never alluded to, and their earlier intimacy was lost. Rebecca missed those easy moments of talk when bits and pieces of Guy would be revealed. If she added them all up together, she knew more about Guy than she knew about any other man. Not that he had talked about his ex-wife or the other women in his life; he was far too reticent for that, but she knew his likes and dislikes, his pet peeves and his favourite things. Blue was his preferred colour, his father had also been trained as an engineer, he had had a motorcycle at fifteen and got his first car during his second year in college, a second-hand red Mustang that had the habit of stalling whenever he tried to act macho and rev the engine. He hated wearing suits and was allergic to green pepper; his ambition was to have his own exploration firm and he liked science fiction. He confessed to having seen *Star Wars* three times.

Rebecca supposed that he knew the same sort of things about her. She had spent a lot of time talking about the hospital and how much she had disliked the autocratic head nurse, but liked the other nurses and the general ambience. She had told him about Fairfax and what it was like to live in a town so small that everyone knew everyone else. Tamara's escapades had always been good for a laugh, and she could sigh over her youngest sister, Celia, who was so withdrawn and quiet. She was an avid reader and loved a movie that made her cry. She had gone to see *E.T.* three times.

As Guy's plans for escape intensified, Rebecca withdrew into silence. He treated her with indifference and never noticed that she hardly spoke any more. But even if he would have been more receptive, Rebecca would have remained quiet. In the face of his drive and enthusiasm, her own fears seemed fanciful and petty. She was terrified of the unknown and afraid that they would get lost. She trusted Guy's abilities and instincts, but she thought the dangers that faced them were awesome. They still had no real idea of the distance or terrain that lay between their camp and the Mackenzie River. Yet, she had to admit that the alternative, staying and waiting for a plane to spot them, was problematic at best. And any rescue party that had been organised to search for them must have given up hope of success long ago.

Sometimes she wondered about her family and how they had responded to her presumed death. She and Guy had talked about that at one point. Tamara, she thought, would be the saddest because they had always been close. Celia was so quiet that Rebecca hadn't any idea what her reaction could be and, as for her mother . . . well, Martine Clark had always been a cold woman. Rebecca couldn't be sure that she would grieve beyond the period required by social standards. When she had expressed this to Guy, he had been shocked.

'Your mother won't care?' he had asked in astonishment.

'There's no love lost between us.'

'But—your mother,' he protested.

Rebecca had tried to explain without going into detail. It was far too difficult for her to talk about her mother. 'She never liked me, not really . . . I guess we were too much alike. We fought all the time.'

'And your father? What about him?'

'My parents are divorced. I haven't seen him in years.'

Guy had shaken his head in disbelief. 'I can't imagine it.'

'Your family must have been close,' Rebecca said wistfully.

'Well, my parents are still married and they're happy together. I'm their only child.' He gave her a rueful grin. 'My mother thinks the sun rises and sets on me.

It's claustrophobic at times, but I confess that I love all the attention.'

Rebecca felt a pang of sympathy for Guy's parents. 'They must be frantic,' she said, 'not knowing if you're alive or dead.'

Guy grimaced. 'I know. I'd give my right hand to spare them this much pain.'

'Is there anyone else?' Rebecca asked delicately, thinking that there must be another woman. Guy wasn't the sort of man who lived without a woman.

'Jake, a buddy of mine and,' his mouth gave a bitter twist, 'there's Maureen, I suppose.'

'Maureen?'

'My wife.' He corrected himself. 'Soon to be ex-wife.'

Rebecca gave him a quick glance; she had sensed that Guy didn't like talking about his wife. 'She's . . . still in love with you?'

'Hell, no,' Guy had said and then added with his usual touch of black humour, 'She's still the benefici-ary on my will. I hadn't known that I was going to kick the bucket quite so soon.'

The fire that destroyed the lean-to and ruined all Guy's plans broke out the night before they were supposed to leave. Rebecca woke up first, the smoke almost suffocating her. She sat up in bewilderment, her eyes already beginning to water, heard the crackle of flames and felt their heat. Gold and orange lights shimmered in the opening of the lean-to, the colours intensified by the black of the sky beyond. It didn't take much deduction for her to realise that the wind must have shifted during the night, lifting a spark from the fire and blowing it on to the tarp. Guy had taken to building the fire close to the lean-to to ward of the chill that came after sunset.

'Wake up!' Rebecca yelled, shaking Guy's sleeping form and coughing as the smoke caught in her throat. 'We're on fire!'

She saw the startled look on his face in the light of the flames. 'Grab anything you can,' he said, pulling himself upright, 'and then get out of here before the whole place goes up.'

Rebecca filled her arms with the sleeping-bag, two cushions and one of the packs they had planned to take with them when they left. Running through the sheet of flames that spanned the opening of the lean-to took every bit of courage she could muster and, even so, she clenched her eyes shut as she threw herself through it. She emerged unscathed into sweet cool-of-the-night air and took several deep and dragging breaths of it before she noticed that her sleeping-bag was smoking. She threw it to the ground and stamped on it, her bare feet smarting from the heat.

Guy came out with a blanket over one arm and a handful of clothes. Sparks seemed to fly around his head, but he brushed them away as he turned back to the lean-to and dropped the blanket and clothes to the ground.

'What are you doing?' Rebecca asked in alarm as he took a step towards the lean-to, his tall form silhouetted against the orange of the dancing flames.

'I'm going back in.'

'No!' She grabbed his wrist. 'You can't. It's on fire.'

'The rest of our packs are in there.'

'You'll get killed!'

He tried to shake her hand off his wrist. 'Let me go, dammit!'

Rebecca now held on to Guy by the wrist with both hands, terrified by this sudden desperation. His face was in shadow except for the glistening reflection of the fire on its planes and angles. The flames accentuated the high ridge of a cheekbone, the deep orbit of an eye, the grim line of his mouth. He pulled at her, all of his concentration focusing on the fire and the loss of their things; their clothes and the supplies for their escape. Rebecca understood that, for the moment, Guy's reason had vanished before his insane determination to breach the wall of fire and save their belongings. He couldn't bear to watch the flames consume almost everything that they owned, and he tugged again, fiercely trying to break Rebecca's grasp.

'No, you can't go in there,' she yelled over the popping sound of the fire. As she spoke, a flame swirled upwards around one of the lean-to's supporting trees, igniting its leaves into a crackling halo.

Guy struggled against her. 'Let go of me!'

'No!' Rebecca braced herself against the pull of his arm.

'For God's sake! Let go!'

Rebecca didn't answer but grabbed at him, throwing her arm around his bare waist and pulling him towards her. He was barefoot and wearing only jeans. She was in a pair of her old slacks which kept slipping down and a blouse so large that it flapped around her. For a few seconds, they struggled silently, their arms grappling with one another, the force of their motions pushing them backwards and forwards. Guy grunted with the effort to break free of her, and Rebecca was panting with the strain of holding him back. In front of them, the tarp of the lean-to finally collapsed sending up a geyser of sparks and flames, the inferno providing a hellish backdrop to their battle.

They were an unlikely but evenly matched pair. A month and a half earlier Rebecca wouldn't have had a chance of keeping Guy within any kind of restraint, but their lack of food played to her advantage. He was weak, disorientated by the fire and his injured leg could not be counted on for support. She could feel him shifting whenever his heel came down hard on the ground, and knowledge of his vulnerability caused her to hold him even tighter.

'Stop trying to protect me,' Guy muttered through gritted teeth as he tried to unwind Rebecca's arm from around his waist.

'And you stop . . . trying to be the . . . Good Samaritan,' she said, panting.

'Don't you realise that we won't be able to leave tomorrow?'

'You couldn't go with third-degree burns anyway.' She was tall enough to put an arm around his neck and their mouths were within inches of one another.

'I'm going to kill you for this,' he hissed, one hand grabbing on to the wrist of the arm that encircled his neck, the other pushing at her shoulder.

'You can't,' Rebecca said, twisting her fingers in his hair and holding on for dear life. 'You need me.'

'The hell I do.' He yanked his head and then swore at the pain in his scalp.

Rebecca tried to get her breath. 'You couldn't get . . . out of . . . here without me.'

Her hair tumbled out of its tie, the waves swirling around her head in the wind. A strand whipped against Guy's mouth, and he let go of her arm to pull it away from his lips. Rebecca took immediate advantage of his lapse to wrap one arm tighter round his waist, tuck a heel behind his injured leg and, using the leverage of her weight, push him over. They fell together to the ground on top of the sleeping-bag, cushions and clothes, Rebecca sprawled over Guy, one leg over his, her cheek against the slickened skin of his bare chest, the tangled mass of her hair resting on his skin. She could hear the rapid tempo of his heartbeat and feel the swift up and down movement of his chest as he sought to regain his breath.

They lay there, both spent from the exertion, the hissing and popping sounds of the fire filling the silence. Rebecca had lost her slacks in the struggle, and she could feel the heat of the fire against one of her bared thighs. But the flames were dying now and they had consumed the lean-to and its contents, the two slender trees which had formed the shelter's support and the fence Guy had built around the opening. Fortunately, they had cleared the ground for yards around the lean-to; otherwise, the fire would have spread into the brush and forest, destroying everything within miles. There was a small crash as one of the trees collapsed and, below her, Guy shifted.

Rebecca rolled off him as she recalled his anger and

irritation of the week before. She steeled herself for his attack, knowing that he would not take her mastery of him lightly. 'Are you all right?' she asked.

His easy tone surprised her. 'I didn't know you took judo.'

'I don't.'

He pulled himself upright on one elbow and stared at her. 'You don't?'

Rebecca shook her head. 'Or karate either.'

'Rebecca, it would have soothed my ego considerably if you'd admitted to even one, small lesson. This is a TKO.'

'TKO?'

'Technical knock-out.' He gave an exaggerated sigh. 'I guess you never took boxing either.'

'No.'

There was a short silence while Guy turned his head and looked to the fire. 'And everything's gone, I suppose.'

'Except for the things we came out with.'

He looked at her then. 'Thanks for saving my life. I went a little crazy back there.'

'Oh,' Rebecca was taken aback by the humility of the apology, 'it was nothing.'

Guy laughed then, a full laugh that seemed to fill the enormous upturned bowl of the sky that hung over them. Thousands of stars winked in its blackness as she stared upwards, amazed at the incongruity of Guy's good humour. They had just lost most of their clothing, their shelter and their tools, and he was laughing. It was as if the burden of problems and responsibilities had become so heavy that he had just flicked it off the way a duck will flick the drops of water off its wings and then fly off, free and light and easy.

'Wrestling a full-grown man to the ground is nothing?' he asked.

'You have an injured leg.'

'And you took advantage of it.'

Rebecca cleared her throat. 'It seemed the right thing to do at the time.'

Guy threw his arms around her, pulled her back down against his chest and laughed again. 'Have I ever told you that I wouldn't want to be marooned with anyone else but you?'

Rebecca could hardly believe her ears as she tucked her head into the curve of his shoulder. 'What?'

'You set legs, chop wood, catch frogs, eat raw fish and wrestle like a pro. Hell, Rebecca, I can think of half a dozen guys who wouldn't be so useful.'

'Oh.' It was a back-handed compliment, Rebecca thought, being compared to other men.

Guy caught the disappointment in her voice. 'And you're sexy, too,' he added with a smile.

This so alarmed her that she tried to wiggle out of his grasp, but his arm tightened around her, and he pulled her closer to him. 'Don't,' she said.

'Why not?'

'Because I don't like it when you . . . please don't say things like . . .'

'Things like you're sexy and beautiful and have a lovely body?'

'Guy!'

'I've noticed, you know.'

'I don't . . .' she almost choked on the words '. . . have a lovely body.'

'Listen, Nurse Clark, you are curvaceous and voluptuous and you've got one hell of a birthday suit. Take it from an expert.'

The fire was slowly subsiding, but it still crackled in front of them and the heat it gave off was enough to warm Rebecca's bare legs. 'How do you know?' she asked suspiciously.

'A small confession—I watched you bathing one day.'

'You didn't!'

'Scout's honour. It was, admittedly, one of the more rotten things I've done, but it gave me such immense pleasure that I couldn't help it. Rebecca, you were fat when we first crashed but, believe me, you don't even look like the same woman.'

'But . . . I am inside.'

Guy let go of her then and, propping himself up on an elbow again, looked down at the pale oval of her face. 'And what does that mean?'

'I'm a fat woman disguised in a thin body.' She tried to explain it better. 'I don't *feel* any different.'

Lightly, he ran one finger down the bared length of her leg, from the edge of her panties to the soft curve of her knee. 'Yes, you do.'

Rebecca swallowed at the sensations that his feathery touch aroused in her, a shivery sort of warmth that ran along the nerve endings on her skin. She pushed his hand away and attempted to turn the conversation in a different direction. 'I don't understand you,' she said. 'You've been so . . .'

'So grouchy,' he returned drily.

'Yes, and now that we've lost everything, you've suddenly become happy again. I can't figure you out.'

He ran his fingers through the tumbled thickness of his hair and, sighing, stared back at the glowing embers of the fire. 'Everything was getting to me, I guess. I knew I was losing ground physically; I could feel myself getting weaker every day. I got desperate thinking about staying here one more day, trying to get food and praying for aeroplanes to fly overhead. So I decided that we'd have to go, but the truth was that I don't have any real idea where we are or even if we'd be heading in the right direction. I just assumed that those planes were flying along the Dempster Highway and that, if we headed north, we'd hit it. But if I was wrong, we'd be heading north into nowhere. And it isn't easy to cross muskeg. I didn't say anything, but I could see the knowledge in your eyes. You knew I was flailing around in the dark.'

'I wasn't sure,' she said. 'You seemed so confident.'

'And then my leg's been acting up, and I knew you were right about the walking. I don't know if I could go a mile without it giving out on me.'

'I worried about it.'

'I know you did,' he confessed. 'And I worried about it and everything else. The rational part of me fought against leaving, the emotional part of me knew I couldn't stand one more day. I was constantly torn, knowing that if I failed, I would be responsible for your death and mine.'

Rebecca felt a pang of guilt. Why hadn't she tried harder to understand what Guy had put himself through? She had never questioned his decisions or helped him talk through his problems. By remaining passive, she had foisted the burden of responsibility on his shoulders and it had not rested there easily. No wonder he had frowned so often and his voice had been quick with anger.

'I'm sorry,' she said.

'Why?'

'I should have discussed the trip with you and asked more questions. We could have been responsible together.'

Guy smiled then and flicked her nose with one finger. 'You were one of my worst problems,' he teased.

'Me?'

'Call it a delicate matter of frustration without the relief of cold showers.'

'Cold . . . ?' Guy's innuendo suddenly became clear to her. 'Oh.'

'Oh,' he mimicked. 'Is that all you can say?'

'I didn't know.'

'I meant it when I said you were sexy.'

Rebecca shook her head. 'It's not me,' she said. 'It's because we've been here so long and . . .' She tried to find the proper word to describe Guy's condition without sounding crude.

'And I'm as horny as hell,' he finished bluntly, his mouth widened in a grin.

She felt the blush heat her cheeks with a greater warmth than the fire. 'Something like that,' she mumbled.

He turned serious then and lifted her chin with his

hand so that their eyes met. 'At first, I thought it was only that. After all, I'm not particularly fond of abstinence. But my feeling went beyond just physical needs. Rebecca, I wouldn't be satisfied by just any woman. I'm not that sort of a man who falls for anything in skirts.'

'Why . . . didn't you say something?'

'Because you were so damn shy of me. You jerked away whenever my hand brushed yours; you looked in another direction whenever our glances crossed. How could I admit that I'd seen you naked and wanted to go to bed with you? I had the feeling you'd take off into the woods and I'd never see you again.'

Rebecca had never really had a man tell her that he found her attractive and lovely and sensual. The words made her feel dizzy as if he were spinning her around and the world had become a swiftly-moving kaleidoscopic blur. She blinked and blushed again. 'I probably would have,' she said. 'Taken off into the woods, I mean. I've never . . . slept with a man. No one wanted me, I was too fat.'

He was silent for a second and then gently brushed a strand of hair off her temple and tucked it behind her ear. 'Rebecca, we may never get out of here alive.'

'I know.'

'And the only thing we have is each other.'

She felt suddenly breathless. 'I know that, too.'

'We like one another and we're both consenting adults.' Guy paused and Rebecca waited in a delicious, trembling anticipation. She wondered how he would make his proposal to her. Would it be lighthearted and humorous? That would be typically Guy.

Or would he take a more serious tack? She had never had a man ask her to sleep with him, and she relished the moment for all it was worth, her eyes on Guy's face, on the stillness she saw there. But when he spoke, it was with such a bitter grimness that she was taken aback and shocked out of the sweet web that his words had spun.

'Will you sleep with me, Rebecca,' he asked, 'before we die in this godforsaken place?'

CHAPTER FIVE

THE words resonated in her ears—*die, die in this godfor-saken place*. They made a shiver run down her spine as the truth of it came home to her. With so many of their belongings burnt to cinders, they really had no way of leaving. And, if they were never spotted by the occasional low-flying plane, they would die as surely as if a gun were being put to their heads, its trigger cocked and ready to fire. They would die of malnutrition, or disease, or simply freeze to death when winter set in with its bitter winds, snow and ice. They weren't equipped to last beyond the Arctic's brief fall, not without heavy clothes, a decent shelter and a good food supply. The odds had always been against them before, but fate's latest blow had almost totally tipped the scales in favour of nature, and Rebecca had already learned that nature was a creature of cruel whimsy and indifferent caprice.

Guy's proposal was pragmatic, unromantic and hardly sensual. It bore no relation to the movies Rebecca had seen and sighed over or the books she had read where heroines were swept off their feet and into the beds of the heroes. It was more like a pact, an agreement, between two people who were arranging as best they could for the future. Guy had laid out the situation with great clarity and Rebecca knew what she was being asked to do; to weigh a certain amount of pleasure against an uncertain death. He wasn't talking about love, and the concept of commitment was ludicrous; he was merely suggesting that they enjoy one another in the short time left to them. It was a relationship that would end either with death or rescue, and the latter was a possibility that seemed more and more remote.

Of course, she was going to say yes; Rebecca knew that. Now that she admitted the truth to herself, she knew that she had wanted to sleep with Guy for a long time. She was attracted to him, physically attracted in a way she hadn't been with any other man. She had never permitted herself to feel the sensations of arousal; she had always clamped down on them, shoved them away, knowing that no man would reciprocate her feelings. But she hadn't been able to do that with Guy; he had somehow managed to penetrate her defences and, for weeks, she had longed to touch him. In their struggle before the fire, when she had grappled with him, her hands on his skin and hair, she had become aware of a warmth, a quickened movement of blood through her veins and pulse that had nothing to do with exertion. It arose in the centre of her, an uncurling of desire that reached in all directions, heightening every sensation, and turning her slowly to liquid.

'Rebecca?'

She blinked. 'Sorry, I was thinking.'

'Look, that was a lousy way to ask you.' Guy gave a small, embarrassed laugh. 'I can do better than that.'

'No,' she said sombrely, 'I don't mind.'

There was already a hint of light in the dark sky, a

harbinger of dawn, and it allowed her to see Guy's face more clearly. He looked weary and drawn, harsh lines cutting from his nose to his mouth, and Rebecca thought she had never seen a man who looked less like he wanted to make love. He had the appearance of someone who desperately needed hours of sleep.

'You're too tired anyway,' she added.

'Too tired for what?'

'To . . . have sex.'

He appraised her. 'Do you need some time to think it over?'

'No,' she said.

'I see.' He seemed to find her amusing because he was smiling now. 'Care to tell me what conclusion you've come to?'

'Oh!' Rebecca had been so sure and so convinced of her answer that she had assumed that Guy knew all along what it would be. She tensed suddenly and her mouth went dry. 'Well, yes . . . I mean I will . . . sleep with you, that is.'

He lay back and stared up at the sky, really grinning now. 'You know something, Rebecca. I just made the most unromantic one-liner of my life and you managed to trump it. I've never had a woman tell me that I was too tired before.'

'Well, you are.'

Her voice had taken on a professional tone and he grinned again. 'Ever the nurse.'

Considering what they were talking about, the conversation had taken an odd turn. Rebecca had just agreed to make love with him, but Guy had not taken her in his arms, kissed her or acted as though her decision was important at all. Instead, he was teasing her and laughing a bit at himself. Suddenly she smiled back at him, realising why he had undercut the heavy drama of the moment. In addition to the fact that this would be a first time for her, their decision to sleep with one another and the reasons for it were so serious and so frightening that neither of them would have been able to perform well. Rebecca knew that she would be stiff and awkward, and the act practical and cold-blooded. She wasn't so naïve that she didn't understand that the atmosphere between them was too uncomfortable for satisfactory lovemaking. It was with gratitude for Guy's perceptive sympathy that she slipped into the spirit of the moment.

'I wouldn't want you to fall asleep in the middle of things,' she smiled. 'I told you, I've never slept with a man before and I want a . . .'

'A good and competent performance.'

'Right.'

He gave her an arch look. 'You don't sound like a woman without any experience.'

She shrugged lightly. 'Tamara's told me a lot.'

'Your sister's had a lot of affairs?'

'A dozen at least.'

'Why?' Guy yawned then and she saw his eyes flutter.

'Why? You mean why has she had so many lovers?' He nodded. 'Because she has this philosophy about men. She doesn't trust them. You see, my father was a very untrustworthy person. He lied to my mother and he lied to us.' A tinge of bitterness entered her voice. 'He was very unreliable and would never show

up when he was supposed to. He missed my grade
school graduation and . . .' Rebecca had been watching the dying embers of the fire as she spoke, but now
she glanced down at Guy and saw that his eyes were
shut and that he was fast asleep. She was right; he had
been exhausted. He no longer had the strength he had
once had or the stamina. The shock of the fire and his
struggle against her had worn him out.

Rebecca rearranged the cushions beneath them as
best as she could and, unzipping the sleeping-bag all
around its perimeter, pulled it over the both of them.
She was starting to get chilled herself and, when she
lightly touched her finger to Guy's chest, his skin was
cold. She tucked a pair of Guy's jeans under her head
and snuggled up against him. Within minutes, she too
had fallen asleep and the sun, when it rose above the
trees, caught them in a pose of contented stillness, its
pale gold and rose rays washing them with the early
morning light. Beyond them, the lake glittered like a
vast blanket encrusted with jewels until a fish leaped
high, breaking the surface, twisting silver in the air as
it fell backwards and sending the water into a miniature cascade, a spray of drops as multi-coloured as a
rainbow.

Rebecca woke with the unexpected sensation of sun
directly on her closed eyelids and the unwanted feeling of water dripping on her chin. She opened her eyes
and stared into Guy's face. He was kneeling beside
her, dressed only in his jeans, water drops making sinuous trails down the bronzed skin of his
chest. It was obvious that he had been washing in the

lake. He looked rested and refreshed, his hair damp and combed back, his dark eyelashes spiky and wet.

She stretched and yawned. 'Are you crazy?' she asked. 'The water must be freezing.'

'I like to be clean.'

She remembered the fire then and glanced at the site where their lean-to had been. There was nothing there but blackened logs and cinders. 'Do we have any soap?'

'The pack you dragged out last night had the tooth-brushes, the comb and soap.'

'That's good,' she answered with a yawn.

'Sorry I couldn't shave though.' He rubbed a hand over the roughness of his chin. 'Most women prefer it.'

'I'm used to it,' she said. 'You haven't shaved every day anyway.'

His dark eyes held a sudden gleam. 'But today is different.'

'Why?' Then she gave him a startled glance. 'You mean . . . now?'

'Well,' he drawled. 'You did say yes.'

Rebecca felt a sudden panic. 'But it's . . . full day-light,' she protested, gesturing at the wide expanse of blue sky.

'The birds don't care.'

'But suppose a plane flies over and . . .'

Guy interrupted her with a shout of laughter. 'And sees us? After all those planes that have gone right over our heads without spotting a thing? Rebecca, sweetheart, if all rescue would have taken was making love to you in the middle of the day, I would have done it long ago.'

She pulled the sleeping-bag up to her chin, her blue eyes wide, her auburn hair falling in tangles on to her shoulders as she stared at him. For a moment, she was tempted to deny her acquiescence of the night before or tell him that she had changed her mind. The idea of making love was frightening enough; the thought of doing it in broad daylight was positively terrifying. Then she remembered that this was Guy who had seen her at her worst. And he was the first man she had ever known who really seemed to understand her and to whom she could speak honestly and frankly. 'I'm . . . scared,' she finally admitted.

His smile vanished and, sliding down beside her, he took her in his arms. 'I think you're lovely, Rebecca. I told you that before.'

'But maybe you'll be disappointed.'

'I don't think so,' he said.

'Guy . . .'

He kissed her softly on the lips. 'We're going to take it easy and slow and gentle. And if you get scared and want to stop, just say so, all right?'

She swallowed and nodded her head.

He reflected for a moment and then added, 'Not that I would, I suppose.'

'Would what?' she asked in bewilderment.

'Stop.' He gave her a rueful smile. 'I've wanted you for a long time.'

But Guy was as good as his word, and Rebecca's initiation into lovemaking was slow, languorous and thoroughly satisfying. He began with kisses, light kisses that touched her closed eyes, the shell of her ear, the corner of her mouth. He pulled away the sleeping-bag as his lips traced a line from the tip of her chin down to the juncture of her throat where her shoulder-blades winged outwards. Rebecca felt only the softest brush when he slid her blouse open and exposed her breasts to the sun. Her head was back, her hair thrown over his arm. She didn't dare open her eyes; she didn't dare move, afraid that if she did, it would break the spell, the lovely, sensuous magic that he was working on her.

Her breath came faster as his lips touched the apex of one breast, causing the nipple to rise upwards as if it sought the damp warmth of his mouth. But she couldn't help gasping when he took it between his teeth and tugged on it slightly. 'You like that?' he asked and then, not waiting for an answer, licked the nipple, the areola around it and then the heavy curve of her breast. A flame seemed to leap from his tongue to her skin, a hot flame that made her arch upwards, raising her breasts to him in invitation.

Guy laughed then, opened her blouse further and ran his tongue down a line from the middle of her breasts to her navel.

'Ticklish?' he asked.

Rebecca still didn't open her eyes. 'Yes,' she said breathlessly.

'If you don't mind then, I'll skip it and go on to other places.'

Her breath caught when he slipped her panties down her thighs, past her knees and over her ankles. He tossed them away and then returned to her side.

She felt the cool length of him against her and realised that he had also taken off his jeans. She opened her eyes to find him looking at her.

'I wondered when you were going to get curious,' he said, smiling.

Rebecca tried to salvage a thread of dignity; she gave a small cough as she cleared her throat. 'I've seen a lot of naked men.'

'Aroused naked men? What kind of hospital *did* you work in, Nurse Clark?'

'Oh, Guy.' She couldn't help laughing. 'Is this how people make love?'

'How?'

'Talking and laughing?'

'Did you expect silence and lots of heavy breathing?'

A small, unexpected tremble ran through her. 'I didn't know what to expect.'

Guy caught the tremble and pulled him up against her so that their bodies met; at the chest, hips, toes. She felt his hardness against her stomach and it was far from cool. The skin there was hot, burning. 'Hey, you asked for a good performance. I was just trying to be accommodating. You want me to cut the comedy routine and go for the serious stuff.'

Her eyes were enormous, blue as the sky as she looked up at him. 'I want you to make love to me.'

Guy was no longer bantering. 'Not afraid any more?'

'No,' she whispered.

He kissed her then, deeply and warmly, their tongues meeting, touching slipping past one another as he sank back with her against the cushions. Over their heads, squirrels chattered as they scampered up the trunks of trees, a hawk swooped in the sky and a slight breeze lifted up the surface of the water, causing it to lap against the beach and the edge of the promontory. The midday sun blazed down as they twisted together, their legs entwined, their skin tones white and gold and bronze in the dappled shade. Rebecca could not get enough of Guy; her hands ran down his back to the hard muscles of his buttocks, over their curve to the strength of his thighs. His breath came in gasps when she stroked him, and in turn, he touched her, deep between her legs, where the sensitive skin was warm, wet and silky.

She ached for him; she burned for him; her body seemed to flow for him. Rebecca had never experienced desire that was so strong or overwhelming. Her head twisted from side to side as his fingers played upon her, and she said his name over and over again, not knowing that she spoke, not knowing that her voice urged him to go on, to continue, to please, please not stop. He knew exactly where to touch her and with what sort of pressure; she opened to him like a blossom, petals wide, scarlet with desire. When he finally slid into her, his hands parting her legs for his entrance, the sense of fulfilment was wonderful, all-encompassing.

She moaned as he pulled her up to him, his hands tight on her buttocks, and she clenched his shoulders with her fingers, her nails digging into his skin. They moved in an entranced unison, oblivious to everything but the motion between them, the slow and then increasing pace, the deep thrusting. Rebecca squeezed her eyes tight as an intense, focused heat seemed to spin her upwards into a dizzying, golden spiral. His hands slid between them , stroked her again and she suddenly bit his shoulder in the sudden ecstasy, at the incredible sensation of release as she fell over the edge and sank deeper . . . deeper . . . into a warm and pulsating blackness.

Guy shuddered above her and then lay still, his head resting on her shoulder, his chest heaving. For a few minutes, they rested and then Rebecca opened her eyes and felt the tears seep out of their sides to run down her temples into her hair. She cried silently for happiness, for the delight of having a man within her and for the years that she had been so alone and so desolate. She had never known the power of sex; she had never even been aware of the passion her body was capable of producing. She had drowned every instinct and desire in ugly, pasty flesh, burying herself alive in her own fat.

Guy shifted, his face against her hair. 'You smell smoky,' he whispered and then, feeling the dampness at her temple, lifted his head. 'Are you all right?'

Rebecca smiled tremulously. 'I'm fine,' she said.

'Disappointed?' he asked.

She shook her head. 'No.'

'Neither was I.' He sighed, a luxuriant, pleasure-sated sigh and, putting his lips to a tear that was wending its way past her eyebrow, spoke the words again, his lips moving against her skin, 'Neither was I.'

*   *   *

Rebecca always thought of the next four days as the happiest of her life. It didn't seem to matter that they had to spend two of them chopping trees so that the tail end of the plane could be brought to the ground and used as a shelter, or that they no longer had the utensils for cooking or eating, or that they barely had enough clothes to keep them covered. She found that she didn't even care about the steady diet of fish and roots, the way her back hurt from chopping or the constant low-grade urge of hunger that had plagued her ever since the crash. Nothing mattered except Guy and their lovemaking and the hours they spent together talking. It was as if the walls they had both erected around themselves had evaporated into thin air. They talked about their childhoods, their adolescence, their parents and their feelings. Rebecca had thought she knew Guy fairly well, but her information had been gained from the façade he had shown to the world; the decisiveness, the humour, the hint of a devil-may-care attitude. The man within was different; he was sensitive, caring, loving and unhappy about the past.

'I don't know why my marriage went on the rocks,' he said one afternoon after they had made love. They were lying in the shade of a tree, Rebecca in Guy's arms, her foot slowly massaging his calf. He was growing ever thinner, and his leanness was the one cloud that marred the happiness on her horizon. She was worried about him; she circumspectly ate less so that he could eat more, but their calorific intake was simply insufficient for his needs. And their diet was so bland and boring that she could understand why he didn't seem to have any appetite. There were times when she thought she could never face another fish again.

'You said you were incompatible.'

He ran his fingers through his hair. 'What does that mean really? That we didn't get along? That our personalities conflicted? It wasn't true. Maureen wasn't hard to get along with. She's basically a nice person. It was just that I didn't care for her any more.'

'You drifted apart.'

A look of frustration passed over his face. 'We both had jobs that we liked; we'd bought a nice house and had a lot of expensive things, but one day I realised that we had *nothing*, no communication, no affection, no love. We were like a pair of strangers who ate dinner together and slept in the same bed.'

Rebecca couldn't comprehend the vehemence in his voice. 'Guy, that happens to a lot of married couples. People change and their partners don't; they grow away from one another; they develop different interests.'

'You don't understand,' he said. 'I fell out of love . . . just like that.' And he snapped his fingers in demonstration.

'Maybe you didn't love her in the first place,' Rebecca suggested.

'Maybe I don't know how to love anyone,' he said in a low voice.

She twisted in his arms and looked up at him. 'What do you mean?'

'I thought I loved Maureen; I was crazy about her and then . . . then the feeling vanished.'

'Because it wasn't love,' she repeated.

'Rebecca, you're not getting it.'

'Getting what?'

He ran a hand over her hair, lifted up a strand and put it to his lips. 'It was me, don't you see? She still cared for me and I hurt her. I was the one who was fickle; I was the one who wasn't . . . steadfast.' Guy grimaced. 'What an old-fashioned word.'

'You mean you slept with other women before you were separated from Maureen?'

He tugged on the strand of hair until she gave a small sound of pain. 'You've got sex on the brain, lady.'

She gave him a teasing look. 'I wonder why.'

He grinned at her. 'It must be because you like my . . .'

Rebecca quickly put her hand over his lips. 'I can always tell when you're about to get crude, Mr McLaren,' she said, and then laughed as he licked her palm.

Guy pulled her hand away from his mouth. 'Don't go prim on me. You liked it when I was 'crude' about fifteen minutes ago.'

She snuggled back up to him. 'Mmmm,' she purred. 'I did, didn't I?'

He grew serious then. 'Do you see what I'm getting at?' he asked.

'Just because your feeling about Maureen didn't last, doesn't mean you can't love anyone. Maybe the real thing hasn't hit you yet.'

'You think there's a real thing?'

Did she? Rebecca wasn't sure whether she did or

not. She had never fallen in love with anyone in her life, and she had watched the so-called love of her parents disintegrate into bitter brawling. She knew that she was developing strong feelings about Guy, but she hesitated to put the label 'love' on them. Who was she to set herself up as an expert? Until a few days earlier, she hadn't even known what it was like to have a man put his arms around her. She was a novice, a rank beginner when it came to the relationships between men and women. 'I don't know,' she finally said. 'I've only read about it.'

He was silent, absent-mindedly twisting her hair around a finger and staring towards the lake.

'Well, did you?' she asked.

'Did I what?'

'Sleep around before you and Maureen were separated?'

He glanced at her with a smile. 'Why do you want to know?'

Rebecca could have responded with a flirtatious or teasing remark, but instead, she said in a serious tone, 'I wouldn't have thought you were the type.'

'Conservative, am I?'

'No, not exactly. It just wouldn't have been an honourable thing to do.'

He laughed then and tugged on her hair once again. 'I've never been called honourable before.'

'But you were, weren't you?'

'I was so damned honourable,' he confessed ruefully, 'that I was too embarrassed to tell my friends.'

*   *   *

If Guy talked about his marriage, Rebecca talked about her fat and her family. She told him what it was like to be a compulsive eater and how she had hated herself. She described what it was like to live in a house where the parents no longer spoke to one another and used the children as message bearers. Celia had withdrawn into silence, Tamara had become more and more eccentric and wild, and she had grown addicted to food, stuffing herself with anything and everything when the relations between her mother and father had grown so bad that it had seemed the house might blow up in an explosion fuelled by anger, jealousy, bitterness and hatred.

'So that's why you wanted to know if I'd been sleeping around when Maureen and I were still together,' Guy said. 'Your father was running around with other women.'

Rebecca sat down on a tree stump and let the axe fall out of her almost lifeless fingers. Cutting the plane down out of the trees was a decision that both she and Guy had agreed upon. They needed shelter and, now that his leg was better, he could help her with the chopping. But it was an enormous undertaking because the ailerons was wide and there were at least twelve trees supporting the plane, some of them large and heavy. And they had had to chop carefully; they wanted the plane to slide forward on to the promontory rather than fall to one side or the other. And if it went backwards into another set of trees, all their work would have been done in vain.

'I don't think my father had ever been faithful,' she replied thoughtfully, sweeping her hair off her forehead and feeling the perspiration on her skin. It was so hot in the midday sun that she had almost given up on clothes, wearing only a pair of panties and a torn-up piece of blouse around her breasts. Guy had cut off the legs on a pair of jeans and used the fabric as suspenders to hold up his newly-made shorts. He had grown so thin, his jeans wouldn't stay up any more. It was too bad, Rebecca had thought, that Sandra's suitcase had burned up. At this point, both of them would have fitted into her clothes.

'Then why are you so bitter about your mother?' Guy asked, taking the axe and starting to chop.

Rebecca watched the long sinewy muscles in his arm as he raised the axe and brought it down, the ringing sound of metal on wood echoing over the lake. 'Because she was so controlling and domineering that sometimes I couldn't blame him. Everything has to be my mother's way. As children, we had to dress in the clothes she liked and behave the way she thought was proper. She didn't treat my father any differently. It's no wonder he rebelled, but I wish . . .' She paused and Guy looked at her.

'Wish what?'

'I wish that he had been different,' Rebecca said slowly, feeling the old, familiar hurt starting to build in her again. She was speaking of events that had occurred thirteen years earlier when she was still a child, but they still had the power to cut her. With the hurt came a sharp pang of hunger, not the insidious ache that accompanied their slow starvation, but the pain she associated with anger, with compulsive eating, with being fat. It was sharp, strong, and insistent, and she knew what it arose from: the memory of her debonair and handsome father standing by the kitchen door and looking down at her as if he wished she didn't exist. 'He couldn't seem to separate his feelings about my mother and his feelings about us. We were all burdens; he was sorry that he'd ever had children. He told me that one day and I ended up eating an entire apple pie, a huge bag of potato chips and a box of Ritz crackers.'

'Did your sisters get fat, too?'

'No, I was the only one. Both Tamara and Celia are skinny as rails.'

'I wonder why you chose that route.'

'I don't know,' Rebecca mused. 'I've never thought about that.'

'It doesn't matter,' he said. 'You're not fat any more.'

Rebecca glanced down at her legs which were stretched out before her. They were long and shapely and tanned, quite lovely if you discounted the occasional mosquito bite and the scratches she had received from running into many thickets in her attempts to find food. No, she wasn't fat any more, and all the exercise; the chopping, the foraging and the swimming, had slimmed her figure into a shape that a model would have been proud of. She wasn't carrying an ounce of extra flesh and, while it made her look quite attractive now, she knew what it meant for the future if they weren't rescued. She was down to the last bit of her own physical resources. As she grew thinner, she would start to look gaunt and, like Guy, her energies would diminish. He couldn't chop as long as she could and, whenever they made love, which was frequently, he fell asleep afterwards. She felt more energised than ever, but the exertion clearly pushed him beyond the limits of his strength. The thought of what the next few weeks would bring was so terrifying that Rebecca pushed it away.

'If we got rescued, I don't know if I could resist the temptation,' she said lightly. 'Think of broiled lobster, dripping in melted butter, garlic bread, brandy alexander pie . . .' She would have gone on, playing the game they had played in the past if Guy hadn't stopped her.

He had put down the axe and come to stand in front of her. 'You'd find the strength to stay thin,' he said. 'You wouldn't want to go back to the way you were.'

'Haven't you heard about dieters?' she asked. 'We play hooky, we obsess about food, we get Big Mac attacks.'

His hands were on her bare shoulders and he shook her a bit. 'I'd hate it if you got heavy again.'

'I'd lose my sex appeal?' she asked playfully. It was easier to tease and flirt with Guy than it was to talk seriously about her weight. Desperate though she was for rescue, Rebecca didn't dare contemplate what would happen when she re-entered society. She was afraid of how she would act when confronted with real food once again.

Guy pulled her up to him. 'I like the woman you've become,' he said, his eyes sombre. 'You were different when we first crashed. You didn't have any confidence; you didn't even think of yourself as female.'

Rebecca skittered away from the dark intent in his

eyes and wrapped her arms around his neck. 'I'm female now,' she said as the fullness of her breasts touched his chest.

Guy buried his face in her hair. 'Mmmmm.'

'And lean and hungry,' she added.

'Not again,' he said in mock-horror.

But she knew that they would make love again. Sex for them was the only outlet they had that did not remind them of where they were and what could become of them. The act was an affirmation of life, of human feeling and of hope. They coupled often and with great urgency, Guy bearing Rebecca down to the ground anywhere; on the beach, on the moss below a tree, on the hard rock of the promontory. And she in turn wanted him with a desperation that was intense and consuming. She stayed close to him; she touched him whenever she could. Despite his thinness, he had not lost one bit of sexual appeal for her, and she clung to him, wanting the ferocity of his lovemaking, begging for it, dreaming about it when she slept. When he was within her, nothing else existed but sensation and pleasure and happiness.

Rebecca wrapped her arms around his neck. 'I want to make love in the lake,' she said.

'The lake?'

'Well, we haven't done it there yet.'

'You'd really be something in a house,' he said. 'You'd want to try the top of the refrigerator.'

'I like variety.'

He nibbled at her ear. 'So I noticed. I think you're trying to cram it in after too many years of abstinence.'

Rebecca had tugged off the hand-made bandeau,

allowing her breasts to sway full and loose, and now she pressed herself against the warmth of his body. 'Guy?'

'Mmmmm?'

'Did you really hate the idea of having children?'

He pushed her away slightly. 'When did I say that?'

'One day when we were stuck in the tent because it was raining. You said that Maureen had wanted children, but you didn't.'

'You think I'm like your father?'

'I . . . don't know.'

'I didn't want Maureen's children,' he emphasised and then suddenly gave her a sharp look. 'Are you trying to tell me that you could get pregnant?'

Rebecca quickly shook her head at the look of horror on his face. 'No, I don't think I could. I haven't had a period since we crashed. That happens sometimes when a woman loses a lot of weight.'

He slid his hands down to the slender curves of her waist. 'Don't scare me like that,' he said and then glanced down at her nipples which were dark-red and swollen to the size of thimbles. 'Have I told you what beautiful breasts you have?'

'Frequently,' she said smiling at him, 'but you can tell me again.'

'You have the best set of mammary glands this side of the Arctic circle.'

'That takes in a lot of territory,' she said in mock-warning.

He bent his head and ran his tongue along her shoulder-blade. 'I've done the research.'

'Really.'

'What's the matter, nurse, can't you take the competition?' His tongue slid down the centre of her chest to the valley between her breasts.

Rebecca gave a soft laugh. 'What competition?' she asked.

Guy straightened up and his gaze went to the huge and empty bowl of the sky, the vast expanse of lake and the wooded forest behind them. 'You have a point,' he admitted. 'You've no competition at all.

The next day, Guy went foraging for food while Rebecca fished. She had the habit when she was sitting at the edge of the promontory and watching their three fishing lines of letting her mind go into neutral. She didn't think about anything but allowed the sound of the water lapping against the shore and the warm rays of the sun lull her into a trance-like state. Therefore, she didn't notice the build-up of clouds on the northern horizon until they had obscured the sun and a cool, gusty breeze lifted her hair off her bare shoulders and chilled her skin.

She glanced up at the sky, saw the dark, swirling clouds and realised that a cold front was coming through. Although they had had days when it rained for hours, most of the time the storms were intense, violent and brief. Rebecca gathered up the rods and ran back to the tail end part of the plane which now provided them with shelter. It was far better than the lean-to had ever been. It was sturdier, drier and not as flammable. She crawled into the open end, scrambled past the torn-up seats and started to pull on extra clothes, a pair of Guy's pants and two shirts. She left jeans and a heavy plaid shirt for Guy, remembering that he had gone out only in shorts.

Thunder crashed overhead and rain began to drum against the top of the plane. The sky had gone quite dark and the air temperature must have dropped ten or fifteen degrees. Shivering from the sudden chill, Rebecca picked up the sleeping-bag and thought of Guy caught out in the storm. She didn't think that he would have gone too far away from the campsite; his leg wasn't that strong. She sat down, her back against a wall and snuggled into the sleeping-bag, tucking her bare toes underneath her. Not even the frame of the plane could keep out the sudden, cold gusts of wind.

Every sound other than the patter of rain or rumble of thunder made Rebecca glance hopefully towards the opening in anticipation of Guy's arrival. After about ten minutes, she started to worry; after twenty minutes she was frantic. She had visions of him hurt and drenched to the skin; she imagined him attacked by a bear or wolf. Perhaps he had fallen and knocked himself out; perhaps he had been standing by a tree and been struck by lightning and . . . the image was so horrifying that Rebecca couldn't sit and wait any longer. The rain seemed to be letting up a bit so she stuck her head out of the opening and called his name.

'Guy!' Her voice seemed to go nowhere, its sound deadened by the mist, the greyness of the sky, the light but steady downfall of rain. 'G-u-y!'

There was no answer so she stepped out of the plane on to the ground and turned in the direction that Guy had taken. It was then that she saw him, on his hands and knees, trying to crawl out of the forest, his body slowly collapsing against the earth.

'Guy!' she screamed, running towards him. Rain wet her hair and fell on her face as she raced to him and knelt down beside him. 'Guy, what happened?'

'My leg,' he mumbled. 'Hurt it . . . trying to get out of the rain. Twisted it in a hole.' He was soaked to the skin, the rain plastering his hair to his scalp, his jeans completely water-logged. He was shaking as Rebecca helped him stand upright; she could feel his arms and legs tremble and his skin was icy-cold to her touch. He had hurt his bad leg and couldn't put any weight on it. She wrapped her arms around his waist and half-supporting him, half-pushing him forward, she managed to get the two of them into the shelter of the plane.

He was shivering uncontrollably by the time she got off his shorts and wrapped him in the sleeping-bag. She dried his hair and face with a shirt and rubbed his hands with hers, desperately trying to transfer some of her body heat to him. His eyes were closed and his lips were blue; the high cheekbones had never looked more prominent or skeletal. She lay down next to him and wrapped her arms around the sleeping-bag that held him, crooning, 'Easy. You're going to be all right. You're back now and it isn't raining any more.'

But Guy didn't seem to hear her although his eyes flicked behind their lids and his lips moved a bit. His lashes were so long and so dark against the pallor of his skin that the sight of them made Rebecca feel like crying. He couldn't seem to stop the tremors that shook him; he didn't even have the energy to open his eyes and speak. She had the terrible feeling that the man she had known was gone from her for ever, leaving this helpless, shivering body in his place. How could she not have seen that Guy was almost nothing but skin and bone? Rebecca didn't know why the truth hadn't come home to her earlier; after all, she had made love to him, she had clasped him in her arms and wound her legs around him. She had thought she knew every part of his body, but his spirit and his intensity had deceived her. She hadn't realised just how frail he had become or how vulnerable he was. She hadn't known how fast he would succumb to the chill and trembling of fever.

As she held him, the brilliance of sunlight filtered in through the overhead trees to pierce the gloom in the plane. The storm had blown to the south of them, its passage marked by fallen leaves and broken branches. In the distance, she could hear the dying rumble of thunder. The man in her arms shook violently, his teeth clenched together so hard that she thought the bone would pierce the skin over his jaw. Rebecca was too much the professional not to know the probabilities, but she buried her face against the damp sleeping-bag, unable to face the horrible reality of it.

Pneumonia, a small, insidious voice whispered in her mind, repeating the horrifying phrases, *he has pneumonia and he is going to die, to die in this godforsaken place.*

CHAPTER SIX

Guy had a classical case of lobar pneumonia; Rebecca could have written a textbook on it. First there was the high fever that made him burn and shake, the racking cough that was so violent in its paroxysms that she was afraid he would crack a rib, the pain in his chest that indicated infection and finally, the onset of delirium. She tried everything she could think of, keeping him warm with the clothes and the sleeping-bag, cooling him down by rubbing his limbs with water from the lake, forcing hot Labrador tea down him that she heated in the washed-out tackle box, and holding him in her arms in a semi-upright position so that he could breathe more easily.

At times he was coherent; at others he rambled and raved. When he was rational, he tried to talk her into fishing, foraging or leaving, saying that she had to eat, that there was no reason for her to stick around and nurse him, thereby endangering her own life. When he was incoherent, his mind seemed to go back to earlier times, touching on childhood and adolescent experiences. He talked about a bike that he had had, a baseball team, a maths teacher. Occasionally, he thought Rebecca was his mother; sometimes he confused her with Maureen. Most of the time she couldn't even understand what he was saying, his words were so confused and jumbled.

But she listened to him, wiping his forehead with a cool cloth or just holding him to her. She knew he was going to die; she had worked long enough in hospitals to know the inevitable course that pneumonia would take. Sometimes when she nursed him, she would cry softly to herself, the tears streaming down her cheeks. She had virtually stopped eating and she slept only in snatches. Without being aware of it, she was slowly losing physical ground, her face starting to be carved in hollows, her hair lank and dull. But she gave no thought to her future without Guy or what survival would mean on her own. She was in a period of mourning, grieving for the man in her arms, his death so real to her that she saw him as already gone.

It was during this nightmarish period that Rebecca realised that she had come to love Guy. It was the emotion that had fuelled the powerful sexual attraction that bound her to him and fed the intensity of her grief. She no longer thought that their relationship was one that could only have come about in the isolation of their camp and under the stress of their survival. She had the feeling that she was losing the one man in her life that she would never be able to replace: her alter ego, her other self. He knew her better than anyone else ever had; he had loved her in return. That's what Rebecca came to believe in the dark hours of the night while she lay in the tail end of the plane with Guy in her arms, feeling him shake and hearing him mutter to himself, that, despite his fear that he would never be able to love anyone, Guy had fallen in love with her.

The hours blurred together, night separated by day

only by the light that made her blink her eyes when she rushed out of the plane to get water or build yet another fire. The irony of Guy's dying did not escape her as she wrung out cloths and chopped more wood. An antibiotic would have healed him in a minute—a medication that could be obtained twenty miles away? Forty? A distance that was nothing by car and insurmountable by foot when it covered marsh, muskeg and mountain. She would have risked it, walking around the clock to save Guy, if only she knew the direction to travel. But she was as helpless as Guy had been earlier, and she didn't want to leave him, his fever blazing high, his thirst unquenchable, his body ravaged by tremors and coughing. She couldn't leave Guy to die all alone.

Every bit of nursing skill that Rebecca had acquired went into her care of him, but he was sinking day by day and hour by hour. His skin was ashen and deep circles had appeared under his eyes. Occasionally, when his fever was very high, his cheeks would flush to an unhealthy red. She would try to get him cool then, rubbing each limb with a damp cloth and wiping the sweat off his forehead. One night when her complete and utter exhaustion had caused her to fall into a light doze, he thrashed around with such frenzy in his delirium that the sound of his arms and hands hitting the plane wall woke her up. And the next day, when light finally filtered into the plane, she saw that he had a bruise on an arm and a deep gash on one hand.

'Hurt . . . myself,' he mumbled as she knelt over his prone body and wiped away the blood. He had thrown off the sleeping-bag and was wearing only a pair of briefs. Although he was coherent this morning, he was so weak he could barely talk, and Rebecca could feel the fever on his skin.

'I'll wrap a cloth around it,' she said, pulling the sleeping-bag over him so that only his shoulders were bare.

' 'becca?' he whispered.

She sat back on her heels. 'Yes?'

'I'm not going to make it, am I?'

She clenched her hands together and willed herself not to cry. 'Yes, you are,' she said vehemently.

His dark eyes were knowing and sad. '. . . lousy liar. Should get . . . yourself a poker face.' His lips curved upwards in a slight smile.

'You're not going to die,' she said furiously. 'I won't let you.'

It seemed as if he were trying to laugh, but the laughter turned into a deep, hacking cough that seemed to tear his chest apart. Rebecca brought a cloth to his mouth and, with a sinking dismay, saw that he had coughed up blood. She hoped that he hadn't seen the stains of red, but after she had crumpled the cloth up in her hands and threw it behind her, she turned to find that he was watching her.

'It doesn't mean anything,' she said in desperation, putting a cool hand to his blazing hot forehead. 'Don't jump to conclusions.'

It was hard for him to speak; she could see that. The words came out between gasps and the effort made him shake. 'I know . . .' he said '. . . what's going . . . to happen.'

'No!' The denial was torn out of her, wrenched out

of her conviction that he might not even last another day.

He lifted a hand to her face and placed trembling, hot fingers to her cheek where tears were falling, curving around her nose and into the corners of her mouth. 'I'm sorry,' he whispered.

His apology and touch of tender pity accomplished what grief and lack of food and sleep had not. All of her rigid composure, the control she had held over her emotions, broke down and her despair spilled out, not only in tears but in heavy, great sobs. She curled up with the pain of it, her arms wrapped around her chest, her head bent so that her hair fell on to Guy's chest. He rested his hand on the back of her head and let her cry, let her body shake with the force of it, let the helpless words pour out of her. 'Don't . . . please, don't die . . . don't leave me . . . I don't want you to die . . . please . . .'

When she was finally quiet, Guy's hand slipped off her hair, and Rebecca lifted her head, her eyes red-rimmed, her face damp, her mouth full of salty tears. 'I'm the one who's sorry,' she said. 'I . . . I didn't mean to do that.'

He had been lying with his eyes closed as if the exertion of the past few moments had completely worn him out. She saw how thin his face had become, almost skull-like as the flesh fell away from the high ridge of his cheekbones. But a spark of life still burned within him for he opened his eyes and, smiling, said in a hoarse whisper, 'Have to . . . improve your bedside . . . manner, nurse.'

Rebecca loved him so fiercely at that moment that

she would have given up her own life for his. She
sniffed and wiped her eyes. 'Oh, Guy,' she said in a
shaky voice. 'Only you would joke at a time like this.'

His whisper was barely discernible, and she had to
bend her head to catch his words. 'Can't . . .' he said
'. . . do anything else.'

When she emerged from the plane, there were sharp
cramps in her calves and her head seemed to swim
from dizziness. She crouched down in front of the
place where they usually built their fires and slowly
put a log on a pile of twigs. She had to heat up some
water for Guy; she wanted to make him more hot tea.
But her eyes wouldn't work right. Dark spots
appeared before her pupils and, although the sun was
shining, her peripheral vision was so dark that she felt
as if she were looking down a long tunnel.

She pulled out the matches from her jeans' pocket
and lit one of the twigs, noting in an abstracted way
that there were only about five matches left. She
wondered if it were really possible to build a fire by
rubbing wood together and, if it did work, how long it
would take. She couldn't imagine surviving without
fire; it would mean a constant diet of raw foods and no
heat for warmth. But she brushed the thought away as
she blew on the small flame that arose out of the twigs.
What was the use of worrying about a future that was
five matches away? That might be tomorrow or the
day after, and Rebecca was unable to think beyond the
minute, beyond Guy's rasping breath in the plane,
beyond the utter stillness of his body when he wasn't
coughing. The fever was like an inferno inside of him,

burning up every bit of strength and life that he had. She knew the next step, the slipping away into unconsciousness and the final coma. She knew it, but she simply couldn't . . . wouldn't accept it.

Strong, hot tea— that's what he needed. She piled on more logs, desperate to build the fire up to an intense heat. Flames fanned her face, but she was oblivious to the way they made her flush and sweat. Rebecca had lost all interest in how she felt or what she looked like. Her hair, longer now, unparted and uncombed, fell in knots and tangles to the middle of her back. Her face was thin and her lips were chapped. She was wearing the same clothes that she had worn three days earlier, a pair of Guy's jeans, held together with a belt of torn fabric, and a plaid shirt that was ripped in the back. She had no shoes and wore socks with gaping holes. Her hands had taken the toughest beating; they were calloused and blistered with ragged, broken nails. Two months earlier, she would have died rather than let anyone see her with hands like that. Like many fat women, she had paid a great deal of attention to her hands, face and hair.

But the old Rebecca was gone, and the new one was different. The new one could kill a squirrel, eat raw fish and wrestle a man to the ground. The new Rebecca was going to have to be tough and strong; she would be forced to watch the man she loved die and then learn to survive without him. As the flames of the fire crackled and hissed, Rebecca looked deeply into their orange centres and wondered if she was going to have the will to live. With Guy gone, there would be nothing left to live for. She would have no one to talk to who understood her so well that he could almost finish her sentences. She would never again feel a man's arms around her, the touch of his face against hers, his hardness between her legs. At his death, she would be losing a lover, a confidant, a friend, a . . .

There was a sudden roaring in her ears and Rebecca blinked, dazed and confused by the sound. She stood up and shaded her eyes, glancing up at the northern sky where a lone heron flew, its elongate shape black against the sun. She turned then and looked to the south, not believing what she saw and not convinced that she wasn't dreaming. A white seaplane had passed right over her head and was heading towards the mountains. A plane that had come so close that she could see the numbers on its side and the seams along the edges of the pontoons. A plane that could rescue them, that could bring them back to civilisation and transport Guy to a hospital where he could get the proper medications that would save his life.

'Come back!' she screamed, running towards the edge of the promontory, her arms waving frantically in the air. 'Don't leave! Come back!'

But the plane appeared to be heading away from her and her voice rose to a higher pitch. She couldn't believe that it had passed by over her head and not seen the broken half of the Twin Otter on the ground or her figure stooped over the fire. Surely, the pilot wouldn't just fly away from such a scene. Surely, he would have enough curiosity or compassion to investigate what had obviously been a crash. But as it flew farther on, towards the end of the lake, Rebecca realised that the seaplane wasn't coming back.

'Bastard!' she cried, shaking her fist at the steadily diminishing plane and feeling the sharp prick of tears in her eyes. 'Guy is dying. Don't you understand? He's dying!'

No one cared; not the heron disappearing over the horizon, the squirrel that scampered up a tree behind her, or the pilot who had so casually flown past. Her arms fell heavily to her sides and her shoulders slumped. The effort of screaming, of running and waving her arms had left her limp and exhausted with legs that shook uncontrollably. Her vision started to darken, and Rebecca realised that she might faint. Quickly, she knelt down and put her head between her knees to hold off the oncoming blackness. There was a roaring in her ears that she attributed to the fainting spell, and she closed her eyes to ward off the sudden attack of dizziness and nausea. She took deep, careful breaths and tried to slow the frantic beating of her heart, knowing that if she did faint Guy would be left unattended and helpless.

It was the sound of water whipped into a frenzy that made her lift her head, and she saw with astonishment that the seaplane had returned. What she had taken to be its leaving was merely a pass over the lake that the pilot had been forced to make before he could land. White-caps spread out from a circle of grey-green froth as the seaplane came down and were then forced into a wake as the plane revved its engines and headed towards her, its propeller whirling into a disk and making that incredible, roaring sound.

Rebecca didn't scream or run this time; she merely stood up, swaying slightly, a lone figure against the backdrop of the forest. The wind lifted up the tangles in her hair and pressed the fabric of her shirt against her slender frame, its back billowing like a sail. She would never know how she looked to the two men inside the plane as they approached close to land —like a wraith; thin to the point of emaciation, her clothes baggy and ragged, her blue eyes dark and enormous in the bony slenderness of her face.

The first one leaned out of the cockpit door as the pilot cut the engines. 'Are you okay?' he yelled.

'There's a man,' she cried out. 'He's very sick. Please hurry!'

Within minutes, the seaplane was brought to the beach and the two men were out and scrabbling up the slate to the promontory. Rebecca stared at them as if she had never seen human beings before, but the truth was that she had quite forgotten what other people looked like. Her world had narrowed to Guy and herself, and she had been living in a population of two for so long that the sight of other healthy men almost struck her dumb. Their faces were so ruddy and well-fleshed, nothing like Guy's gaunt appearance, and they had an awesome amount of energy.

As they came up to her, the black dots swam before her eyes and she stumbled a bit as she stepped towards them. The shorter one with brown hair caught her by the elbow. 'Are you all right?' he asked.

Rebecca swallowed and stood up straight. 'I'm fine,' she said, 'but Guy has pneumonia.'

'Where is he?' asked the other one. He was taller and burlier with a reddish beard.

She waved her hand to the tail end of the plane

which sat at the edge of the promontory. 'He's in there.'

'We'll get him,' the brown-haired one said as the other one took off at a run. 'Now, you just sit down and relax.'

Rebecca obediently sat down on the rock while he crouched down beside her. Although she knew the ordeal was over, she couldn't quite take in the men's presence and what it meant. She and Guy had been isolated for so long that she barely remembered any other way of life. And she had been so convinced that he would die and that she might die along with him. 'Are you,' she asked carefully, 'the rescue party?'

'Rescue?' He shook his head and smiled at her. 'We were just flying over and saw the plane on the rock. That's why we came down; we didn't know if there would be any survivors.'

If only they had cut down the plane earlier, she thought, and then remembered that Guy's leg had been so bad that he hadn't been able to wield an axe until recently. It would have taken her weeks to cut it down by herself, but if she had known that the downed plane would bring them rescue, she would have . . . Rebecca shook herself as she realised the futility of hindsight. 'You didn't know that a plane had crashed here?'

He shook his head. 'We'd heard there was a plane lost a couple of months ago. A Twin Otter with three passengers. Was that you?'

Rebecca nodded.

'And the guy in there—is he the pilot?'

'No, the pilot's dead and one of the passengers—a

woman named Sandra.' She pointed to the wreckage
of the fuselage in the lake. It had sunk down so low
that the torn edges of metal were barely visible above
the water. For long periods of time, she had forgotten
that it even existed.

The brown-haired man had turned in the direction
of her pointed finger. 'God,' he swore under his
breath. 'Poor bastards.'

'Rick!' The other man was standing in the opening
of the plane. 'We need the first-aid kit and some
blankets. We've got a really sick man on our hands.'
He turned to her. 'Are you Rebecca?'

Rebecca stood up slowly and ignored the way the
world swivelled in a dizzying fashion. 'Yes,' she said.

'He's calling you, ma'am. I think you'd better go
back to him.'

For Rebecca, the rescue and their flight back to Inuvik
went by in a blur. Guy was wrapped in blankets and
placed in the back of the plane. Because there were
only two seats, the brown-haired man named Rick
wanted to sit on the floor in the back with Guy and let
Rebecca have the comfortable bucket seat beside the
pilot, but she refused. No one could have separated
her from Guy; the ties that connected them together
were so strong that she couldn't bear to leave his side.
And she saw that he was delirious again and realised
that he wasn't even aware that they were no longer at
the promontory. They had given him aspirin and an
antibiotic from the first-aid kit, but he wasn't respond-
ing to the medication yet. He muttered to himself and
his skin was hot to the touch. Rebecca clutched on to

his hand, massaging the taut tendons on its back, and prayed that he wouldn't die before they reached help.

An ambulance met them where they landed, at a river near the town of Inuvik. They were taken immediately to the airport where Rick and the pilot of the seaplane held a hasty conference with a doctor right on the tarmac. Guy had already been given an injection and was hooked up to an intravenous and oxygen supply when he was wheeled up to a larger plane that would take them to Edmonton. Rebecca didn't question the decisions; she was simply grateful that Guy's care had been transferred over to someone who was better trained than she was and fully equipped to handle such emergencies.

They placed Guy on a stretcher in the aisle of the plane, and she sat near his head, sipping slowly and with the most intense pleasure the thermos of soup the doctor had handed to her when she entered. It was only canned beef broth but she didn't think she had ever tasted anything quite so wonderful. It was hot, salty and rich with flavours her tongue hadn't experienced in months. Her dizziness began to dissipate and her vision brightened as if she had gone through a darkened tunnel and was emerging into daylight on the other side. When she had finished the soup, she put down the thermos and closed her eyes, putting one hand on Guy's shoulder and leaning her head back against the seat. She tried to listen to the conversation between Rick and the doctor, but their words were only murmurs as waves of exhaustion carried her into sleep.

'Slow starvation,' the doctor was saying. 'They must

have been on a severely limited diet.' He was sitting on the other side of the aisle from Rebecca, and he held Guy's wrist in his hand, his fingers constantly monitoring his pulse.

'Think he'll make it?' Rick asked, staring down at what was visible beneath the oxygen mask that covered Guy's face.

The doctor sighed, his eyes worried behind the tortoise-shell frame of his glasses. 'It's touch and go, although he must have had a strong constitution to get this far.'

Rick gestured at the sleeping Rebecca. 'She's in better shape.'

'Wasn't she fat before the crash?' the doctor asked. 'I remember seeing a picture of her. Or was that the other woman?'

Rich shrugged. 'I don't know. She sure isn't fat now.'

For a moment, they both looked at her. Her head had fallen slightly to one side and heavy strands of hair covered one cheek. Sleep had softened the lines of strain on her face, but it didn't hide the gauntness or the pallor. 'They've had it rough,' the doctor said. 'She looks as if she's been nursing him night and day.'

Rick glanced at the way Rebecca's hand rested on Guy's shoulder. Even in sleep, her air of possession was obvious. 'They seem to have got attached to one another.'

'Isn't he married?'

'Don't know,' Rick said with a shrug. 'But it could cause complications if he was.'

The doctor made a grimace. 'If there's one thing this

man isn't going to need it's complications. He's in bad shape.'

'We've radioed the Edmonton airport and they're supposed to have an ambulance ready and waiting.'

'I hope the press hasn't caught wind of this yet. These two need some seclusion and rest before civilisation hits them. It isn't going to be an easy adjustment.'

'Well, the families have been notified and the hospital has been contacted. If the press is there, we'll know there's been a leak.'

The doctor held Guy's wrist in a firmer grip. 'Let's just hope it's nice and quiet when we arrive. He's going to need all the help he can get.'

Rebecca woke as the plane began its descent and, raising her hand to her neck, rubbed sore and aching muscles. For a second, she had no idea where she was and then the memory of the rescue came rushing back to her. With a sudden, frantic motion, she turned towards the aisle to see how Guy was doing. The doctor noticed her concern and gave her a reassuring smile. 'He's okay,' he said.

Rebecca's deep inhalation and exhalation of breath was shaky. 'His infection is so widespread. I think both sides of the lung are involved.'

'You sound like a doctor.'

'I'm a nurse,' she corrected.

'He was a lucky man then. You knew what to do.'

'I couldn't do much without antibiotics,' she said. 'I couldn't keep his fever down.'

The doctor acknowledged her difficulties with a slight inclination of his head. 'He's a bit cooler now, I think.'

Rebecca reached over and touched Guy's forehead. The skin was not so hot and dry, and she gave the doctor a tremulous smile. 'I think you're right.'

'And what about you?' he asked. 'We haven't heard a complaint out of you.'

'There's nothing wrong with me that a little food and sleep in a comfortable bed wouldn't cure.'

'We'll run some tests anyway and check your blood. You may feel fine, but I don't want you leaving the hospital until you're in such good health that I'd let you run a marathon.'

Rebecca smiled at him as she slipped her hand down Guy's arm to his wrist where the pulse was beating. It felt stronger under the tips of her fingers, steady and insistent. He was going to live, she thought with a glorious surge of happiness. He wasn't going to die after all. They had removed the oxygen mask, and she stared down at his sleeping face, the harsh, thin profile and the heavy wave of dark hair that fell over his forehead. She imagined him as he had been, healthy and strong, and her heart contracted with love. She thought of the life they would have together; living in a house, waking up in the morning next to one another, sharing dinners over candlelight, their fingers entwined. She thought of Guy introducing her to his friends, his hand lingering on her waist. 'This is my wife, Rebecca,' he would say and she knew he would be proud of her prettiness, the rich lustre of her hair, the slender curves of her body.

'Yes,' she said slowly. 'Maybe I will take up jogging.'

The ambulance ride from Edmonton airport to the hospital was uneventful except that Rebecca was stunned by the noise, the traffic and the sight of people and buildings crowded upon one another. She had forgotten what a big city was like, and her senses felt assaulted as the ambulance's siren screamed, horns blared and people gawked at them as they passed. She wouldn't have believed it possible to miss their camp, but she suddenly had an intense longing for the quiet rustle of trees, the soothing sound of water lapping against rock and the haunting cry of the loon. She had never realised how harsh the glare of the sun could be when it glinted off the windows of buildings instead of the surface of a lake, and she had got so accustomed to the silence of the wilderness that she had forgotten how jarring urban sounds could be.

The cars in front of the ambulance parted before them like a metallic Red Sea, and they raced around corners, brakes and tyres screeching. Rebecca held on to her seat with one hand and on to Guy's hand with the other. His closed eyelids twitched occasionally, but he was sleeping through all the noise and motion with all the placidity of a baby. As the ambulance drove up to the emergency entrance of the hospital, Rebecca saw a large crowd gathered before the doorway.

'Damn,' the doctor exclaimed.

The ambulance driver shook his head in annoyance. 'I don't know how they got wind of it.'

'Of what?' Rebecca asked.

'You,' the doctor replied. 'It's the press.'

'Press?'

'Newspapers, radio and television.'

Rebecca glanced out at the crowd as they pulled closer. Now, she could see cameras and microphones. 'No,' she said, shaking her head. 'I don't want to talk to anyone.' For the first time in days, she thought about her appearance and touched her hand to her tangled hair. She hadn't seen herself in a mirror for months but she had a good idea how she looked; gaunt, dirty and tousled. The thought of her image on millions of television screens made her heart sink.

'Can we get in some other way?' the doctor asked the driver.

He shook his head. 'All the equipment is ready here.'

The doctor turned to Rebecca. 'We'll get you in quickly, just grin and bear it.'

'But I . . .'

It was too late. The ambulance pulled up to the door and the crowd was already milling around the vehicle, lights shining in the windows. Several figures emerged from the hospital and started cordoning the mob away as the ambulance doors were opened and the stretcher with Guy was borne out. Rebecca could hear the murmur of the crowd get louder when he appeared, and she prayed that he was still asleep and wouldn't be conscious of the prurient curiosity of the faces hovering over him as he passed by.

The doctor took one of her arms and the ambulance driver the other. She felt their bodies protecting her as she stepped down from the ambulance, her eyes blinking as a strobe light flashed in front of her. The murmur of the crowd had now grown into a roar at her appearance. She swallowed nervously as she looked around and her body tensed.

'Easy,' the doctor murmured.

A microphone was shoved in front of her. 'How does it feel, Miss Clark, to be back in civilisation?'

And then another voice chimed in and another.

'What did you eat out there?'

'How did it feel when the plane went down?'

'Did you realise Mr McLaren had pneumonia?'

The voices overwhelmed her and Rebecca shrank backwards, unable to take in the sounds, the shoving and pushing, the quick flashes of light that blinded her every time they went off. She was slowly being walked through the mob as the doctor and driver elbowed the more aggressive out of the way, but they couldn't shield her from the avid eyes, the thrusting microphones and the mouths that screamed at her. She would have liked to cover her face, but both her arms were being held and she was forced to keep her chin up and paste a smile on her face. They were within a foot of the hospital door when a question came that made her gasp in shock and almost caused her knees to buckle. The doctor felt her sway and held her up more firmly.

'Don't give up,' he said. 'We're almost there.'

But she couldn't get the words out of her mind as the automatic doors parted before them, and she barely noticed when she was handed over to two compassionate nurses.

'Did you develop a romantic attachment to Mr McLaren?' the voice had yelled over the rest. 'Did he tell you about his wife?'

Rebecca was given the royal treatment by the hospital staff. The nurses took pity on her physical state, and she was allowed a luxurious soak in the bath-tub and had her hair washed and then trimmed by one nurse who had once been a hairdresser. They brought her a delicious lunch of veal parmigian that she was sure had never come from a hospital kitchen, but when she asked if they had ordered it from a restaurant for her, they had merely smiled and told her to enjoy it. They gave her lotions to heal skin that had been damaged by sun, wind, hard work and general deterioration, and another nurse gave her a manicure, exclaiming over her broken nails and the calluses on her palms and fingers. She knew that the staff were curious about her, but she appreciated the fact that they didn't ask her questions or push her in any way. The technician who took blood samples and the doctor who gave her a check-up were gentle and kind. And when she asked about Guy, they were quick to reassure her. He was doing well, they said. He was in the intensive care unit where his condition was being monitored constantly. Although he was under sedation at the moment, they thought she would be able to see him in the morning.

Rebecca was given a private room and a telephone. It was a while before she could bring herself to make the calls to her family. She knew that the authorities had already notified them so that their shock and surprise would be abated by the time she reached them, but a certain reluctance held her back from picking up the receiver. She sat and stared out of the window for a while, thinking about her family and realising that hearing her mother's voice would be her true initiation into normal life. It would mean that she was once again caught in the web of connections; that uncomfortable and upsetting mesh of family that had forced her to leave Fairfax two months earlier.

She called Tamara first who started to cry when she heard Rebecca's voice.

'I thought you were dead,' she wailed.

'I'm fine.'

'Really? Really fine? You're not sick.'

'A little food will help.'

'Did you lose a lot of weight?'

'About sixty pounds.'

'My God! Rebecca, I don't think I'd recognise you.'

She gave a little laugh. 'I don't recognise myself.'

'Was it . . . terrible?'

'Pretty awful,' she confessed.

'And what about the man you were with? Is he okay?'

'No, he got pneumonia. I thought he'd die, but he's going to be all right.'

'You can't imagine the things I thought about; starvation and wild animals and ice and snow.'

Rebecca couldn't help smiling. 'We didn't have any ice and snow.'

'When will they let you out of the hospital?'

'A couple of days, I think.'

'Are you coming back East?'

'I don't think so.'

Tamara's voice rose to a pitch of astonishment. 'You're not thinking of going back to the Arctic, are you?'

'I . . . don't know. I can't leave right now.'

There was a moment's silence and then Tamara said, 'It's that man, isn't it?'

'Yes,' Rebecca admitted.

'Did you . . . look I don't want to be nosy, but it sounds as if you got involved with him.'

Rebecca cleared her throat. 'That's putting it mildly.'

'But he's *married*. I read about his wife in the newspaper.'

'He's separated.'

'Are you sure?'

'Of course, I'm sure.' All of a sudden, she remembered the words of the reporter and a sudden doubt gripped her. 'That's . . . what he told me.'

Tamara's sigh was deep enough to carry the two and a half thousand miles of telephone cable. 'Look,' she said. 'Just take care of yourself, will you?'

'I always do, don't I?'

'No,' Tamara said firmly, 'you don't. You're a nitwit about men.'

'What men?'

'That's the point. You don't know the first thing about them.'

Rebecca couldn't help coming to the reluctant conclusion that Tamara might be right. Compared to her sister, she had had little experience with the opposite sex. 'Don't worry,' she sighed. 'I'll manage.

'You'll phone, won't you? And let me know how you're doing?'

'I will.'

'Have you called Mother?'

'No.'

'Are you going to?' Tamara asked cautiously.

'Do you think I can avoid it?'

'No, sweet sister of mine, I don't. But listen, don't let her get to you. You know how she is.'

'I know,' Rebecca said flatly, 'how she is.'

The phone rang ten times before Martine Clark picked it up, and Rebecca couldn't help the way her insides seemed to shrivel when she heard that cool, elegant voice. 'It's me, Mother, Rebecca.'

'Well, you've given us quite a surprise.' There wasn't a hint of emotion in her mother's words; not happiness, not regret, not excitement.

'I suppose I have.'

'Are you all right?'

'The doctors seem to think so.'

'They said you were in very good shape.'

'I'm just hungry and tired.'

'Did you lose some weight, Rebecca?'

Rebecca gritted her teeth against a sudden surge of appetite. She had forgotten how hungry she got whenever she talked to Martine. 'I only weigh about nine stone.

Her mother's laughter had a way of sounding brittle and sharp. 'I really can't quite imagine you that way.'

'I think that . . . I look very nice.'

'Don't get defensive, darling. I'm sure you do.'

There was an awkward moment of silence. 'How have you been—and Celia?'

'It's been a difficult summer.'

Rebecca recognised her mother's statement for what it was—the only acknowledgement she would make to the strain Rebecca's presumed loss had imposed on her. 'Is Celia there?'

'She's at the library desperately cramming in her summer reading list before school starts. She's looking forward to seeing you.'

Wasn't that like Martine, Rebecca thought, using Celia as a way of finding out what she herself wanted to know. 'I . . . I won't be coming home yet.'

'No?' Martine wasn't like Tamara; she wasn't sensitive enough to guess at Rebecca's reasons for staying in western Canada.

'I thought I might . . . go to that job in Fort Good Hope if it's still open.'

Martine didn't speak of her former opposition to Rebecca's new job. She merely said, 'I would have thought you'd have had enough of the Arctic by now. At any rate, the hospital here would like you back. I spoke to your supervisor this morning after I got the phone call that you'd been found.'

Rebecca tried desperately to ignore the severity of her hunger pangs. Martine had always attempted to dominate her life: to tell her what to do and how to do it. She could just imagine the satisfaction Martine must have had approaching Rebecca's old supervisor and getting her hired again. It was precisely that sort of manipulation and interference that had, in the past, set Rebecca off on a course of compulsive eating. Now, she steeled herself for the forthcoming battle.

'I don't want to work there,' she said. 'Tell her the answer is no.'

'Honestly, Rebecca, you're so short-sighted. You haven't committed yourself to anything; I was just making sure that you had all your options open.'

Rebecca had forgotten just how slippery Martine was. 'You should have consulted with me first.'

'I was just doing you a favour, darling. Don't be so prickly.'

'I'm not being prickly, Mother, I'm just trying to make my own decisions.'

'And I'm not stopping you,' Martine responded in her most reasonable tone. The vision of a black forest gâteau passed through Rebecca's mind, a chocolate layer cake rich with kirsch cherries, dark frosting and whipped cream. Her mouth watered; her stomach made a furious grumbling sound. 'I'm afraid,' she said desperately, 'that I have to get off the phone now. A . . . the doctor just walked in.'

'Please make sure that they check your sugar level, will you? Remember how high that used to be?'

Rebecca clenched her teeth. 'That was when I was *obese*, Mother. I'm not fat any more.'

'Of *course*, I'd forgotten.' Martine gave a little laugh. 'Well, take care, Rebecca, and I'll phone you tomorrow to see how you're doing.'

Rebecca would have given her right arm for food, any sort of food, after that phone call, but she willed herself to lie down on the narrow hospital bed. She knew how dangerous it would be if she allowed

Martine's manipulative behaviour and thinly-veiled insults to get to her. Her relationship with her mother had always been rocky, difficult and destructive; it was the main reason why she had left Fairfax for a job four thousand miles away. She had wanted to put as much distance between Martine and herself as possible.

Now, she closed her eyes, turned over on her side and plumped the pillow under her head, determined to sleep and to forget Tamara's disturbing suggestions and her conversation with Martine. Instead, she concentrated on Guy who was sleeping two floors below her, imagining the strength that the drugs were giving him and the steady, watchful care of the hospital staff. She tried to envision what she would say to him when she saw him; what he would say to her. She knew how much a shampoo, haircut and bath had changed her. The woman she had seen in the mirror before going to bed bore little resemblance to the Rebecca she had seen reflected in a mirror two months earlier. When she had pulled the masses of her auburn hair away from her temples, she had looked like the little girl of eighteen years earlier who had smiled out of the pages of the *Fairfax Gazette*; slender, smiling and very, very pretty.

Rebecca took care with her appearance the next morning, despite the disadvantages of wearing a hospital gown and a borrowed blue quilted bathrobe that had seen better days. She brushed her hair until it shone in burnished waves and used eye make-up that had been donated by one of the nurses. Her hands were still a mess, and her skin tone was going to require a lot of loving care before it regained its former creaminess, but she thought she looked quite nice as she headed down the elevator to Guy's floor.

She had, with all the energy and optimism that a good night's sleep can bring, brushed off the problem of Martine and discounted Tamara's concerns, coming to the confident conclusion that her sister didn't know Guy and couldn't begin to understand what he and Rebecca had shared. Theirs was a unique relationship, forged in unusual circumstances and strengthened by experiences that rarely touched other people. Guy had said that he was separated from Maureen, and Rebecca had a guilty feeling of disloyalty for even listening to Tamara's doubts. She trusted him, Rebecca thought, as the arrow on the elevator pointed to Guy's floor. Of course she did.

Rebecca was so eager to see him that she flew out of the elevator when the doors opened. There was a smile on her face when she asked an orderly where intensive care was and happy anticipation in her heart as she approached the desk before its doors.

'Yes?' a nurse asked.

'I've come to see Guy McLaren. He's up, isn't he?'

'You must be the woman he was found with.'

Rebecca fidgeted with impatience as she nodded.

'You'd better keep your eye out for reporters. We had a couple hanging around here this morning and had to kick them out.'

Rebecca couldn't have cared less about the press. 'Is he awake?'

The nurse frowned. 'He is, but he has someone with him.'

Rebecca barely heard her words. 'Can't I see him?'

'Well . . .'

She was through the double doors in an instant and almost running past the beds. She had to slow down for an orderly wheeling a cart of medical equipment, and it was then that she heard his voice coming from a bed cordoned off by a screen. She couldn't decipher his words, but the woman who answered him spoke in a loud, clear voice.

'And the house is fine,' she said. 'I had the patio finished. Remember how much you talked about the patio? I really didn't know if you cared any more, but it was a sort of lucky talisman. If the patio is completed, I thought, Guy will come home.'

Guy's voice was still weak. 'Maureen . . .' he said.

'And your parents are fine now. Your father had . . . a heart attack a week after you were lost . . . no, darling, don't try to sit up . . . there.' A short pause. 'He's fine now and, of course, ecstatic that you've been found. Your mother's been bearing up well considering the stress and she's dying to see you. I think they're going to fly up some time today. I'll meet them at the airport so you don't have to worry about your father driving.'

Rebecca had come to a full stop by the screen. Guy was hidden by its frame, but she could see the woman who was sitting by him, an attractive woman with curly blonde hair and a pair of thickly lashed, tilted brown eyes. She appeared to be holding Guy's hand in hers and was hovering over him with a concern that appeared to be quite genuine and very loving. She didn't seem at all like a wife who had been separated from her husband for two years; to Rebecca, it looked as if Maureen was very much in the centre of Guy's life.

As Maureen went on to talk about Guy's office, his car and the cat, all of Rebecca's earlier ebullience drained away, leaving her strangely empty and numb. Slowly, she backed away from the screen as the reporter's words and Tamara's advice came back to her. Although she knew she should confront Guy and ask him what the truth was, she was suddenly reluctant to have that face-to-face meeting. Suppose he didn't want her any more; suppose he wanted his old life back without her presence. He had never said that he loved her, she realised; even on his deathbed, he had never mentioned the word 'love'. He had joked instead; a typical Guy reaction. She could imagine what he would say now when he saw her. *Hello. Well, it was great knowing you. Hope you have a good life.*

The delicate fabric of her self-confidence tore under a sudden avalanche of doubt and bewilderment. She had been so sure that she would spend the rest of her life with Guy that Rebecca hadn't made any contingency plans. She had simply viewed her future through the rosiest of glasses and assumed a state of happiness that was ephemeral at best and non-existent at the very least. Like many fat women who lost a great deal of weight, she had thought that when she was thin, the world would be hers for the asking, but now she realised that certain aspects of the old Rebecca had not been shed along with those extra pounds. She was still shy, unable to deal with men and gullible. Oh, so very gullible.

She turned then and fled from intensive care, her hands hiding the misery on her face. She didn't answer the startled inquiry of the nurse at the desk or notice the curious glances thrown her way as she ran, a slender figure whose hair rippled behind her like a mass of dark flame against the billowing blue bathrobe.

PART TWO

CHAPTER SEVEN

A TALL, broad-shouldered blond man stood on the
tarmac at the Calgary airport, watching a small plane
land and then taxi to a space near the terminal. He
shifted impatiently and nervously from one foot to the
other as an interminable amount of time seemed to
pass before the doors of the plane opened and an
airport attendant wheeled up a mobile staircase. He
then chewed in an agitated fashion on his dashing
reddish-brown moustache, his eyes intent on the lean,
dark-haired man who slowly descended from the
plane, one hand raised in a gesture of refusal as he
turned down the attendant's offer of help while the
other was gripping on to the rail as if he were afraid
that he would fall or collapse on that short staircase.

Jake DeBlais knew better than to step forward and
offer assistance. He had known Guy McLaren since
childhood. They had played Cowboys and Indians
together, had been on the same high school football
team and had shared some memorable nights on the
town together. Guy had studied geology in college;
Jake had gone in for economics. After graduation they
had joined forces and gone into business together,
starting a seismic exploration company from scratch
and working night and day to make it a going concern.

It would have been difficult to find two friends or
business associates who were more suited to one

another in temperament and personality. Guy was shrewd, incisive and witty; Jake was expansive, amiable and fun-loving. Guy had the ability to put even the most complex business ideas into words while Jake could reduce them to understandable numbers. Together, they were capable of putting together an exploration proposal that had brought them more business than they were capable of handling. They agreed or amiably squabbled on large and small issues; politics, religion, business acumen and the world at large. Their lives only seriously diverged when it came to one thing: the female sex. Guy had always been a 'one woman' man; even after his separation he had been faithful to a single woman at a time. Jake, on the other hand, didn't feel the limits of morality. He adored women and they adored his good looks, his enthusiasm, and his overwhelming admiration for anything female. He went through girl-friends with gusto and energy, sometimes dating two or three women simultaneously, and his escapades in juggling 'bed' dates were hair-raising and legendary. He had yet, he once declared to Guy, to meet the woman who was capable of tying him down.

The most enduring relationship in Jake's life was his tie to Guy. Although he wouldn't have been able to articulate it, both because he wasn't the introspective type and because such an admission lacked the usual masculine edge, Jake had feelings towards Guy that went far deeper than mere friendship. They were more than childhood playmates, college drinking buddies and business partners. Guy had played many roles in Jake's life; the brother he had never had, the father whose advice was far sounder than his own father's drunken ramblings, the confidant who understood the very workings of his mind. While most men turned to a woman for affection and trust, Jake had turned to Guy and never been disappointed. His reliance on Guy was so strong that the disappearance of the Twin Otter and the presumed death of his closest friend had cast Jake into a mind-reeling grief.

Only the business had kept him sane enough to live on a daily basis. He had mourned with an extravagance that had shocked even himself, living daily with a sensation of emptiness and of loss hollowing out the very core of his heart. He missed Guy's conversation, his presence and their easy camaraderie. He became morose and unsociable, and for the first time in his adult life, stopped seeing women. His world had become dark and uninhabitable when the news of Guy's rescue entered it like a brilliant ray of sunshine. In a roaring celebration, he had gone out that night and painted the town red, waking up the next morning to find not one, but two women, in bed with him. His only regret was that he couldn't remember, for the life of him, what he had done with them!

Although Jake was warned about Guy's condition and repeatedly told by the doctors that Guy's convalescence would be long and his adjustment to civilisation difficult, nothing could dampen Jake's buoyant belief that all was right and proper in his life again. He had anticipated Guy's return to Calgary with high expectations. Happily he had contemplated the plans he had made for Guy and himself; they would have dinner and talk shop, he had got tickets for the next football game between the Stampeders and the Argonauts, and he would introduce Guy to his latest love of a month's standing, the voluptuous Sophia who was bound to elicit a few well-deserved turns of phrase.

But as Jake watched Guy come down the staircase, his exuberance died a quick and painful death. The other man's obvious fragility brought a lump to his throat, and he had a totally unmasculine and embarrassing urge to rush forward and take Guy in his arms. But Jake knew Guy too well to make any sloppy or sentimental gesture. From the rigid way Guy was holding himself, Jake realised just how important it was that he get down the staircase and across the tarmac by himself. Instinctively, he waited as Guy walked towards him.

Then he stepped forward slightly, smiling with his hand outstretched, trying hard not to show the depth of his shock at Guy's condition, at his old-man shuffle and his pallor. Guy had yet to gain back all the weight he had lost. His face was all bones and planes, the shaven cheeks still hollow enough to give him a gaunt appearance. He wore a new jacket and slacks that fitted him well but Jake, taking his hand, could feel the skeletal thinness of the fingers and the slight tremor in them. For a second Jake couldn't help believing that this man with the slumped shoulders and silver hair at the temples was surely someone else who, although he bore a semblance to Guy, was in fact a pale facsimile, a shadow, a faded image of the real flesh-and-blood man.

He cleared his throat and shook that delicate hand.

'They gave you an honourable discharge?' he asked.

The humour was still there, albeit as strained and fragile as the skin that stretched so tightly over Guy's high cheekbones and straight nose. 'Dishonourable. They kicked me out for bad behaviour.'

Jake didn't think that Guy looked capable of raising hell in their favourite beer joint. 'I'll bet you were the worst patient they had ever had. Chased nurses up and down the halls.'

The rakish look was incongruous on that weary face. 'Hell, no,' Guy replied with a forced grin. 'The nurses couldn't keep *their* hands off *me*.'

Jake aimed for a laugh of appreciative camaraderie, but Guy had bent his head and started walking towards the parking lot, his shoulders hunched in his sheepskin jacket. He seemed exhausted by the small effort of talking, and he held himself stiffly as if he were brittle and only barely anchored to the ground. As Jake stepped into stride next to him, he had the horrible feeling that the cold and omnipresent Calgary wind was capable of tossing Guy up to the blue sky as if he were a dry brown stem of prairie grass.

Although his shock dissipated a bit as they got into the car, Jake couldn't help being uneasy about Guy's silence and the way he slumped in the seat as if the energy that had sustained him after the plane ride had completely drained out of him. In the past, the two of them would have fallen into the type of conversation where each could finish the other's sentences and there was an immediate and strong mental rapport. Now, there was only the sound of the motor revving and the rush of street beneath quickened wheels as the car swung out of the airport parking lot and on to the road into Calgary. In unhappy desperation, Jake made several valiant attempts to engage Guy's interest.

'You know the economic climate is beginning to look up. We might consider this a good time for expansion. For example, Delta Gas is just begging for a buyer, and we've got enough cash flow to look into stock-takeover. If we took them on, diversification would show us a good profit a couple of years down the line.'

He took his eyes off the windscreen and glanced at Guy, but the other man was staring at the passing streets as if he had never seen them before.

Jake cleared his throat. 'See that poster? Simpson is running against Candell for mayor and it's been a hot campaign. Name-calling, dirty linen, hints of bad practices at city hall. Of course, I don't think Candell is really to blame for all the excess spending; he had to deal with policies set years ago and . . .'

Guy rubbed his temple with a weary, circular motion as if there were a throbbing pain at that location, and Jake abruptly stopped speaking. He felt helpless and impotent, and he suddenly wanted to slam his hand on the steering-wheel in an inarticulate and raging fury against the unfairness of life and the heavy blow of fate that had changed his closest friend into a sick and apathetic stranger. He would have given his right arm to find one subject that would make Guy sit up and take notice, to come alive again, to laugh with that slow and lazy smile.

'There's a woman living with me,' he said. 'Her name's Sophia.'

It worked as Jake had thought it would. For the first time since they had left the airport, Guy turned and looked at him. 'You're kidding.'

'She lost the lease on her apartment, and I took pity on her.' Jake grinned with a sheepishness that would have, in the past, elicited at the very least a laugh and an obscene comment. Jake almost never invited a woman to stay with him. His last attempt at cohabitation had been six years earlier and had ended in disaster after two months. 'I don't know what prompted me to do it,' he went on. 'Maybe the single life was getting to me and she is great in the sack. Of course, she can't cook worth a damn and she won't iron my shirts, so I'm not sure how long . . .' He would have gone on had Guy not turned away and stared out of the window again. The rage came over Jake again, almost blurring his vision of the street, but this time it was tinged with an unutterable sadness, and he was horrified to feel the prick of tears behind his eyes.

They were driving now into the southwestern section of Calgary and entering a wealthy suburb where the houses were large, luxurious and often ostentatious. A sudden movement on the seat next to him made Jake give Guy an uneasy sideways glance, and he was suddenly apprehensive about the arrangements that had been made for Guy's return. For the first time, it occurred to him that Maureen had swayed him against his better judgment. Her reasoning had been impeccable, her arguments sound and everyone had agreed with her; the doctors, Guy's parents, even Jake. He knew Guy couldn't take pressure or stress; he

knew that surgery still needed to be done on Guy's leg;
they were all aware that Guy's mother was incapable
of caring for him with his father still recovering from
the heart attack. Jake couldn't nurse Guy himself, not
considering the fact that he had to head up north in
two weeks to assess the latest exploration project. And
yes, he had to agree with Maureen that Guy's apartment was large and prohibitively expensive when you
considered that he wouldn't be able to live in it for the
next three or four months. Still, Jake was now wishing
that they hadn't jumped to conclusions so quickly,
that they had waited a bit before subletting the apartment, that they hadn't made decisions for a man who
was accustomed to being in control of his life. No
matter how dull and apathetic Guy seemed, Jake had a
strong suspicion that he wasn't going to like the course
of action they had planned out for him.

Even though he had fortified himself, Jake couldn't
help wincing when Guy said angrily, 'What the hell
are we doing here?'

Jake had pulled into the curved driveway of a large
house with an artificial Tudor façade, replete with
wooden beams to hide the ubiquitous Calgary stucco
and windows with narrow crossbars to imitate old
English leaded panes. He turned off the ignition and,
turning to Guy, said carefully, 'We thought you'd be
better off staying with Maureen for a while.'

'Who's we?' Guy demanded.

'Myself, Maureen, your folks.'

'My parents!'

'Your Dad is still a sick man, Guy. Your mother
couldn't take care of both of you.'

Guy spat out his reply. 'I don't need someone to take *care* of me.'

'The doctor told us that you . . .' Jake sought for the right words '. . . that you shouldn't be left on your own right away, that you . . .'

Guy gritted his teeth. 'Take me to my apartment.'

'I . . .'

'I won't stay with her. We're divorced, remember?'

'Guy, she doesn't mind having you here. In fact, it was her idea.'

Emphatically. 'No.'

'What if you got sick again? What about the surgery on your leg? The doctor said you won't be able to walk for a month.'

'My apartment, Jake.'

Jake ran his hand over the steering-wheel. 'It's been . . . rented.'

'What!'

'Sublet for four months.'

Guy sat back as if he had sustained a blow to his solar plexus, but when Jake tried to explain, the look he received was positively malevolent.

'God, Jake, did you really think I'd want to stay with her?'

Jake was cautious. 'Maureen still . . . cares for you. She never wanted the divorce.'

'I don't want to be married to her.'

'Staying with her while you're sick isn't being married. It's only temporary.'

Guy was impatient with this line of reasoning. 'We both know what she's after.'

Jake twisted his hand around the steering-wheel.

'Would it hurt to try, Guy? Maybe the divorce *was* a mistake.'

'You always were on Maureen's side, weren't you?'

Jake was stung at this hint of disloyalty and, not being used to having Guy attack him, he swung his head unhappily like a bull at a bullfight, confused and disorientated. 'Maureen's a . . . fine woman,' he answered slowly. 'I've always liked her.' There had been some who had thought that Jake would view Maureen as competition after Guy married, but he didn't have a possessive bone in his body. He had simply seen Guy's wife as a part of Guy and enfolded her in his affections. And being a man of habit, his affection for her had remained after the separation.

'If you don't get me out of . . .'

But it was too late. The front door to the Tudor house opened and Maureen stood there with a welcoming and anticipatory smile. They could see her mouth forming the words 'Guy' and 'I've been waiting for you.' Jake turned to beg Guy to give his stay here a second thought and was shocked to find that no persuasion would be required. The anger had drained out of Guy in an instant and, with it, the spark that had brought him to life again. The dark head was bent and a weary hand was rubbing his eyes. His body slumped against the bucket seat in apathy and helpless acquiescence. Jake hadn't liked Guy's anger but it was preferable to this, he thought with a sinking dismay. Infinitely preferable to this.

Guy had known his recovery from pneumonia would be slow. You don't stand on the threshold of death for days and just walk away with body and mind intact. And the doctors had warned him that his adjustment back to ordinary life would be complicated by his illness, but he hadn't counted on the irritability that plagued him or the bouts of apathy or the sleepless periods that alternated with days in which he could barely stay awake. He hadn't counted on the frustrating, infuriating and maddening weakness that would catch him so suddenly that he thought he could feel the very beat of his heart slow to a snail's pace.

He supposed he was lucky to have Maureen nursing him although the knowledge of his dependence on her grated hard. She did her level best to make him comfortable and happy, although the latter was an impossible task, particularly when the surgery on his leg cut his already limited mobility to the narrow confines of a bed or chair. She brought him tasty meals to whet his appetite, played cards with him, took books by his favourite authors out of the library. She chatted to him lightly and without any seeming intent, her voice high and happy, her blonde head tilted like a bird's, her brown eyes bright. She straightened his bed, smoothed the pillowcases, eased down the edge of a blanket that was sticking out at one corner. She fussed over him endlessly until Guy had to clench his teeth to keep from being rude. He had forgotten the way Maureen could fuss and how much he had always hated it. Guy needed a woman whose presence was soothing, whose hands were gentle and easing, whose eyes were the colour of the Arctic sky.

He dreamed about Rebecca endlessly, in the troubled, shallow sleep of an afternoon's nap, in the heavy, dark curve of the night. Although she was often naked in his dreams, the content of them was not erotic. In them, she would walk towards him, away from him, her hand touching his forehead and then moving to stroke the bark of a tree. The dreams were a crazy *mélange* of images of the lake, the lean-to, the promontory, all containing Rebecca in constant motion. She was never close enough for him actually to hold her; she slipped away into the water, the shadows, the trees. In one dream when he touched her, her skin was cold and slippery, like that of a snake or the side of a swiftly-moving fish. He had woken up after that dream, sweating and exhausted, only to stare up at the dark ceiling and wonder for the millionth time, why. Why had she left the hospital so abruptly? Why hadn't she come to see him? Where had she disappeared to?

Guy had been far too weak and sick after the rescue to be aware that Rebecca was gone. He had been awake for such short periods and so busily cared for by the hospital staff when he was conscious that he had had little time for contemplation. He couldn't keep track of the days, the hours or even the minutes so it wasn't until a week after the rescue that Guy suddenly realised that he hadn't seen Rebecca at all. It had been a shock to discover that she had disappeared without a word to anyone. In fact, her disappearance had caused something of a scandal since she had been under surveillance. The doctor had been furious and the nurses on her floor had come in for a tongue-lashing. The only evidence of her departure had been the missing white outfit from the nurses' station.

Shock had yielded to unhappiness which had given way, in the moments when Guy felt strong, to a raging anger. These were the times when, had Rebecca suddenly appeared before him, Guy would have strangled her with his bare hands. Had she held their relationship so cheaply that she could walk away from it without a word? Had their lovemaking meant nothing to her? Had she cared so little about him? Had she not realised the depth of his feeling towards her?

The questions raced around his brain and, when he spoke them in the emptiness of his room, they bounced off the walls, echoing and unanswered. Had he been healthy, Guy would have gone to his club and smashed a squash ball against a wall or jogged around the track until he was running with sweat and mindless from the exertion, but he was barely strong enough to make it from Maureen's kitchen back to his bedroom. He hated his weakness; he railed against it, but he was helpless to stop it from undermining his resolve and determination.

It wasn't until two weeks after his arrival at Maureen's house that Guy managed to make the phone call he had been thinking about for days. Maureen worked part-time as an interior decorator and had left the house at midday. Guy pulled himself out of bed, cursed the trembling in his legs and slowly walked the short distance to the telephone. It didn't take him long to get the number from the long-distance operator, and he took a deep breath as he listened to the phone ring.

The voice that answered was adolescent and timorous. 'Hello?'

'Is Rebecca there?'

A pause. 'Who's calling, please?'

'Guy McLaren. Rebecca and I were . . . we crashed together.'

'Oh! I think you'd better talk to my mother.'

Martine Clark was cool and aloof.

'Mr McLaren? How nice of you to phone. Are you in town?'

'No, I'm calling from Calgary.'

'Really. Is it cold up there?'

'No, we've been having a mild . . . Look, Mrs Clark, I'd like to talk to Rebecca.'

'I'm afraid that isn't possible.'

'Is she staying with you?'

'No, she isn't.'

'Has she left Fairfax?'

'Yes.'

Guy had the frustrating feeling that he was pulling hen's teeth. 'Could you give me her new number?'

'She's unlisted, Mr McLaren.'

'But I know she'd like to hear from me.'

'Well, she hasn't *mentioned* you.'

His anger was rising, but so was the headache that plagued him incessantly. He tried to be calm. 'Mrs Clark, is there any way you can help me get in touch with Rebecca?'

Martine was reasonable. Too reasonable. 'Of course, and I'm sure once she knows you've phoned she won't hesitate to call you.'

'You'll tell her then?'

'Certainly. Give me your address and telephone number.'

Guy complied and then made one last desperate plea. 'Where has she moved to?'

'I'm sure Rebecca will tell you when she calls you back. Goodbye, Mr McLaren.'

Guy had hung up the phone and was staring malevolently down at the innocent black receiver, understanding for the first time Rebecca's description of her mother as a cold woman with a polite veneer that masked a will of iron. He had wanted to ask her a thousand questions: Is Rebecca all right? Is she happy? Does she talk about the crash, the Arctic, me? But they had all died on his lips when he realised that she wouldn't have answered any of them. He could only pray that Rebecca would phone him as Martine had promised.

For the first time in his life, Guy discovered what it was like to be in a position that was familiar to women and alien to men. His natural masculine aggression was blunted; he could only be passive and expectant. He had never before waited for the telephone to ring with the right person at the other end. His pulse raced whenever Maureen picked up the receiver, the ringing of the phone tied him in knots when he was alone in the house. He tried not to let his nervous anticipation show, but he wasn't quite successful.

'Who was that?' he demanded one day when Maureen came into his room with a lunch tray. He had recently had surgery done on his leg to repair a tendon and his calf and ankle were back in a cast. Rebecca's handiwork had been much admired by the orthopaedist, but Guy had injured a tendon when he had twisted his leg the day of the rainstorm.

Maureen gave him a surprised look. 'Jake calling to say he'd drop by later. Are you waiting for someone else to phone?'

'No,' he said.

Maureen looked suspicious but shrugged as she perched on the end of the bed. She smoothed down one corner and rearranged the cup of coffee on Guy's tray so that it was symmetrical with the napkin, a gesture that made his teeth tighten together. He could smell the perfume she wore and could see how carefully she was made up. Although they shared the house, Maureen never, metaphorically speaking, let her hair down in his presence. She always dressed impeccably, even now she was wearing an attractive blue tweed skirt and soft matching silk blouse, and she looked as if she had just come from the beauty salon. It was as if she felt it necessary to have her best foot forward for his appraisal. Guy felt alternately sorry for her and irritated by the constant pretence. Although Maureen was a very pretty woman, he felt absolutely no sexual interest in her at all and he had, he discovered, developed a taste for a woman who didn't look artificial, whose hair wasn't held stiffly in place with spray, whose mouth hadn't been altered by a line of lipstick.

'It's a roast beef sandwich,' she encouraged.

Guy looked down at the tray on his lap without much enthusiasm. 'Thanks,' he managed.

Maureen flourished the pad she had carried in. 'Guy, I really wish you'd back down on the decision to avoid the press. The world is just dying to know your story. You don't realise what a celebrity you are. And

I'm not just talking about the Calgary or the Canadian papers. The television people in the US are just fascinated by what you've been through.' She paused to give extra weight to the words that would follow. 'Merv Griffin phoned. He wants you on his show.'

'No.'

Maureen sighed. 'I've been fending off everyone, saying that you're too ill, but really you're not any more.'

'It never had to do with my being sick. I'm not interested in being a three-day wonder.'

'But Guy, think of the opportunities, the exposure. You'll be famous.'

'Famous for what?'

'For being a survivor.'

'I told you; I'm not interested.'

Maureen leaned forward, her brown eyes intent. 'The nurse has completely dropped out of sight and the public is starving for you. You know how the phone's been ringing. Everyone wants to see and hear you.'

'No.'

Her lips pursed in that old, familiar way. 'I think you're making a big mistake,' she said angrily. 'I think you're letting life pass you by.'

Guy picked up the sandwich. 'Maureen, it's my decision.'

She stood up abruptly, jerking the blanket with one hand to straighten where his foot had kicked it out. He could see how furious she was and how hard she worked to contain that fury. 'We'll talk about it some other time,' she said.

'Maureen . . .'

But she was gone, the door shutting with a bang behind her as Guy sighed. The conversation was not a new one and they had covered the same ground before. Maureen, Guy had discovered after moving in, had acted like a quasi-press agent on his behalf, granting interviews and busily arranging television appearances. He had gone through with a few of them for the sake of keeping the peace and refused the rest, hating the way the reporters sought after the intimate details of his life with brazen questions that were asked without the restraints of common decency. But Maureen had thoroughly enjoyed the exposure and had played, to the hilt, the role of spokesperson. He came to realise that she had been involved in the same sort of self-aggrandisement before the rescue, talking to the media and implying that she and Guy were still married instead of separated with the divorce papers imminently on their way.

Being in the limelight had given her a new brittleness and artificiality. She had become manipulative and aggressive, and Guy had often wondered if she were the person who had leaked news of the rescue to the press in the first place. He had heard over and over again from the hospital staff how hard they had tried to keep his arrival a secret so that he and Rebecca wouldn't be bothered by the press. But someone had spread the word, and reporters had invaded the hospital, sneaking in by back corridors, dressing in medical clothes, pretending to be orderlies for the sake of getting a hot story. Guy couldn't help feeling that Maureen's obvious desire to erase their two-year

separation and start a relationship all over again arose,
not from any love for him, but more from a driving
urge to stay in the spotlight, to be on the front page of
the newspaper and have the phone ringing off the
hook with calls from magazine editors, radio stations
and television anchormen.

Her moment of greatest triumph had been the
photographing of the house by a national women's
magazine. Being a decorator, she had preened herself
over that coup while Guy had remained silent. Early in
their marriage, he had yielded to her desire for a large
and grandiose house that she could decorate to her
heart's content, but he had come to hate it. Their taste
was totally different, and the brightly coloured knick-
knacks, the dark wallpapers, the art deco mirrors still
bothered him intensely. He longed for his own apartment with its casual leather and tweedy furniture, the
walls of bookshelves, the fireplace piled high with
logs.

Slowly, Guy gained weight and strength, his rest-
lessness increasing with each gain, the weakness and
irritability disappearing. After his cast came off, he
began to go to the office for half a day at a time,
chauffeured by an optimistic Jake, and took part in
business decisions again. The sublet was almost over
and he began to make plans to move back into his
own place. Maureen came into the kitchen one day
as he was phoning a painter and making arrangements to have the place painted before he got back
in.

That bird-like chirpiness had left her and her eyes
were wary. 'So you're moving back,' she said, sitting

down in the cane chair by the table as he hung up the receiver.

'Yes.' He smiled at her. 'I don't know how to thank you for all you've done.'

She lined up the salt and pepper shakers and put the sugar bowl between them, her nails gleaming a deep red. 'I don't suppose you'd change your mind and think of staying.'

Guy suddenly understood another reason why Maureen had wanted to nurse him. She had been lonely in this mausoleum of an over-decorated house and now dreaded being on her own again. 'Maureen, I . . .'

She threw her hands out. 'You don't have to say anything, I just thought I'd ask. I guess I've known all along that there's no real spark between us any more, and you've made it perfectly clear that, if you feel anything about me, that it's . . . well, sisterly.'

He had once thought he loved her; he had certainly felt an intense sexual desire for her. Not all her flaws and his complete indifference to her femininity could erase what had existed in the past. 'If I thought there were a chance, Maureen, if there were even an inkling of something between us, I would have tried.' He spoke with conviction, suddenly realising that it was true. He had not completely understood his reasons for leaving Maureen; he had believed with a strong sense of guilt that boredom had lain behind his decision. This guilt about the past had been one of the reasons why he had not fought harder against staying with her for his convalescence. An uneasiness about his own motives had made him willing to see if his feelings towards Maureen had changed. But now he realised with far greater clarity why the divorce had come about. They had little in common except for a set of shared memories and, if any emotion existed between them, it was formed of a tepid sort of affection. Neither of them was to blame, nor had any particular bitterness or battle marked the end of their life together. Their passion towards one another had simply not withstood the test of time, its fire burning out, the ashes to remain forever cold.

Her mouth turned down. 'You were always kind. I'll give you that.'

'Hasn't there been anyone else?'

She shrugged. 'One man, about a year ago. It didn't work out.'

Guy reached out and gently touched her hand which was nervously fiddling with the edge of a black lacquered placemat. 'You're a very lovely woman,' he said with total sincerity. 'I'm sure someone will turn up.'

She smiled at him then, a small and unhappy smile. 'That's what I keep telling myself.'

Guy's move out of Maureen's house and back into his own apartment coincided with a determination on his part to forget that Rebecca had ever existed. No one had guessed the agonies he had gone through, certainly not Maureen or Jake who had asked him a few questions and been put off by his casual answers, or the few reporters who had been rebuffed by his coolness. He had suffered through disappointment, despair and an impotent raging fury. Now he was aiming for complete disinterest. Rebecca had never phoned him, and Guy could only assume that either Martine had not passed along the message or that Rebecca had ignored it. Of course, he preferred to think that the former was the case, only because it assuaged his hurt ego. He was more convinced, however, that it was the latter. He had no belief in the ESP phenomenon or mental telepathy, but he had a deep gut feeling that Rebecca was hiding, not from the world or the curious press, but from him. For some reason, she didn't want to see him again.

He thought he could understand why she had wanted to distance herself from the experience of the crash, their survival in the Arctic, his illness and the final rescue. He had the same instinctive withdrawal from memories of that time. They were intense and overwhelming, the kind that make you shudder in retrospect and haunt you in your dreams. Both he and Rebecca had come a knife's-edge close to death several times. The emotions that had fuelled them were intense enough to burn. In order to heal from the suffering, the fear and the uncertainty that had been constant companions for two months, he wanted to put that time at arm's length, to perceive it in the proper perspective, to adjust back to civilised life with both mental and physical health.

Although he longed for Rebecca, although the remembered touch of her body was enough to stir him immediately, Guy was aware of a hesitancy in himself. While one part of him felt a strong and driving urge to find her again; another part resisted the return of those remembered emotions. He felt too fragile; he wasn't sure he could withstand them. And then his rational side wondered if his feelings had survived the rescue intact. He had come to believe that he loved Rebecca, but realised that his love for her existed in another time and place, grown and nurtured by isolation and the ever-present awareness of death. Perhaps, it would have no reality in a world not encompassed by a lake, trees and mountains.

Still, Guy missed Rebecca with a physical sensation of aching that was as real as any other kind of pain. He felt that part of him was gone, as if a surgery had been performed on his very soul. There were a thousand and one things he would have liked to share with her; the reporter who had gone green around the gills when he described their meals of raw fish, the dreams he had about the camp, the déjà vu feeling he had had when he caught sight of an axe in a store window. No one could have appreciated those events and his emotions the way Rebecca could have. No one but she could understand their experience and its after-effects: those extraordinary and unexpected moments when he suddenly felt an intensity and power of living that only comes from having been a hair's-breadth away from dying.

Despite his gut feeling, however, that Rebecca was sharing the same emotions of longing and doubt, her disappearance into the woodwork and the way her family had erected such a protective shield around her had brought Guy around to another and even more painful way of thinking. Two beliefs warred within him. One was that Rebecca had found another man;

the other was that she had succumbed to temptations and gained back all the weight she had lost.

He wavered between these two thoughts, each bringing its own specific feelings of hurt, anger and helplessness. The idea of another man possessing her roused a jealousy in him that he had never felt about another woman. He found that it tore at him like some sort of wild beast, destroying his calm, his peace of mind, his own confident belief in his masculinity. There were moments when he lay alone in bed, the dark night pressing all around him, and his imagination would run riot with visions of Rebecca being kissed by another man, held in strange arms, caressed by hands that were not his. Sleep eluded him then, and he would find himself lying rigid, his teeth grinding together, his hands clenched into white-knuckled fists.

Yet, his second thought was equally as torturous. While he could try to compete with another man, Guy knew that he was impotent in a battle against Rebecca's compulsive eating. Its origins arose in her childhood and were reinforced by patterns of behaviour she had established as an adult. If she had gained back all the weight she had lost in the Arctic, the woman that he had known would no longer be in existence. The physical Rebecca who had stirred his blood and caused him to tremble within her arms would be gone, trapped within herself, and the other Rebecca, the woman who had discovered her femininity and an unexpected happiness in her ability to please him would have disappeared.

Guy had vivid memories of Rebecca as he had first

seen her; she had been withdrawn, frightened and insecure. She had been unable to take a compliment and recoiled from the slightest hint that she was a woman. She had preferred to think of herself as a body with a neuter gender. Nothing had existed between them at that time but a buddy-like camaraderie, a sexless and bland connection. Guy knew he could never return to that sort of a relationship. He wanted Rebecca as the person she had become, but he was afraid that the woman whose body he had taken with such passion and whose mind he had known with such pleasure would be buried deep in the oblivion of fat.

It was these thoughts, fears and hesitancies that held Guy back from a search for Rebecca. He didn't try to phone Martine again; he never tried to reach Tamara. Instead, he was determined to pick up the broken threads of his life and, if that meant erasing the memory of Rebecca from his mind, then he was prepared to do it. He allowed work and the move back into his apartment to occupy him. He bought a new couch and had the carpets cleaned. He purchased several new suits and threw himself into the finishing details of the exploration project he had been en route to visiting when the Twin Otter went down. For a while, these activities were sufficient to distract him from thoughts of the past, but in time the novelty of new things and being back at the office waned. He became restless and plagued by the physical need for a woman. He thought any woman would do and accepted, much to Jake's delight, an invitation to meet a friend of the voluptuous and sexy Sophia.

CHAPTER EIGHT

SARAH Downes' back ached like the dickens, but the hands that were massaging the painful muscles were gentle, soothing and skilful. They seemed to know, without her help, exactly where the spasms were and the tight, knotted places. She sighed and thanked her lucky stars that this nurse had turned out to be so wonderful. It hadn't been easy for her to admit to the need for full-time care, but the doctor had finally insisted that she get off her feet and into bed. The relief had been almost instantaneous. She was immensely pregnant and in her eighth month of carrying quadruplets, the result of taking fertility drugs. In addition to being enormously large, she was suffering from water retention that made her fingers, feet and ankles grotesquely swollen, severe leg cramps and the constant pain of stretched back ligaments.

'You give the greatest back rubs,' she praised. 'Is that what they taught you in nursing school?'

The voice was equally easing. 'It comes with the diploma.'

'I could become addicted to it,' Sarah added. 'It feels terrific.'

'I'll give Dave some pointers.'

Sarah smiled when she thought of her husband. 'He's a sweetheart, isn't he? Imagine putting up with all this and still keeping in a good humour.'

'You're a lucky lady.'

'He's got a brother.'

'Uh-oh, I think I hear the sound of matchmaking.'

'Why not? I have nothing else to do.'

The gentle hands pulled down the quilted fabric of her bed-jacket. 'Yes, you do. It's time for lunch.'

Sarah turned over on to her back with effort, the mound of her pregnancy lifting the blankets. She was a slight woman with curly dark hair and a slender face that would have been pretty had she not looked so exhausted. She looked up with a weary smile. 'What is it?'

'Tuna fish and tomato salad, a piece of toast, an apple and skimmed milk.'

'When this is all over,' Sarah vowed, 'I'm going on a high-carbohydrate and sugar diet. Lemon meringue pie, baked Alaska, chocolate-chip cookies.'

'When this is all over, you're not even going to have time to eat.'

Sarah groaned. 'Don't remind me.' She closed her eyes and said in a wondering voice, 'Four babies. *Four babies.*'

Rebecca was smiling to herself as she walked out of the bedroom and into the kitchen. Nursing Sarah Downes was her third private nursing job, and she had discovered that she liked the independence and anonymity that working free-lance gave her. And she liked maternity care so much that she had promised Sarah that she would help out with the babies after they were born. The knowledge that she had several months of guaranteed work ahead gave her a secure feeling. Her life was finally in a calm equilibrium after weeks of manic highs and depressed lows, days and nights of hiding out in Tamara's apartment and trying to recover from the panic and misery that had forced her to sneak out of the hospital and flee Edmonton as if all the mythical Furies were pursuing her with a vengeance.

The media had been the catalyst that had sent Rebecca into a dizzying spin of hysteria. If it hadn't been for the press, Rebecca might have stayed at the hospital to find out precisely what role Maureen would play in Guy's life, but when she had returned to her room, running away from the sound of the other woman's voice with its combination of affection and intimacy, she had found a reporter waiting for her, a woman with glossy, platinum hair and bright red lipstick, who had come into the hospital through a service door and was dressed in a nurse's uniform. Not being used to dealing with the press, Rebecca hadn't known how to get rid of her and had agreed to an interview. It began politely enough and then deteriorated into a series of questions so personal and leeringly suggestive that Rebecca had finally fled. Since most hospitals were the same, she had found where the nurses kept their uniforms. With an audacity she hadn't known she possessed, Rebecca stripped off her bathrobe and hospital gown, stuffed it under a bench and climbed into a strange woman's clothes. Her hands shook as she buttoned up the bodice and laced up a pair of shoes on her bare feet, but she managed an air of confidence when she stepped out into a corridor and almost collided with an orderly.

'Excuse me,' she said and he nodded.

She went out the back entrance of the hospital and found herself in a parking lot. People passed her as she stood in the middle of the pavement and wondered where she would go and what she would do without any money or knowledge of the city. A cool breeze lifted up a strand of her hair and she shivered a bit. The outfit she had stolen only had short sleeves and her legs were bare. The courage and bravado that she had mustered to make her break swiftly drained out of her as she contemplated the immediate future. She hadn't really thought about the actual means of getting away from the hospital—like taking a taxi to the airport and having the money to phone Tamara who could get her a plane reservation. She had simply panicked and run, stealing only clothes and no money. Not that she thought she could have actually rummaged through another woman's purse and lifted even a dollar.

Rebecca was never sure later whether she would have continued on into a highly uncertain future or gone back to the safety and security of the hospital. The choice was made for her by a tiny, elderly lady by the name of Crazy Maude.

A small finger poked her arm and Rebecca jumped in alarm.

'I know you,' an old woman said with a shrewd look in hooded blue eyes. 'Saw you on my shift yesterday. You're the one from the rescue, ain't you?'

Rebecca's heart was beating so loud she thought the woman would hear it over the sound of the cars passing by. 'No,' she answered, trying to hide her fear. 'I'm not.'

The old woman ignored her and pursed her lips. 'Never forget a face, I do. Got the memory of an elephant.' She grinned, revealing five teeth, her own face a web formed of a thousand wrinkles. She was wearing a shapeless brown coat and a knitted red toque that barely covered her wisps of grey hair. In one hand she carried an old needlepoint canvas bag that sprouted a salami and bread, a trailing scarf and a bent twig wrapped in yarn.

'I . . .'

'Skipped out, have you?'

'Certainly not . . . I wouldn't think . . .' Rebecca stammered as she glanced wildly around her and wondered if, should she run for it, this half-crazy individual would alert the police.

'Don't like doctors much myself,' the old woman went on in a confiding tone. 'A bunch of quacks with airs, that's what they are.'

Rebecca stared at her.

'Don't suppose you got even a cent on you.' The old woman shook her head and then gave a little cackle. 'Well, Crazy Maude has a few tricks up her sleeve that those doctors don't know about. Stepped on my mop, one of them did. Big feet too. Didn't think much of that, I didn't.'

There didn't seem to be any proper response so Rebecca said nothing.

'Well, can't have you live here in the parking lot. Come with me then. I'll get you straight.'

Maude lived in a run-down building in a tiny one-room apartment with two cats and a parakeet. She had a rickety bed and chair, a two-burner cook-top and a huge television set. Rebecca gingerly sat down on the chair, watched Maude fuss about, talking incessantly about people at the hospital as if Rebecca knew who they were, and wondered, with a slight tinge of hysteria, if the television had been stolen.

'. . . can't stand Mrs Ross neither. She's a sneaky one, always staring at a person's back. I can feel her eyes, I can.'

Rebecca cleared her throat. 'Maude. I'd like to call my sister. Is there a phone here?'

'Can't stand it when a person just stares. It gives me a heap of the willies.'

Rebecca spoke a bit louder. 'Maude. Do you have a phone?'

Crazy Maude turned and looked at her. 'Me? What would I have with a phone? Ain't nobody to call.' She cackled then as if it were all a big joke. 'Of course, there's a phone downstairs, but I wouldn't trust it. Nope, I wouldn't trust it.'

Rebecca had more confidence in the telephone company. 'Is it a pay phone?'

'Eats quarters.'

'Could I borrow a quarter?' Rebecca asked and then added hurriedly, 'I'll pay you back.'

Maude blinked at her. 'Well, of course you will. I trust you.'

It was a relief to get Tamara on the first ring and, when she explained what she had done, to discover that her sister was sympathetic. She gave Tamara the number of the pay phone and waited until she called back to say that she had made a plane reservation for Rebecca that left Edmonton at ten o'clock the next morning and arrived in New York at seven in the evening.

'How are you going to get to the airport?' Tamara asked in concern after Rebecca had described her situation.

'I'll get there,' she said fervently, 'if I have to walk.'

But she hadn't counted on Crazy Maude's resources and upside-down version of generosity. The old woman distrusted most people and hated the rest, particularly the hospital workers. But she had a soft spot for anyone who stood against the medical establishment and she seemed to think that Rebecca had taken a wonderful stand. Their unexpected alliance gave Crazy Maude a lot of pleasure, and she regaled Rebecca with stories of doubtful nefarious medical practices, rotten personalities and downright swindling. Rebecca was unable to discover if Crazy Maude's attitude was based on any experience or if it was simply a part and parcel of an obvious senility and paranoia.

The old woman made her a dinner of fried salami and egg, which they ate on odd plates which looked as if they had been scavenged at a jumble sale. They watched the news, Rebecca sitting on the bed, Maude perched on the end of the rickety chair like some bedraggled sparrow, her head cocked at an angle when a picture of the hospital flashed on the screen. Maureen then appeared looking self-confident and poised as she spoke into a bank of microphones, explaining that her husband was too ill to speak to the press himself, that he was still on the critical list, but she and the rest of his family were praying for . . .

'Hypocrite,' Crazy Maude mumbled. 'Seen her type before.'

Rebecca gave her a startled glance but was distracted when her own face filled the screen. It was a picture that had been taken of her the night before when she had entered the hospital from the ambulance. It was a shocking image of a woman on the verge of collapse, her arms supported by two men, her hair hanging in ratty coils, her clothes in tatters, her face caught in an expression of utter weariness. 'My God,' she whispered to herself as the announcer spoke.

'Hospital officials said tonight that Rebecca Clark, another survivor of the Twin Otter crash, has mysteriously disappeared from the hospital and her whereabouts are uncertain. Our own reporter, Cynthia Mallory, spoke with her earlier today.'

Cynthia Mallory, her hair glittering like a silver cap under the television lights, had her moment's-worth of glory while Rebecca cringed. She speculated on the disappearance, hinted at an affair with Guy and cast innuendoes in every direction about the tragedy of disappointed love under the bright glare of the world's attention. She had also interviewed a psychiatrist who discussed, in a highly academic fashion, the reactions of survivors, their disorientation when they returned to civilisation, their potential craziness. At the last word, Crazy Maude looked at her and gave another cackle, and Rebecca wondered if the old woman now thought they were truly kindred spirits.

Somehow, the whole experience of the hospital, her escape from it and her sojourn with Crazy Maude seemed to be happening to someone other than Rebecca. She felt aloof from it all as if she were viewing herself from a long distance away, from a mountain top perhaps or through the small end of a telescope. Later, Rebecca was to realise that this was one of the ways her psyche had worked to protect itself. It would have been far too easy to succumb to panic or to an underlying misery over her separation from Guy or to indulge in a bit of the old woman's lunacy. In order to maintain her sanity, it was necessary for Rebecca to hold the part of her that was real in a protected seclusion, waiting for the moment that she could be herself again.

It was easy to let Crazy Maude insist that she sleep on the bed even though Rebecca said she could manage in the chair, and she didn't mind the way the old woman muttered and fussed over her as she slipped off the nurse's uniform and slid in between old, mended but thankfully clean sheets. Her eyes closed almost immediately and she fell into a dreamless, refreshing sleep, waking at dawn to the sound of a tuneless humming. She could never be sure if Crazy Maude had slept at all because she was sitting by Rebecca, stroking her hair, her almost toothless mouth stretched in a contented smile. For a moment, Rebecca wondered if she should be frightened of what she had deemed a harmless old eccentric, but Crazy Maude moved away when she realised that Rebecca was awake.

They had the ubiquitous salami and eggs for breakfast and Rebecca tried to clean herself in the tiny sink in one corner that served for dishes as well as personal needs. She was worried what Crazy Maude would do when she said she was leaving, but the old woman merely nodded, her grey wisps bobbing in the air.

'Need money. Can't get to the airport without money. Lend you a sweater, too.'

The sweater was old, green and smelled of mothballs, but Rebecca obediently put it on over the nurse's uniform. The money came from a huge wad underneath the bedstead, a thick roll of twenties, fifties and even hundred dollar bills. Crazy Maude muttered over the money and pursed her lips as she slowly but carefully peeled off two twenty dollar bills and handed them to Rebecca.

Rebecca was intensely relieved that she would now be able to make it to the airport and extremely touched by Crazy Maude's generosity. She knew how paltry the old woman's salary must be, and she suspected that her forty dollars came from a carefully saved nest-egg. Crazy Maude wasn't the type who would trust banks either.

'Thank you,' said Rebecca. 'I'll repay you. I promise I will when I get home.'

If a heart of gold truly existed beneath Crazy Maude's unbalanced exterior, it was blocked by her next gesture. With a quick motion, she grabbed back one of the twenty dollar bills, giving Rebecca a suspicious glance. 'You going to a hospital?'

Rebecca suddenly realised how lucky she was that Crazy Maude had never actually seized on the fact that she was a nurse. 'Never,' she vowed with absolute sincerity. 'I'll never go near a hospital again.'

*   *   *

According to the news, the police had been alerted to Rebecca's disappearance, but somehow she had managed to travel the two and a half thousand miles east and cross into the United States without detection, merely walking through the gate that said for 'US Citizens' only and meeting a relieved Tamara at the other end. And Rebecca had kept both her promises to Crazy Maude. She had repaid her with a sum vastly greater than what had been given, and she had not gone back to work in a hospital. She hadn't wanted to be recognised and she hadn't been sure she could handle the pressure of a complex working environment. The shock of her re-entry into society had been severe. She had suffered from confusion, disorientation and depression, finding it not only difficult to make major decisions such as those concerning a job and an apartment, but being totally lost on such minor issues as what to wear or what to have for lunch. It was as if all the responsibilities she had endured in the Arctic and the immense energy it had taken to escape from the hospital had left her without vigour or resources.

For weeks after she had left Edmonton, Rebecca virtually hid out in Tamara's apartment, staring out of the window or lying in bed looking up at the cracks on the ceiling. Sleep either eluded her or held her in a tight grip from which she would awake with her heart thudding loudly and her body sweating. She felt then as if she were drugged by the play of her imagination and could remember only in brief images what must comprise the vast, intertwined plots of her dreams; the tangle of trees, the flash of the axe, firelight on Guy's dark hair, his face skeletal and gaunt.

Tamara was, fortunately, understanding and sympathetic. She took Rebecca shopping, leading her from store to store, and helping her choose a new wardrobe. She didn't hurry or push her into any particular lifestyle, assuming that the passage of time would eventually wear off Rebecca's particular brand of shellshock. Her one intrusion was finding her sister a job, and it was done in such an off-hand manner that Rebecca accepted it without undue agonising or uncertainty. It was arranged by Tamara's doctor and was a private nursing job for a small boy who had required leg surgery. That referral led to another job and word of mouth accomplished the rest. Without any particular exertion on Rebecca's part, she discovered that she was employable in situations that guaranteed anonymity and didn't require the stress she associated with working in a hospital. Moreover, the ability to control her own working and leisure hours gave Rebecca her first small taste of independence and was her first step towards regaining her mental health.

Jogging was the second. She had never forgotten the doctor's assertion in Edmonton that he wouldn't let her go until she was fit enough to run a marathon. In her desire to hold down her weight and keep fit, Rebecca began running. At first, she hated it; truly hated it. Her feet hurt, her heart pounded, her chest felt as if it would explode. She did it for her body; she did it so that she wouldn't gain any weight, but after a while the running became almost pleasurable, the distances goals worth achieving. Ironically, she had less appetite when she ran although she wasn't sure whether the lessening of desire for food was mental rather than physical. It seemed absurd to sit down and eat a box of cookies after she had worked so hard to run five miles.

After the crash, Rebecca had thought that the temptations of available food would overwhelm her, but the type of hunger that had forced her to eat obsessively rarely appeared and, when it did, she was able to ignore its pangs. She loved the taste of food and savoured every morsel, never forgetting the blandness of the diet she had been forced to keep in the Arctic, but the habit of compulsive eating seemed to have been broken for good. She had no idea whether the experience of survival or her distance from her mother and Fairfax had cured her. Rebecca only knew that as long as she kept jogging and held her life to an even emotional keel, she was able to remain slim.

Rebecca carried the tray into Sarah's room and saw that the other woman was awake.

'Hungry?' she asked.

Sarah sighed. 'Starving. It must be a condition of pregnancy.'

'Well, you're feeding four extra hungry mouths.'

Sarah allowed Rebecca to put the tray down on her lap but she didn't begin eating right away. 'I hope they all make it,' she said slowly, fear making her eyes darken.

Rebecca quickly sat down beside her on the bed and gently took her hand. 'Of course they will,' she encouraged soothingly. 'Dr Michaels says they're all healthy and have strong heartbeats.' She had discovered that a private nurse did more than just look after a patient's physical health. In the hospital, she had barely been able to spend more than five minutes with any one individual. Working in a private home and spending hours with a sick person meant that she was responsible for mental comforting as well as looking after physical needs. Sarah was a relatively easy patient as far as actual nursing went, but she was plagued by the fears of any new mother magnified four times and intensified by the fact that babies of multiple births were more likely to suffer from disease, defects and death. Rebecca could understand her need for solace.

'But . . . oh, hell, let's talk about something else.' Sarah picked up a fork and determinedly dug into her tuna fish. 'Tell me about your love life.'

Rebecca flushed and embarrassment made the lie come automatically. 'I . . . don't really have one.'

Sarah looked at her in astonishment, taking in the lovely oval of Rebecca's face, the tilted blue eyes, the fall of auburn hair. 'You're too pretty not to have a boy-friend.'

She would go to extreme lengths, Rebecca thought wryly, to distract Sarah from fearful thoughts of the impending births, but a detailed exposé of her emotional life was not part of the bargain. 'You'll be the first to know if anything exciting turns up.'

Sarah waved a fork at her in a chiding fashion. 'You're holding out on me,' she reproved. 'I'll bet you have three lovers going at one time.'

'Jealousy,' Rebecca smiled, 'will get you nowhere.'

'You're right,' Sarah said, heaving a huge sigh. 'My sex life went the way of the mammoth—it's extinct.'

*   *   *

Rebecca had moved into an apartment four months after the rescue when she felt strong enough to be on her own, when the dreams had lessened and she was less confused and bewildered by the rush of humanity around her. News of Guy waned within weeks after her return to New York. The media's desire to discover all the small and intimate details of their life together was initially thwarted and, by the time Guy emerged from the hospital, an event that was broadcast internationally and seen by both Rebecca and Tamara on a small set in Tamara's apartment, their interest had already focused on other, more recent and newsworthy items. As far as Rebecca knew, Guy must have refused interviews, book offers and movie deals, because she never heard anything further about him. And, over time, the bombardment of her own family had slowed to a trickle. Her mother had been contacted by all sorts of agents and entrepreneurs who had wanted to make a million dollars out of Rebecca's story and Martine, under instructions from Rebecca, had turned them all away. For once, Rebecca had been thankful for her mother's hard, cold demeanour. Not even the most obnoxious and persistent reporter had dared to call back twice.

It wasn't until Rebecca had passed through the period of disorientation and lethargy that had plagued her after the return to New York that she was able to think clearly about Guy and her reasons for leaving the hospital. What had at first seemed liked unwarranted panic on her part seemed far more logical to her now that she had had time to reflect on her actions. Nothing in her life had ever given Rebecca a reason for trusting men. Her father had been an absentee parent; her mother had let her daughters know in depth the extent of his philandering. And obesity had given Rebecca a view of men that most women didn't have. She had rarely been at the receiving end of male charm and attentiveness, and it wasn't until Guy had entered her life that she had realised precisely what she had been missing.

Although she desperately missed him, and the sight of a dark-haired, broad-shouldered man passing by on the street made her heart lurch in her chest, Rebecca could not bring herself to take the first step towards contacting him. She knew Tamara's insinuations that Guy had gone back to his wife might be wrong, and she felt ashamed of the way she had acted after seeing Maureen by his bedside. Nothing in that conversation had given any hint that Guy reciprocated his wife's feelings. Yet, Rebecca's hand was stilled whenever she thought of calling him, and she could not bring herself to sit down and write a letter. It took months before she was able to pick out the threads of reason and emotion that kept her from yielding to a strong and sometimes overwhelming urge to see him again.

She was, of course, terrified of rejection. The very thought of Guy telling her that he was no longer interested made her cringe inside and, even if she had just eaten, an unappeasable hunger would come over her. In order to protect herself from this, Rebecca pushed thoughts of Guy away and, with every bit of will power she possessed, ignored the fact that *he* had made no effort to contact her. Yet, she wasn't quite successful. It was a long time before her hands stopped trembling when she opened her mailbox and her heart didn't assume a furious pounding when the phone rang. And, as the days, weeks and then months went by, his silence had the effect of reinforcing her original fears, her lack of knowledge about him feeding her own dark fear of rejection.

She also no longer knew whether her feelings towards Guy had been real or fantasies she had constructed in the Arctic, in an environment so artificial that their passion might have been a hothouse flower, beautiful in its place, but fragile and unable to survive in any other locale. Her time there had receded from her consciousness and become relegated to some place in her psyche reserved for experiences that were so intense and frightening that she must be protected from their memories. Rebecca wasn't aware of the way her mind worked to heal itself, she only knew that when she tried to remember the Arctic, the images seemed shrouded in a mist, the events losing their clarity. She could recall believing that she loved Guy, but the feeling seemed distorted and hazy. Whether she could still love him now in ordinary surroundings, in the midst of the humdrum aspects of daily life, was questionable. The relationship she had had with Guy after the crash bore no resemblance to any sort of relationship she could have with him when life would consist, not of survival, but of jobs, groceries, a mortgage and visits to the dentist.

Logic and pragmatism were the crutches that Rebecca used to support the fragile construct of her life. She jogged, she worked, she ate carefully, she tried to maintain a balance that kept her from spinning into another depression or, even worse, being pushed into a bout of compulsive eating. Rebecca had a fear that the slightest emotional breeze would break down what she had so carefully erected, and her time, even her thinking, was organised in such a way that nothing would jar the orderliness of her existence. She tried not to think of Guy, she rarely talked to Martine, she only took on jobs that she thought would be pleasant. Generally, Rebecca was successful, but in one area of her life she was an abysmal failure.

Guy had given her the gift of sensual sensation and, try though she might, she was unable to obliterate it from her mind. Vivid sexual memories came to plague her when she least expected them; images coming unbidden to her mind of flesh against flesh, the softness of a mouth, the lick of a tongue. She would be caught unawares, forced to pause no matter what she was doing and wait helplessly while the warm flush of desire washed over her. Her own sensuality, awakened and now knowledgeable, could not be put aside or ignored as it had been in the past. Rebecca was now alive to her body; to its needs, its demands and its wishes. In the past, she had been able to forget that she was a woman for long periods of time; now, she was aware of it constantly. Guy had taught her that she was desirable, and this knowledge made Rebecca respond to men differently from the way she had and with an instinct that was purely female. It was her glance, unconsciously flirtatious and just the slightest bit wistful, that had caught the attention of Brian Ross.

She met him on the jogging path in an early hour of a December morning when the sun was just beginning to rise, turning the streets a pale grey. The air was so cold that morning that a person's breath issued in plumes of steam. It was the time of day when strangers said hello and struck up conversations, and joggers who might otherwise run side by side in silence were apt to look at one another in sympathy and commiseration. Rebecca had stopped at a cross-street and was running lightly in place, waiting for the traffic light to change, when Brian ran up to her and stood beside her, also jogging in place.

'Hello,' he had said. Rebecca recognised him from other mornings when she had run the same route. He was a tall man with sandy hair that was held back with a red hairband and a craggy, comfortable sort of face with laugh wrinkles around his blue eyes. He also wore a distinctive jogging outfit; a violet sweat-shirt with a pink and kelly-green Smurf design and a lavender pair of running pants. When she looked down, she noticed that his sneakers were tied with pink laces.

She couldn't help smiling. 'Hi,' she replied.

'Can you hear through those things?' he asked.

Rebecca nodded. Running kept her warm but she usually wore mitts and a pair of white fluffy ear-muffs to keep her ears from freezing.

'Go far?'

'About two miles today,' she answered.

'You run at the same time as I do.'

'I noticed,' she said as the light turned green.

Brian kept by Rebecca's side as she made her way across the street and picked up her stride, her ponytail swinging back and forth as she ran.

'You did?' he asked.

'You're hard to ignore. A vision in violet.'

Brian looked down at himself and then grinned. 'My niece picked it out for me,' he said. 'She's five.'

'I suppose that also accounts for the pink shoelaces,' Rebecca smiled.

'Pink is her favourite colour,' he replied, 'but I tried to hold the line to purple.'

'And I suppose she loves Smurfs.'

Brian had given a rueful pat to the front of his shirt where the Smurf smiled in idiot bliss. 'They're my favourites, too,' he confessed then added, tongue in cheek, 'I also have a Smurf bedspread.'

Rebecca fell in with the game. 'And sheets?'

'Sheets, pillowcases, wallpaper and curtains.'

'Cute,' she said. 'Does your niece sleep over a lot?'

Brian's face dissolved into a wry grimace. 'She's the only one who will,' he had moaned sadly.

Brian was an economist with the Securities and Exchange Commission, and he lived several blocks away from Rebecca in an old high-rise building. He was also training to run a short marathon and, like Rebecca, alternated long jogs with short ones. She began to meet him on the running path at first twice a week, then every other day and soon every morning. Brian could never be called handsome and he didn't have Guy's sex appeal, but he was likeable and had a great sense of humour. Rebecca welcomed his company and, on the one or two mornings when he didn't appear, she discovered that solitary running wasn't half as satisfying as it had been in the beginning.

They discovered that they had a fair number of

things in common: non-violent movies, avocado salad, divorced parents, favoured authors, theatre, a dislike of loud personalities and overbearing bosses. They began going out for lunch at weekends and occasionally seeing a movie together on Saturday nights. Rebecca learned that Brian had recently come out of a long depression when a relationship with a live-in girl-friend had ended after five years. The problems he mentioned were similar to those that had afflicted Guy's marriage; disinterest, loss of love and incompatability. The difference was that Brian had been at the receiving end, not aware that his girl-friend had been unhappy until the day she had sat him down and laid out the facts for him.

'I was devastated,' he had said one night as they walked back to Rebecca's apartment. 'I hadn't even known anything was going wrong. No, that's not quite true. I suppose if I'd thought about it I might have noticed that she'd seemed sad and down in the mouth. And our sex life wasn't so great.' He glanced at Rebecca then and added, 'You don't really want to hear all this, do you? It's pretty boring stuff.'

'I don't mind,' she reassured him.

'You're a nice person, Rebecca. Has anyone told you that recently?'

She smiled and shook her head.

'No old boy-friends calling up to give the message?'

Rebecca recognised the angle of Brian's approach. 'No old boy-friends,' she replied.

'That's hard to believe. You're too pretty.'

'Flattery,' she said with mock-severity, 'isn't going to get you very far.'

Brian snapped his fingers. 'Damn.' He looked crest-fallen. 'Most of them fall for that line.'

'I've been around.'

'Yeah?' he drawled. 'Where?'

'New Jersey, Brooklyn, the Bronx.'

'Come on. I know you're from some hick city up-state.'

'I think you're insulting my birthplace.'

'What's it called?'

Rebecca had linked her arm through his. 'It doesn't matter,' she shrugged. 'I hated living there anyway.'

The only drawback in her relationship with Brian was Rebecca's instinctive withdrawal when he questioned her about the past. She had a strong desire to be accepted for who she was right now, not the woman she had been five years ago or even two months ago. She didn't want Brian to know that she had been fat, unloved and unwanted. She was desperate that Brian not connect her with the woman who had crashed in the Arctic and been a minor sensation for a few days. So she lied and prevaricated, keeping her background somewhat mysterious. She kept his interest a secret from Tamara and didn't tell Brian that she had a sister living in the city. Rebecca didn't put her experience with Brian into the category of experimental, but that was precisely what it was. For the first time in her life, she was actually dating, and the man who was taking her out did not pity her or feel that she had once been repulsive. Guy had been different; Guy knew what she had been and what she could become again. Brian didn't have any such hang-up; he accepted her for what she appeared to be on the surface: an ordinary

woman with an ordinary shape who didn't have the
spectre of obesity hanging over her head at every
moment.

They hadn't slept together yet although Rebecca
suspected that an affair with Brian was inevitable. She
neither hated the thought of it nor was especially
moved by it, but she did think that, when it finally
happened, their physical relationship would be a comfortable one. Brian didn't excite her the way Guy was
capable of doing, but the slow growth of their
friendship suited the quiet pace of her life, and he was
the sort of person that Rebecca wouldn't hesitate to
rely on in an emergency or seek help from during a
crisis. Of course, she didn't love him, nor did she
expect to, but then Rebecca had an instinctive distrust
of love. It was an emotion that couldn't be controlled
or restrained, and she knew that it had the ability to
take charge of her in unpredictable and frightening
ways.

Sarah dozed most of the afternoon and then Rebecca
helped her with a bath at the end of the day before
her husband came home. By common agreement, the
two women had decided that if nothing else got
accomplished all day, Sarah should look appealing for
Dave. Although Sarah argued that 'appealing' wasn't
the word that could be applied to a woman whose
body was swollen, whose waistline had disappeared
and whose toes looked like miniature sausages,
Rebecca insisted that, when Sarah's hair was clean
and blown dry, her nails manicured and she had put
on a modicum of cosmetics, she looked positively

attractive. And Dave certainly seemed to think so. He was a tall, slender man with a kind face who was devoted to his wife. Rebecca couldn't help a twinge of envy when she watched Dave enter the bedroom at the end of a day, his face lighting up with love when his eyes met Sarah's, his concern for her touching to see.

Rebecca was pulling on her coat and beret in the foyer of the Downes' apartment when Dave came up to her. 'Everything okay?' he asked. 'Did she have a good day?'

'She's doing fine.'

Dave's face crinkled with worry. 'She had a few twinges the other night.'

'I know,' Rebecca reassured him soothingly. 'False labour—it's not uncommon. I talked to the doctor about it this afternoon.'

His expression eased. 'You're doing a great job,' he said. 'Sarah and I really appreciate it.'

Rebecca knew how much her moral support meant to both of them, but they would never know just how much pleasure nursing Sarah was for her. 'I enjoy it,' she smiled. 'And I can't wait for the babies.'

Dave rolled his eyes in mock-horror and threw his hands up in the air. 'I can,' he said. 'It's going to be bedlam.'

A sweet bedlam, Rebecca thought as she took the bus into town to her own apartment and watched the snowy streets pass by. She had always loved working in the maternity ward, holding and feeding those tiny, demanding morsels of humanity. As the bus pulled to her stop, Rebecca got off and wondered if she would

ever have any children of her own. It was an idle
speculation, but she found herself thinking of a baby
with an unexpected yearning. She had often thought
that she could not be a good mother, having no real
experience of good mothering herself, but her experiences in the Arctic had taught her that she had capa-
bilities she hadn't known to exist. Martine was cold
and hard, but then—she wasn't Martine. Perhaps she
could bring to a child all the love and warmth that it
deserved. A child with dark hair and eyes—the sort of
child that Guy would . . . The thought came unbidden
and unwanted, and Rebecca tried to shake it off, but it
clung to her, a wisp of longing, the slender web-like
strand of a wish.

The telephone was ringing when she entered her
apartment and, as she flicked on the lamp by the sofa,
she picked up the receiver. It was Tamara at the other
end, her voice a bit breathless.

'Bad news,' she began.

'Tam, I just walked in the door,' Rebecca said
reproachfully. 'I haven't even taken off my coat.'

'Sit down. You're going to need the chair.'

Rebecca obediently sat down, although she grimaced into the phone. She was used to Tamara's drama-
tics. Her sister rarely presented a new idea, a new
boy-friend or a new event without giving the telling far
more theatrical flare than it deserved. 'It can't be that
dreadful. What's happened? Didn't Rob ever phone
you?' Rob was Tamara's latest lover in a soap-opera
affair that involved passion, jealousy, infidelity and
the constant threat of a break-up.

'It isn't Rob.'

'Well, what is it then? Broadway has been shut down and there'll never be another audition?'

'Becks, this is serious.'

There was something in Tamara's voice that made Rebecca suddenly straighten up. 'What?'

'Martine is moving to Manhattan.'

Rebecca found that she could barely breathe. It was as if a weight were pressing her on the chest and suffocating her.

'She's got the house on the market,' Tamara went on, 'and is planning to move here in March.'

'Oh, no.'

'I couldn't believe it when she told me. She said that since both of us were here now, she couldn't see any reason to stay in Fairfax. She's always wanted to live in the city anyway.'

There was a silence as both sisters contemplated the fact of Martine's presence within hailing distance. Rebecca was the first to speak. 'I don't think I'm going to be able to stand it,' she said in quiet desperation.

'You'll have to.'

'Tam, what am I going to do?'

'You're going to be strong,' Tamara declared firmly and then her voice changed as if she couldn't quite imagine Rebecca carrying it off. 'Stronger than you've ever been.'

CHAPTER NINE

THE evening had, so far, been a smashing success. Jake was his usual *bon vivant* self, Sophia was glamorous and sultry and her friend, Anya, was everything a man in Guy's position was looking for. She was attractive with blonde hair that cascaded down her bare back, curvaceous in a sleek black dress, flirtatious with just that right amount of subtlety and quite obviously willing to go to bed with him when the evening was over. She was, Guy thought wryly as he drove Anya to her apartment, just what the doctor would have ordered.

He glanced over at her. She had a small, patrician profile with a straight nose, and her eyes were a dark blue that tilted tantalisingly into a fringe of long eyelashes. Jake had winked when he made the introductions as if he were presenting Guy with a delicious morsel, a confection that was meant to be savoured and then devoured. He had made it clear that he thought all of Guy's problems boiled down to one thing—a lack of sex. In typical Jake fashion, he had come up with the solution: Sophia's friend, Anya, who was free, over twenty-one and, while she didn't quite come under the category of a call-girl, was known to be extremely available.

'No social diseases?' Guy had asked sarcastically when Jake had proposed the double date to him.

'Sophia swears by her,' Jake had said.

Well, Guy thought, as he turned his attention back to the traffic in front of him, she isn't infected and at least she doesn't talk too much. He didn't think he could handle a date who chatted and expected him to respond in an interesting and intellectual fashion. Anya was the first woman he had gone out with since his illness, and she represented to him a complete return to physical and mental health. For months, he had been without any strong sexual urges, and going to bed with her would prove to Guy that he was once again a man in the full sense of the word. For that, he decided, he didn't need conversation.

He parked his car in front of the house and walked Anya up to the door. The overhead light made her eyes look enormous.

'It was a lovely dinner,' she said.

'I'm glad you liked it.'

'And I enjoyed the show.'

'So did I.'

She glanced at him then through those incredibly long eyelashes and gave a small shiver. 'Brrr—it's freezing out here. Would you like to come in for a nightcap?'

I thought you'd never ask, Guy thought with a tinge of self-mockery, but all he said was, 'Why not?'

Her apartment was small, but furnished with an eye to expensive and highly feminine decorations; pastel colours, ruffles, soft cushions. Guy couldn't for the life of him remember exactly what she did for a living, but it was obvious that she was doing well. For a second, he wondered if she would want money afterwards or,

at least, the hint of a gift delivered the next morning for
the use of her more than ample charms.

She was making the most of them at the moment,
having shrugged off her fur coat and flipping her long
hair behind her. The way she stood revealed to Guy
the high lift of her breasts and the long, slender line of
her thighs.

'Cognac?' she asked. 'Whisky? A liqueur?'

Guy pulled off his coat and sat down on the curved
love-seat. 'Cognac,' he said.

She poured the drink into a bell-shaped glass for
him and one for herself and then sat down next to him,
the sound of stockings making that sheer sliding
sound as she crossed her long, shapely legs. 'You look
tired,' she said.

An echo came to him of Rebecca, but he shoved it
aside. 'It's the light in here,' he replied, lifting his glass
and sipping at the fiery liquid.

She lifted a finger and stroked the skin by his
eyebrow. 'Perhaps we should turn them off then.'

He looked into her eyes over the rim of his glass.
'Perhaps we should.'

With the lights dimmed, it was easy for him to pull
her close to him and tangle his fingers in the seductive
length of her hair. One small movement brought their
mouths together, and he tasted the cognac on her
tongue. He ran a hand along the edge of her cheek, to
the curve of her throat and then down to the swell of a
breast. She sighed when his hand brushed a nipple,
and he could feel its hardness beneath the silk of her
dress. In turn, he felt his body swell in anticipation of
her.

He kissed her more ardently, liking the feel of her as she pressed up against him, liking the bold touch of her hand on the zipper of his pants. Guy wasn't interested in shyness, coyness or any female modesty. He wanted to accomplish a sexual connection; quickly, efficiently and thoroughly. He wanted to know that special and unique moment of triumph that comes of entering a woman's body, her silkiness enclosing him in an erotic warmth. He wanted to bury himself in the oblivion of desire, the intense and driving urge towards orgasm that blinded him to all else but the sheer pleasure of fulfilment.

'This couch is a bit small,' he murmured.

Anya smiled up at him. 'I have a bed.'

'How clever of you.'

The bedspread was white and quilted, the pillows had eyelet covers, and the headboard a rococo pattern of royal blue rattan. A small lamp in one corner shed a dim glow of illumination. Guy slipped off his jacket and slacks as Anya slithered out of her dress. Her back was turned towards him, but he saw one white breast swing slightly as she leaned forwards to take off her stockings. She had a narrow back, delicate buttocks and, when she turned, a small, blonde triangle of pubic hair. Guy finished undressing as Anya curled up on the bed.

'Nice,' she said when his briefs hit the floor.

'What's nice?' he asked as he sank down beside her.

'You.'

'Hey, you're making me feel like a sex object.'

Anya laughed a bit. 'That's what you are.' And began to kiss him.

For the first time that evening, Guy was curious about the woman he would be sleeping with. Unlike Jake, he wasn't the sort who liked or desired a one-night stand, and he wanted to know what caused Anya to sleep with a stranger, to seek intimacy in the midst of what could be nothing more than an anonymous encounter. He was going to speak, but her kisses distracted him and finally he forgot what he had been about to say. Her nakedness touched him at the chest, hip and toe, and he felt the heat surge within him as his hand ran down her side to the soft skin of an inner thigh. She was so accessible, so soft, so . . .

Guy was turning over on to his back and pulling her willing body on top of him when his eyes encountered the mirror on the ceiling. What he saw there held him motionless; a couple entwined together, blonde hair spilling on the pillow beside his dark head, long white legs curving on top of his. The mirror had been put there for an obvious reason; it was meant to titillate the viewer, to add an extra fillip to the lovemaking that was taking place below. But instead of turning Guy on, it had exactly the opposite effect. To his horror and embarrassment, he felt the passion drain out of him, his erection slowly wilt.

A hand touched him. 'Guy?'

He took a deep breath, but the coldness was stealing over him and he knew it was hopeless. 'I'm sorry,' he said.

Anya pressed herself against him. 'We'll start again.'

Abruptly he pushed her off of him and sat up. 'I'm sorry,' he said again, running fingers through his hair in a frustrated and angry gesture. 'Look, this is a mistake. I should never have let it start.'

'But Jake said . . .' she began and Guy suddenly understood the motives behind her seduction. Sophia, using all the wiles of her sexuality, had ensnared Jake, and Anya had been prepared to do the same with Guy, trading sex for gifts, a constant escort, perhaps even a meal-ticket.

'Damn Jake,' he growled as he pulled on his clothes.

Anya was now sitting up against a pillow, her nudity covered by the hem of the bedspread, her fingers clutching on to its ruffled edge. 'Is it anything I did?'

She might have been the most cold-hearted of gold-diggers, but she looked so wistful that Guy took pity on her. Kneeling beside the bed, he took one of her hands, lifted it and kissed the inside of her wrist. 'You were fine,' he murmured. 'It's me.' He reached into his pocket and took out his wallet. 'Can I give you something, some money?'

'Money?'

She sounded innocent enough, but Guy suddenly remembered that she was a secretary and knew that her salary couldn't have bought her the furnishings in the apartment or the fur coat she had worn that night. 'Money,' he repeated. 'In place of the gift I would have sent you tomorrow morning.'

Anya looked down at her entwined hands. 'Well . . .'

Guy was firm. 'It would be a pleasure.' He pulled a generous number of bills from his wallet and laid them on the night-table. 'Buy yourself something pretty.'

He fled then, stuffing his feet hastily into his shoes, shrugging on his jacket and grabbing up the coat he had left beside the love-seat. When he was out of the building, he took a deep breath and glanced up at the star-studded sky. It was bitterly cold, a true Calgary winter's night, and the chill in the air stung his skin. Guy shivered as he pulled on his coat, but he felt the cold as a penance, as a punishment. He had failed abysmally at his test of manhood; for the first time in his life, his body had not performed the way he wanted, and with impotence came a crushing sense of humiliation.

'Damn you,' he cried to the unheeding stars, his eyes blurring as he stared up at them. 'Goddamn you!'

Anyone watching the taut line of his profile as he stared up at the cavernous black dome of the sky, the tears turning his lashes to spikes, might have thought he was damning fate or the body that had failed him or his all too enterprising friend Jake or even the woman whose caresses had failed to rouse him again. But they would have been wrong. Guy was cursing the absent Rebecca who had come between him and another woman, who had so effectively turned off the source of his desire that he wondered if he would ever be able to make love again. He had not been thinking of her in that ultra-feminine bed; his mind had been on the woman in his arms. Yet Rebecca's image had superimposed itself over the one in the mirror, erasing the couple below, and Guy had seen her, not as she had been during their lovemaking, but standing at the edge of the lake innocently drying herself as he secretly looked on, her whiteness shimmering in the grey-

green water, breaking and merging under the glitter of
the Arctic sun.

'Have you eaten? Did you have lunch?'

'I'm not hungry.'

'Guy, you're not sleeping well. You can't be. You
don't look good.'

Guy smiled down at the woman who was confront-
ing him, a frown on her face, her hands on her hips.
She was short, grey-haired and had a pair of snapping
blue eyes. There was only one woman in the world
who could fuss over him without driving him up the
wall and that woman was his mother.

He bent down and kissed her cheek. 'And you're
looking great.'

'Don't try to diffuse the issue. I'm talking about *you*.'

'Feed me then. If that's what will make you happy.'

'If you weren't my pride and joy,' she said in a
scolding voice, 'and a good six foot, I'd take you over
my knee and spank you.'

'Mom, you're all heart.'

Guy followed Cordelia McLaren through the small
but impeccably clean living room and dining room and
into a kitchen where it looked as if all hell had broken
loose. There were recipe books everywhere, dishes in
the sink and counters piled high with chopped vegetables. A huge pot of broth bubbled on the stove and
the air was so steamy that Guy had to force one of the
windows open slightly to clear the atmosphere.

'What are you doing?' he asked.

'Trying to feed your father. The doctor wants him on
a no-fat, low sodium, non-cholesterol diet. And no

carbohydrates. That leaves the kind of food that rabbits like and the trouble is your father is human. I've spent weeks already trying to find ways to make vegetables taste like steak and potatoes.' Cordelia flung her hands into the air. 'But I'm not a magician!'

'How is he doing?'

'Sleeping like a baby this afternoon,' she sighed and they both smiled at one another in a conspiratorial sort of way. The doctor had said that Franklin McLaren should rest every afternoon, but getting a once-vigorous man to admit that he was too tired to make it through a day was a major undertaking.

'I refuse to eat green mush,' Guy said, lifting up the lid to a saucepan and grimacing at the mixture within. 'If this is what you're offering for lunch, you can count me out.'

Cordelia grabbed the saucepan away from him. 'I made my lamb stew for you. You look like you could use some nourishment. Now sit down and stop complaining.'

Guy obediently took his place at the table, a small amused smile on his lips as he watched his mother fix lunch. Despite the smallness of her stature, Cordelia had a personality that packed a wallop. As a child, she had been loud, as an adolescent, 'sassy', and as an adult, she was known for the sharpness of her tongue. She had run the McLaren family, wrapping her husband around her little finger and keeping Guy in line with an approach to motherhood that combined quick punishments with equally quick forgiveness. By the time Guy had grown up he had discovered that he not only loved his mother, in fact he also liked her.

'How's your bridge group?'

'That Essie is a dodo. I don't know why I put up with her. She can't tell a heart from a spade.'

Guy's smile widened. Essie and Cordelia had been playing bridge together for thirty years. 'What's she done now?'

Cordelia waved a wooden spoon in the air. 'Don't ask. It would take me all afternoon to tell you, and I don't want to talk about me. I invited you over because I want to talk about you.'

'That sounds dangerous.'

'You're still too thin, you have circles under your eyes, you look rotten and you've been moping from Christmas to Easter.'

Guy shook his head in mock-admiration. 'You have a way with compliments.'

'Is it Maureen? I thought that was over.'

Although Cordelia had never said a word to Guy about his decision to marry Maureen and she had been a model mother-in-law, Guy had been aware that she had, for some reason, not quite approved of his wife. 'It's over,' he said.

'Is it the business? I thought it was going well.'

'We're doing fine.'

'Well, then?' She turned to face him, her eyes determined.

Guy shrugged. 'It's nothing.'

Cordelia examined the ceiling and spoke to it in a disgusted voice. 'Nothing.'

Guy had forgotten how obstinate Cordelia could be when she wanted to find something out. 'Post-rescue depression,' he said lightly. 'I'm getting over it.'

Cordelia eyed him the way she used to when he was a small boy, caught out in some infraction and about to have the moment of truth fall upon him. 'It's the woman you were with in the Arctic. I can tell, you know. I've known for a long time that something went on up there even if you don't want to talk about it.'

'Cordelia . . .' he began in a warning tone, and his mother knew that she had overstepped the boundaries of his privacy. Guy never called her by her first name unless he was angry.

She put her hands out defensively in front of her. 'Shoot me,' she sighed, 'for being too nosy. But there is something wrong, isn't there?'

From the concerned look on Cordelia's face, Guy could see that her questions stemmed from real worry instead of any idle curiosity, and he relented a bit. 'I haven't heard from her.'

'Did you expect to after the way she disappeared?'

He shrugged unhappily. 'I thought she might call me. I tried to reach her but it didn't work.'

'Why not?'

'I don't know. I gave the message to her mother but I'm not sure it was passed on.'

'Have you tried anyone else in her family?'

'No.'

Cordelia gave her son a puzzled look. 'Haven't tried very hard, have you?'

'I think she's made it clear that she doesn't want to see me.'

'And why would she do that?'

Guy looked pointedly at the stove. 'Lamb stew,' he said. 'I've discovered I'm famished.'

'Hmmmph,' replied Cordelia, although she reached for a plate and dipped a ladle into a large pot that was simmering on the stove. 'Why do I get the feeling that I'm hitting the jackpot?'

Guy sighed and surrendered. 'I don't know why Rebecca doesn't want to contact me. I can only guess at the reasons and I've been through them a million times.'

Cordelia put the plate of stew in front of him and said, 'Were you lovers?'

'Cordelia. Really.'

'I wasn't born in prehistoric times,' she commented drily. 'I'm aware that sex exists between consenting adults.'

Guy leaned back in his chair, his face resigned. 'All right, we were lovers.'

'And . . . ?'

'And I want her back.'

'So . . . ?'

'She obviously doesn't want me.'

Cordelia appraised her son with a judgemental look. 'Since when do you give up so easily? You don't actually know a thing. The woman took off without a word and is probably trying to put her life together somewhere. She may wonder why you haven't contacted her; she may be as depressed and unhappy as you are.'

'Maybe she has someone else.'

Cordelia shook her head. 'You're fighting shadows.'

The next was harder to say. 'Maybe she's obese again.'

'Ah,' Cordelia said in sudden understanding. 'She was heavy, wasn't she? The press made an issue of that.'

'So you see . . .'

'No,' she replied forcibly, 'I don't see it at all. Everything you've said is conjecture. This isn't like you, Guy.'

He sighed. 'What *am* I like?'

Cordelia leaned forward intently. 'You're like me. You're a fighter; you don't give up, you go after the things you want.'

Guy sat silent for a second and then said with sudden insight, '*You* want me to find her, don't you?'

Cordelia gave him a grin. 'Of course,' she uttered tartly. 'I have an intense curiosity to meet the woman who's finally ensnared my son's heart.'

Tamara Clark lived in a brown-stone house in Brooklyn, a narrow building sandwiched between other narrow buildings that all had the same curved bay windows at the front and wrought iron railings on the porch. She rented the top apartment on the third floor and, as he approached her door, a strange scent came wafting out from under its sill. Guy sniffed, thought of incense, and wondered about the woman inside. He had talked to her on the phone the day before when he had arrived in New York and, following Cordelia's advice, had refused to take 'no' for an answer. Tamara hadn't given him any information about Rebecca, but she had finally agreed to see him and had given him her address. She had sounded a bit strange over the phone, but Guy remembered the way Rebecca had described her sister; as different, as eccentric, as unique.

The woman who opened the door to his firm knock more than adequately fitted Rebecca's description. She had long red hair—the colour of carrots—that fell below her waist in a curly mass, a headband in screaming scarlet, a bolero top decorated with multi-coloured sequins and a pair of black leather jeans with silver studs on the back and side pockets. She was liberally covered with jewellery; three ear-rings in one ear, two in the other, bracelets that ran up her left arm to the elbow, four strands of purple beads, rings on every finger. She was a tiny woman with a slender nose covered in an arc of freckles, a small, determined chin and blue eyes set in dark lashes. Only the eyes reminded Guy of Rebecca; the rest of Tamara was so exotic and peculiar that he had a strong temptation to turn on his heel and flee.

'Guy? Hey, man, come on in.'

Reluctantly, he crossed the threshold and walked into her apartment. Used furniture of the Salvation Army variety was crowded together with dozens of throw pillows, lampshades draped in red and blue scarves and at least twenty incense-burning candles. He took a breath and then sneezed, causing Tamara to throw him an amused, but concerned look.

'Allergic, right? You'd be surprised at the number of people who are allergic to incense. It's a shame, because incense really puts you in a mellow, laid-back mood, if you know what I mean. I always burn incense when I'm meditating.'

Guy sneezed again and then said, 'I hope I didn't interrupt you.'

'Hey, no sweat, man. I'm easy, really easy.' And, as if to prove her point, Tamara went round the room, snuffed out all the candles and jerked up a window. When she walked the room was filled with the sound of bracelets jingling together and beads knocking on one another. It wasn't an unpleasant sound but combined with the muted light from the lamps and the rainbow-mix of cushions, it gave the room a peculiar air of mystery and deception.

'Sit down,' she invited, 'make yourself at home.'

Guy had been trying to find a place to sit other than on the floor. He had come to this talk with Tamara dressed in a charcoal-grey suit that was impeccably pressed, and he had the uncomfortable feeling that he would look ridiculous sitting on one of Tamara's vividly coloured pillows. The Salvation Army furniture, however, was comprised of several dressers, a rickety table without chairs and an old rocking-horse with a mane that had seen more luxurious days. He cleared his throat. 'I think I'd prefer to stand.'

'Okay by me,' Tamara nodded, sinking to the floor and folding her legs in the lotus position, her small hands resting loosely on her knees. She looked up at him. 'Are you a Leo?'

At first, he didn't get the connection, and then he shook his head. 'Pisces.'

Tamara bit her bottom lip and tilted her head as she appraised him. 'No kidding! I wouldn't have thought that.'

'Look, I've come to . . .'

'I'm a Gemini. That's the twins, you know. They say that it helps an actress if she's a Gemini because she has to play two roles, herself and someone else.' She tilted her head in the other direction. 'But there's also a militant feel to the Gemini. That's because the twins were Castor and Pollux. They were Roman warriors and . . .'

Tamara prattled on as if she were a child in arrested development, and there was something artful about her, something fey that made Guy uneasy.

'You don't look militant,' he said.

Her laughter was like the sound of water in a brook. 'You wouldn't know it to see me, would you? But I can be quite ferocious when roused.' Suddenly she curved her hands into claws, the red nails long and menacing, and then laughed again when she saw Guy's instinctive move backwards. 'I didn't mean to frighten you,' she said and added, humming as if to herself, '''When the moon is in the seventh house and Jupiter aligns with Mars, then peace . . .'''

Guy wondered if Tamara were crazy. 'I want to know about Rebecca.'

Tamara closed her eyes. 'Rebecca of Sunnybrook Farm had blonde hair in pig-tails.' She opened her eyes and went on, 'With little red bows that danced on her shoulders and . . .'

Was she crazy? Stark-raving mad? Guy tried to remember what Rebecca had said about Tamara, thinking that nothing she had ever told him could justify this insane behaviour. On the other hand . . . Guy's eyes narrowed to dark slits . . . she might just be having him on. This whole thing; the run-down room, the weird clothes, the incense, the speech pattern and song from the 'sixties, might all be part of a charade to dupe him, confuse him and lead him astray. He suddenly remembered what she had said about being a Gemini, about playing two roles.

'Where is she?' he asked grimly.

Perhaps it was typical of Tamara that she didn't live up to anyone's expectations. Instead of answering, she dreamily shut her eyes and seemed to go off into a trance. She ignored Guy's restless shifting and didn't speak for several minutes. Finally, she said, 'Conceal-ment is camouflage.'

'What the hell are you talking about?'

Tamara shrugged and opened her eyes. 'I'm not my sister's keeper.'

Guy's anger was building, slowly but surely. 'Is this a game?' he demanded.

'Games are for up-tight people. I'm loose, I flow with the wind and the tide.'

'I would just like some straight answers.'

'Straightness is only a perception. Decisions are made in curves, circles and mazes.' She put her hands together as if she were an oriental potentate and bowed her head.

Guy stared at the vivid orange of her hair and clenched his teeth. 'Don't speak in riddles.'

'It's no riddle,' she replied softly. 'Rebecca's decision to stay hidden did not come easily.'

'Where is she hidden? Has she taken another name?'

Tamara shook her head in reproof. 'Your impatience

is an offence to the universe. The world revolves at its own pace.'

His anger had reached boiling-point, and Guy had the insane urge to take Tamara in his hands and shake her violently until she said something that made sense. He took one threatening step towards her and then checked himself, but it must have been the grim set of his mouth or the way his hands were curved into fists that suddenly let Tamara know that she had gone too far.

'Rebecca's doing fine.'

It was the first honest statement of the afternoon, and Guy pressed his advantage. 'Is she working as a nurse?'

'Yes.'

'Where?'

Tamara dropped her eyes and her voice subtly altered. 'There is sickness everywhere. It pervades the . . .'

'Cut the crap!'

Tamara blinked. 'I can't tell you where she's working.'

'It's here in New York, isn't it?'

'I told you. Rebecca prefers . . .'

But there was something about the way she spoke that gave Guy the hint that he was on the right trail. 'I've called every hospital in the city, and none of them has a Rebecca Clark in their personnel files so I think she's changed her name.'

'You have a right to your conjectures.'

'Come on, Miss Clark, give me a hint. Am I hot, cold or lukewarm?'

Now, it was Tamara's turn to get angry, and she completely dropped the façade of the 'sixties' flower child. 'This isn't a game,' she cried heatedly. 'My sister's life is involved.'

Guy glared at her. 'I *want* to see her.'

Tamara glared right back. 'I'll let her know.'

'How can I be sure that you will?'

Tamara gave him a level look. 'Because I said so.'

Guy sensed that he had pushed Tamara as far as he could. 'Tell me about Rebecca,' he encouraged.

'She's happy; she's got a job she likes.'

'Why did she leave the hospital so abruptly?'

'She needed private time to adjust.'

'Why didn't she ever get in touch with me?'

Tamara lifted her chin. 'This isn't an inquisition, Mr McLaren.'

'Did she tell you we were lovers?'

'I don't think . . .'

'Did she?' he demanded.

'Your relationship with Rebecca isn't any of my business.'

Guy ignored her. 'And you've convinced her that I'm not to be trusted. She told me all about you, Tamara. She told me about your father and the way you feel about men. You've been giving her advice, haven't you? Isn't that the reason she won't see me?' Guy had hit pay dirt. Tamara flushed, opened her mouth as if to refute him and then shut it again. 'So I'm right,' he added softly.

'I think you'd better leave now,' she suggested tightly.

'Hey,' Guy jeered, mocking her, 'what happened to

"flowing with the wind and the tide"?'

Tamara ignored him. 'I'll let Rebecca know that you were here,' she returned coldly.

'I'm at the Hilton, room 1228.'

Her eyes were a chilly blue. 'You haven't told me,' she said, '*why* you want to see her.'

Guy was heading for the door, but now he turned around. There were so many reasons why he wanted to see Rebecca that it would have taken him hours to tell her all of them. Love was one of them, but somehow he couldn't say it in this strange room to a woman he had sparred with for the past half-hour. Tamara was quite capable, he thought, of twisting his words, putting them in a different context and repeating them to Rebecca in a peculiar and distorted way.

'Rebecca,' he finally answered as he took a step across the threshold, 'knows why.'

Guy had planned to give Rebecca two days to call him. At first, he hung around his hotel room, but when he realised that he had paced the same short distance between the bed and the window for the hundredth time, he gave up and went out for a walk, reasoning to himself that she could leave a message with the hotel operator, that if she really wanted to speak to him she would find a way to reach him. He tramped through sections of New York City that he hadn't even known existed; he went to a movie in the middle of the day and a Broadway play at night. Later, he would confess that he couldn't remember either the names or the plots of what he had seen but, at that point, anything was preferable to his own vivid and unhappy conjectures.

He imagined Tamara talking to Rebecca, describing their confrontation; he imagined them laughing over him. The longer he waited for a phone call, the more vicious and cynical this imaginary laughter became. It drove him crazy with frustration and rage to the point that, one afternoon when he was lying on his bed in the hotel, staring at the ceiling and hearing the laughter as clearly as if the two women were standing right next to him, he blindly groped on the night-table for anything, an object, an ashtray, and ended up with the lamp which he would have thrown right through the window if it hadn't got tangled up in its own cord. This unexpected surge of violence was so irrational that Guy forced himself to calm down, determined not to let his imagination get the better of him again.

Anger alternated with misery and apprehension. The two days extended to three, and Guy spent Saturday wandering through the streets, trying to avoid the crowds that were out shopping and enjoying the spring-like balm of an unusually warm April day. He visited the Museum of Natural History, looked at the stuffed representation of an extinct mammoth and tried hard to put his own problems into the perspective of millenia. Somehow, the concept that he was but a speck in the universe and that his unhappiness was as trivial as the workings of an ant failed to console him. Wherever he looked, there were lovers, holding hands as they walked through Central Park; kissing, laughing and smiling. The whole world seemed rosy except for his bleak, dark corner.

Although he didn't want to admit it, Guy was humbled by the treatment he was receiving at Rebecca's hands. He had lived, he now realised, a lifetime of successful masculinity. His parents had adored him; women had been easy to obtain and easy to leave. Even in his marriage, he had had the upper hand emotionally. Guy had never had an experience of rejection and, for the first time, he had an inkling of what Rebecca must have gone through during her adolescence. Misery didn't drive him to food, but it did force him to keep moving, to walk endless miles of hard pavement, his hands jammed into his pockets, his dark head bent against the cold April wind, a tall and solitary figure lost in the crowds.

Late that afternoon, Guy returned to his hotel room, stared at his drawn face in the mirror in the bathroom and decided to call it quits. Rebecca had had adequate time to phone him, and her continuing silence was the final proof of her intentions. He was tempted, for a moment, to call Tamara once more, but his pride stopped him. He had, he thought bitterly, crawled enough. He phoned the airlines, made a reservation for the next morning and packed his bags. When he was done, he threw himself down on the bed and turned on the television and stared sightlessly at a show called Sports Week Round-Up. He barely listened to the announcer as his mind went relentlessly over an already well-trampled and desolate path. Why? Why wouldn't she want to see him again? Even if she had met another man or had gone heavy again, it wouldn't have hurt her to call him and let him know. What, in God's name, motivated her to hide behind her mother's and sister's skirts? What had he done to her that had been so damaging and hurtful that she didn't even want to hear his . . .

'Runners from all over the country came to Central Park last Sunday for the spring's first women's twelve-mile marathon,' the announcer was saying as pictures flashed across the screen in rapid succession. There was an overview of the race from the perspective of an aeroplane, showing hundreds of tiny, colourful figures running along the western edge of Central Park. The announcer droned on about times and speeds while the camera switched to ground level and panned to individuals, to women straining in the last moments of the race, their headbands darkened with sweat, the muscles in their legs visible and pulsing. A face here. A face there. A familiar face with tilted blue eyes and a remembered mouth parted in a grimace of physical exertion. Guy sat up suddenly, a trembling hand running through his thick dark hair. An auburn pony-tail with tendrils escaping at the temples. *Rebecca*, he thought, his heart beginning to pound intensely in his chest. Long legs, broad shoulders, breasts that strained against her red T-shirt. *Rebecca*, Number 112. *Rebecca*.

CHAPTER TEN

THERE were babies everywhere or, at least, that's the way it seemed. Four dark-haired, blue-eyed babies wearing tiny white T-shirts, nappies with yellow-checked rubber pants and booties. One small Downes was asleep in a car bed, another was lying in its crib, its eyes following a mobile made of pastel zoo animals, while a third was in Rebecca's arms intently sucking on a bottle. Sarah held the fourth over her shoulder and burped her energetically. The nursery, decorated with blue and pink wallpaper, white cribs, and curtains of plump teddy bears, smelled strongly of baby powder and formula.

'I still can't tell which of the boys is Ellenor's fraternal twin and which are the identical twins,' declared Rebecca, frowning at the baby in her lap. 'They all look alike to me.'

'Ben has a mole on his rear and his face is a little narrower,' Sarah answered proudly.

'You mean I'm going to have to take off their nappies every time I want to make an identification?'

'Don't bother,' Sarah said. 'Just call them all "baby". That's what Dave does. He can't always tell them apart either.'

'Ellenor is more delicate. She looks like a girl.'

Sarah held out the baby that had been nuzzling her neck and stared into its face. 'She does, doesn't she?'

She kissed the baby's round cheek. 'Mmmm, has Mommy told you that you're delicious today?'

'Five times,' Rebecca teased with a smile. 'I counted.'

Sarah gave her a weary grin. 'I love them even if they are driving me crazy.'

'Well, at least they're past the two feedings at night stage.'

'But I'm still getting up at an ungodly hour in the morning and I'm asleep by eight thirty. Dave insists that he can handle the ones that want a ten o'clock feeding. That's usually Conrad and Julian; they're always hungry.'

Rebecca looked down at Conrad who was guzzling his second bottle, his eyes slightly crossed at the effort. 'I noticed,' she said. 'This one's going to be a bruiser.'

'Did you look at that rash on . . . ?'

This was how Sarah and Rebecca spent most of their time; feeding, washing, caring for and talking about the babies. Rebecca usually arrived at nine in the morning and took charge while Sarah had two hours off to shop, go back to bed or just put up her feet and rest. By the afternoon, she had recharged her energies and joined Rebecca in the nursery. For a while, the Downes had also hired a night nurse, but with some of the babies sleeping through, they had recently discharged her. In addition to Rebecca, Sarah had been helped by friends, relatives and a supportive association for the mothers of twins and multiple births.

Sarah put down Ellenor and picked up Ben who had

started to fuss, his small fist alternately waving in the air and then being pressed frantically against his mouth. 'How's things with your mother?'

Rebecca gave an uncertain shrug. 'So far it's been all right. She's having a brunch tomorrow.'

'Already!'

'There are family friends in the city, and I suppose she wants to show off the apartment.'

'She can't have finished decorating it yet. She's only been in for about three weeks.'

'She hired a decorator before Christmas.'

Sarah made a whistling sound. 'Expensive.'

'My mother's family always had money and, when my grandmother died a couple of years ago, she left everything to my mother who was her only child. And Martine got a good price for the house. Even with the cost of renting here, she's well off.'

'I wonder why she never remarried.'

Rebecca gave her a startled look. 'My mother!'

'She is human, you know,' Sarah replied.

Rebecca shook her head vehemently. 'Not my mother, not after what my father pulled on her.' Over the months that she had nursed Sarah and then the babies, Rebecca had come to think of Sarah more as a friend than a patient. Although she hadn't told her about the Arctic or Guy or her previous obesity, Rebecca had confided in the other woman on such subjects as Tamara's insane love life, Martine's unwanted arrival in Manhattan and her own slowly growing attachment to Brian Ross.

'You mean she never even had a boy-friend?'

'No.'

'Maybe she didn't let you know.'

'I'm sure she didn't.'

'You know, Rebecca, many children can't face their parents' sexuality.'

'Yes, Dr Downes.'

'All right, all right,' Sarah gave way. 'I'll shut up on that subject. What's happening with Brian?'

'Well . . .'

'She's blushing,' Sarah informed baby Ben with delight, 'so it must be good.'

'He took me to a show last weekend after the marathon.'

'And . . . ?'

'And we're going out tonight.'

Sarah's face assumed an expression of dismay. 'I didn't know you had a date tonight. I wouldn't have asked you to work on a Saturday if I'd . . .'

Rebecca put up her hand. 'I don't mind, Sarah, and I know how hard it is when Dave has to go out of town for business. Besides, Brian and I aren't planning anything spectacular.'

'Is he going to the brunch with you tomorrow?'

'No.'

Sarah gave her a curious glance. 'No?'

Although both Sarah and Tamara now knew about Brian, Martine had no idea of his existence. 'I'm . . . not quite ready to introduce him to my mother.'

'I'm sure he's presentable enough.'

Conrad had finally stopped sucking so Rebecca gently pulled the bottle out of his mouth. 'He is but . . .' She couldn't explain why she had such a reluctance to introduce Brian to her mother; she just had a strong suspicion that the outcome of such a meeting would be dangerous.

'But she might not like him?'

Rebecca lifted her shoulders in a gesture of uncertainty. 'I don't know.'

'You know, Rebecca, I can't get a fix on how you feel about Brian.'

'He's . . . nice.'

'Nice? That's all you can say? You've been going out with this guy for almost four months. How about passionate, intense, romantic?'

'He's not like that.'

'What's wrong with him?'

'Nothing. He's just coming out of a relationship that went sour and I . . . well, neither of us was ready for an affair.'

Sarah shook her head in disgust. 'Take it from a very married lady. Make hay while the sun is shining.'

Rebecca gave her a startled look 'You don't mean that.'

'Oh, yes I do. You have to live it up while you're single, experience all kinds of men, find out what you want. That way you won't have any regrets when you're married.'

'You regret marrying Dave?' Rebecca asked in surprise.

'I love Dave,' Sarah stated firmly, 'but he wasn't the first man in my life. I'd had two affairs before I met Dave. But the moment he walked through my door, I knew he was what I wanted. Even so we lived together for a year before marrying, before making such a huge commitment.'

'But you might have made that commitment if Dave had been the first one,' Rebecca pointed out. 'He was the man you fell in love with.'

Sarah didn't look convinced. 'But I might not have recognised it then. What I'm trying to say is that it's so easy to make a mistake and so hard to undo it once it's done. You may not be sleeping with Brian yet, but the two of you are so sober that you sound like an old, married couple to me. I can just see you falling into a lifetime relationship with him, and you haven't really even lived yet.'

It was ironic, Rebecca thought, that she should give the impression of inexperience when the truth was she had packed a lifetime into a mere two months. 'We haven't talked about marriage,' she revealed.

'But it looks like it,' Sarah said and then, cupping her hand around the soft, downy head of Ben, gave a small contented sigh that belied all of her earlier advice. 'And this is the reality after the romance. Babies—lots and lots of babies.'

Rebecca got ready for her date with Brian that night, pulling the thick waves of her auburn hair into a chignon and darkening her eyes with mascara. It was not a fancy occasion; they were merely going out for dinner and then taking in a popular movie. It would be one of their more typical dates; inexpensive, comfortable and unexciting. Not that Rebecca sought any thrills, on the contrary, she quite liked the predictability of the evening ahead. That was one of things that made her happy when she was with Brian; there were never any threatening surprises.

They must appear, she supposed, remembering Sarah's words, as a dull couple who acted as if they had been married for twenty years. Yet, there was a contentment in that sort of relationship that had a solid core to it, a centre that would support a long-term commitment, a family and a mortgage. Sarah might advise her to seek melodramatic entanglements and affairs, but Rebecca could see the way such a lifestyle affected Tamara. Her sister lived on a roller-coaster of emotions, ranging from passion to anger to depression, each successive man making her more and more miserable once the first thrill of desire had passed. Sarah might suggest experimentation, but Rebecca couldn't see the point of it. She already knew that she would take Brian Ross over any of her sister's artistic, moody, sexy, sultry men.

Even the lack of sex in their relationship didn't bother her. It wasn't as if Brian hadn't made any of the appropriate passes; he had and she had begged for time. He was more understanding than most men; the failure of his recent relationship had caused him to be sensitive to her wishes and far less aggressive than he might have been in the past. He was thirty years old and had been through several women. He was no longer brash and impatient. Although he hadn't spoken about it yet, Rebecca sensed that marriage was in the back of his mind. The thought of it made a small part of her feel warm and wanted.

Neither Dave nor Sarah would ever know the impact that their lives had on Rebecca's thoughts of the future. She had always believed that she would be single, not only because of her weight but also because her parents' divorce had scared her away from marriage. She had no experience of love, of stability, of commitment; she didn't know what made a good marriage work. But her hours with Sarah, Dave and the babies had altered her perception. She had learned a lot from the Downes, watching the interaction between Dave and Sarah, the sensitivity, the caring, the ease that came from compatibility. Her hours in the nursery had taken on a magical aura; it was a place that the outside world could not touch, where the gentle rhythms of infancy were predominant. She knew that babies didn't remain small for ever and that life always intruded with its discordant demands, but somehow the essence of love was encapsulated in that small pink and blue room.

Rebecca had come to understand that she was, by nature, a nurturer. She had become a nurse because she liked to care for people. She thought she could be happy spending the rest of her life caring for one man and their children. She wasn't like Tamara; she didn't have that driving urge for an all-encompassing career. She sought, not acclaim or wealth, but a family, and she saw that this goal could be accomplished with a man like Brian. He was gentle, understanding, loving and stable. He didn't excite her, but then a good marriage wasn't built on excitement; it was solidly supported by the very qualities that made up Brian's personality. Rebecca could see herself growing old with Brian, and it was an image that was important to her. She didn't want to end up like Martine, middle-aged, solitary and bitter about life's offerings. Nor did she want to be like Tamara, clinging to men whose sex appeal was strong but whose staying-power was minimal.

Guy was everything Brian was not; dynamic, good-looking and aggressive, but he was also elusive and mysterious. Rebecca had never known what he was thinking; she had never been able to predict what he would do. Marriage to him, she now thought, would have been like building a house on shifting sands, its very foundation dangerously fragile. It didn't really matter that there was a part of her that still longed for him or that her nerve endings trembled simply at the memory of his touch. The Arctic now seemed as far away in remembrance as it was in distance, an episode in her life that had been tucked away, its contents out of sight as if they had been packed in a trunk and relegated to some far corner of an attic to gather dust and oblivion.

Rebecca forced herself not to think of Guy and, if his image came to her mind, she was able to push that aside as well, letting newer and seemingly more important considerations take his place. She had run a marathon the previous week and was now in training to run a longer one. She and Brian spent hours discussing schedules, shoes, diets. Although she hadn't won the race and hadn't expected to, she had beaten her own previous best time, an incentive to go for bigger and better goals. And there was her working week with Sarah and the babies and, of course, there was Martine.

Rebecca had helped her mother and Celia move in

and, so far, her mother's presence in the city had not yet impinged heavily on her life. Martine had been far too busy decorating to focus on her older daughters. Both Tamara and Rebecca knew that this was only a temporary breathing-space, but they made the most of it, calling her only rarely and sounding as if they were very busy. It was easier for Tamara than it was for Rebecca whose job was strictly nine to five. Tamara had landed a small part in an off-off Broadway play and was in the middle of rehearsals, took acting and dance lessons, and worked as a cocktail waitress until all hours of the morning. In fact, it was so hard to get hold of Tamara and Rebecca saw her so rarely that, when the doorbell rang almost an hour before Brian was due to arrive, the last person she expected to see was her sister.

'Tam, what are you doing here? I thought you had to work tonight.'

Tamara walked in through the opened front door and pulled off a scarlet beret that clashed wildly with the long swathe of her red hair. 'I called in sick,' she answered and, throwing off her jacket, plunked herself dramatically down on Rebecca's small couch. Although she was a tiny woman, Tamara had a way of taking over the room, her surroundings fading around her. She was usually dressed outrageously and tonight was no different. She was wearing drab green army fatigues, laced-up hiking boots, and a navy-blue silk jacket with enormous padded shoulders. On any other woman, the outfit would have looked absurd; on Tamara, it looked stylish. Rebecca never understood how she did it.

'Are you? Sick?'

Tamara shook her head. 'Distraught and distressed but not sick.'

'I thought the thing with Rob was over.'

'Weeks ago.'

'Is there someone new?'

'The leading man made a pass but I turned him down.' Tamara blinked her huge blue eyes at Rebecca. 'Frankly, I've . . . well, I've done something I shouldn't have.'

Rebecca repressed a smile and sat down in a chair opposite her sister. She was used to hearing about Tamara's transgressions. 'Will it take long?' she asked. 'I have a date tonight.'

To her surprise, Tamara went rigid. 'With whom?'

'Brian, of course.'

Tamara slumped down again. 'Oh.'

'We're going to Celino's for dinner.'

Tamara studied her long, red nails. 'It's pretty good. They've got great antipasto.'

Rebecca gave her sister an indulgent look. 'Come on, Tam. What have you done? It can't be that bad.'

'*You* might think so.'

'Think of the things I've forgiven you for. Remember when you stole my best blouse and stuffed it for a scarecrow at Hallowe'en? Remember the time . . .'

'I saw Guy McLaren.'

Why was it that the world seemed to stop turning? It had not, of course, but to Rebecca, all motion had ceased as if time itself were no longer ticking on or the earth had momentarily halted in its inexorable circular path. For a second, her heart had quite literally stopped beating, her breath caught somewhere in her chest, and the air had become so still, she thought she might be suffocating. There was a dead silence in the room and nothing, not even the faint rumble of traffic from the street below, could break the heaviness in that utter lack of sound as the two sisters looked at one another.

Rebecca swallowed in the dryness of her throat. 'What do you mean?'

'He called me up and I agreed to meet him.'

'*Here?* Here in New York?'

Tamara nodded, her long ear-rings swaying against her cheeks. 'Two days ago.'

'And you didn't tell me.'

Tamara threw her hands out. 'I didn't know what to do. I've spent two sleepless nights worrying about it. Becks, I didn't want to upset you.'

Rebecca had pressed two cold, trembling hands to the sides of her face. 'Oh, God,' she breathed.

'You see?' Tamara demanded. 'I knew how you would feel.'

'Does he know where I live?'

'I didn't tell him; I just promised that I'd give you his number.'

'He's still here?'

Tamara gave an unhappy shrug. 'I don't know.'

The first wave of shock had receded, and the panicked beating of her heart slowly eased. Rebecca could breathe now, at least the air seemed to move in and out of her lungs, but there was a quivering sensation in the pit of her stomach as if she had been hit there, hard, and the muscles still shook with the impact.

'What did he say? How did you . . . ?'

So Tamara told her the whole story, the recital acted out and embellished with the usual Tamara-like touches. Rebecca could see it all, the incense-filled room, her sister dressed in bizarre clothes, the Salvation Army furniture and Guy, in his charcoal suit, taking it in, suspicious and angry.

'He was so furious that I thought he would wring my neck. He was fooled for a while, but when he caught on . . .' Tamara didn't finish her sentence; she merely shivered.

'Tam, how could you? It was a horrible thing to pull on someone.'

Tamara's shrug held both bravado and shame. 'You can't imagine how much fun it was to dig through old chests and stage properties to put the room and that outfit together. And the incense was the perfect touch even if it did make him sneeze.'

Rebecca took a deep breath. 'What do you think I should do?' she asked.

'It's in your ball park. The man is waiting to hear from you.'

'I guess . . . that he's not with Maureen.'

'You know him better than I do,' Tamara replied, but Rebecca could see that she wasn't convinced.

Since she had moved to New York, Rebecca had discovered that her sister's distrust of men was extensive. Tamara had developed a strong streak of cynicism and a hard core of toughness since she had run away from home and struck out on her own. And eight years of hand-to-mouth living in New York City hadn't softened her outlook. Sometimes Rebecca wasn't sure that the sister she remembered had survived at all. As a child and adolescent, Tamara had always been independent to a fault, but she had also had an appealing vulnerability that let one know that her tough talk was part of a façade, her protection against the outside world. Now, the gentle edge had disappeared, burned away by hard experiences and disappointments.

Rebecca tried to sound positive, but the words were tentative. 'I'm sure he's no longer married.'

Tamara lifted her pale orange eyebrows into disbelieving arcs. 'It took him long enough to look for you.'

Nine months had elapsed since the rescue. Nine long months, some of which had been eaten up by fear and uncertainty and depression. When Rebecca looked back on the time when she had first come to Manhattan, she saw it as a long dark tunnel, one that she had crawled through slowly and painfully. Emerging from it had been like undergoing a birth of sorts, a coming alive, a release into life-giving sunlight. In some ways, Rebecca was newly-born, having shed the patterns and habits of a former life and established a different one. But she was still a novice, untried and untested, and Guy's sudden arrival threatened the structure that gave her days meaning, his presence pressing her backwards into that frightening black void.

'So, what are you going to do? Call him?'

'I . . . don't know.'

Tamara's glance was speculative. 'He's very attractive.'

Rebecca looked down at her clenched hands. 'I wonder what he wants.'

'He told me that *you* knew why he was here.'

'But I don't . . . not really.'

This wasn't strictly true, because Rebecca's thoughts had taken a sudden flight of fancy. Guy might have come because he loved her, but she couldn't say that to Tamara, knowing how amused her sister would be at the word 'love'. Tamara was far too cynical about the opposite sex to believe that such an emotion existed.

Tamara's look was knowing. 'I can think of a lot of reasons.'

Rebecca's innate pragmatism reared its sensible head. 'Maybe he's just curious and wants to talk about old times, maybe . . .'

'He wants to get laid,' Tamara finished for her.

Rebecca winced at Tamara's deliberate crudity. 'He wouldn't come all this way . . . just for that?'

'Hon, you'd be surprised what men will do for their libidos. Did I tell you that Charles . . . do you remember Charles?'

'The one before Simon?'

'The one before Simon who was before David who was before Rob.'

'Do you keep charts?'

Tamara ignored the sarcasm. 'Charles once bought a little whip. Whips really. A leather thong with three whips.'

Rebecca stared at her sister in horror. 'He wanted to whip you?'

'Hell, no. He wanted *me* to whip *him*.'

'God, how awful.' Rebecca paused. 'You didn't, did you?'

Tamara grinned. 'Are you kidding? Can you see *me* whipping some guy's naked quivering hulk? I ran so fast, he didn't see me going. But the point is, Becks, that he couldn't do it without a little torture.'

'But I don't think that Guy . . . no, I can't see . . .'

Tamara leaned forward. 'Maybe he couldn't handle sex with his wife; maybe his illness made him impotent and he wants to see if . . .'

Rebecca had her hands over her ears. 'I'm not going to listen to this,' she cried. 'Just because you keep running into every wierdo in New York, doesn't mean that Guy is peculiar.'

'I'm only trying to help,' Tamara said airily.

Rebecca lowered her hands. 'You don't think I should call Guy, do you?'

Tamara suddenly grew serious, and her eyes were gentle as they appraised her sister's face with its wide-set, trusting blue eyes and gentle mouth. 'I know,' she answered carefully, 'the battle you've been fighting, and I know it hasn't been easy, but I've never seen you so content. You like what you're doing, you like how you feel and I know how happy you are about your appearance. It may be that Guy will raise your level of contentment to sheer ecstasy, but suppose he doesn't? Suppose he's using *you* to solve his own problems. Suppose he doesn't give a damn what's going on in your life.' Tamara paused and, taking a deep breath, went on, 'I'm not saying that Guy is guaranteed to make you unhappy; I'm just telling you that it's a possibility. And if he does, then what will happen? Becks, you know what that will do to you, don't you?'

Rebecca ran her finger over the upholstered surface of the couch in her small living room, feeling the bumps and nubbles with the skin of her forefinger as her mind touched on the texture and substance of Tamara's words. When she finally spoke, it was in such a low voice that her sister had to lean forward to catch her words.

'Yes,' she said slowly. 'I know what it would do to me.'

Rebecca finished getting ready for her date with Brian after Tamara had left, carefully applying blusher and lipstick. Although she knew what her hands were doing, her mind was elsewhere, jumping from one thought to the next, from one memory to another, inevitably returning to the fact that Guy was in a hotel only blocks away, sitting by the telephone and waiting for her to call. There was nothing stopping her from going to her phone, sitting down next to it and making that connection to a man whose image and memory had obsessed her for months. But Rebecca didn't go near her phone. She changed the dress she had put on; she decided to wear her hair down instead of up. She could not bring herself to phone Guy and take that first step out of the orderly scheme of her life and into the unknown.

Indecision held her in its painful grasp for the entire evening. Although she welcomed Brian warmly, smiled and talked to him over dinner and leaned against his shoulder in the cinema, she would never be able actually to recall what she had said and done for those four hours. Brian's image blurred before her, the food had no taste and, as for the movie, she didn't even see the screen. The past had come back to her with such immediacy and vividness that it obliterated the present.

The haze that had obscured the memories of the Arctic lifted so that Rebecca could re-live certain moments; setting Guy's leg, a day of rain, she and Guy huddled together in the lean-to, the heat of the fire, wrestling Guy to the ground, making love in the dappled shade of the soaring lodge pole pines, Guy sweating with fever, his skin pale and ashen. Manhattan receded as each memory surfaced and the old emotions swept over her. Rebecca fought them with every ounce of strength that she had, her mind whirling with confusion, resentment and yearning.

Her anger at Guy for his long silence mixed in a nightmarish *mélange* with the old attraction. Who did he think he was to march back into her existence as if he belonged there, as if her life were a door open to every shifting breeze? She was furious at the arrogance that enabled him to seek her and expect that she would be free, available and ready for his casual beck and call. A part of her hated him with such an intensity that she felt she would burn up with it, glow with the incandescence of her fury.

But a part of herself, treacherous and undermining, yearned to see him again, if only for one second, one small moment in which she might feast her eyes on a face inscribed in her mind for all time. And that small wish flourished as if nurtured on ripe soil, growing and expanding, branching into demands, desires, a passion she had almost forgotten existed. To touch him again, to feel his mouth on hers, to press her body against the length of his, to know the melting sensation that came from his lovemaking. Rebecca felt her body grow hot as she and Brian emerged from the cinema and, in her desperation to stop it, she unwittingly gripped hard on Brian's arm.

He looked down at her. 'Is anything the matter?'

Rebecca shook her head. 'No.'

'Having a good time?'

She smiled up at him. 'Of course.'

Rebecca had never known that she could be such a consummate actress. While her face smiled and her mouth spoke placid words, her mind was travelling a twisted, torturous path. Although her anger seemed to know no bounds and remembered passion could still make her dizzy, the underlying truth was that Rebecca was terrified of seeing Guy again. She didn't know whether she loved him or not; she only knew that meeting him would put her into a position of terrifying vulnerability. Guy had taken a long time to look her up and, if his desire to see her was motivated by curiosity, by nostalgia or even, as Tamara had suggested, by a need for sex, Rebecca knew how she would feel. Nothing in her life at the present was capable of stirring up the old emotions of her childhood and adolescence. She rarely spoke to Martine; she avoided thoughts of the past. But love, unreciprocated love, was different and powerful. It could plunge her into the depths of a misery so profound that Rebecca knew only food would fill the aching void. Food—sugary cakes, dark and rich candies, swirls of ice-cream, available and tempting, whose sweetness would protect her from the hurt Guy was capable of inflicting.

Rebecca was so afraid to be left alone with her own thoughts that, for the first time since they had started dating, she invited Brian into her apartment after a date, and he accepted with alacrity, sitting himself down on her small couch and stretching his long legs out in front of him, his size thirteen loafers peeking out from under the coffee table.

'You don't fit in my apartment,' Rebecca said from the small kitchenette where she was preparing coffee and arranging a small tray of cheese and crackers.

'I didn't know a place could be so small,' he marvelled, surveying the one-room apartment with its alcove for a kitchen. Rebecca had done her best to make it look bigger, decorating it in light colours, a white carpet, oatmeal-coloured sofa bed, white shelving, sheer drapes.

'It's affordable,' she explained, putting the tray down on the coffee table and then catching a lamp that Brian almost knocked over as he straightened up.

'I'm getting that bull in a china closet feeling,' he said.

'Oh, nothing's expensive.'

'Do you sleep on the floor?'

Rebecca sat down next to him. 'The couch folds out.'

'And where do you eat?'

'On my lap.' She handed him a cup of coffee. 'Sugar? Cream?'

'Black,' he said.

'I like the place,' she declared defensively. 'It suits me.'

Brian raised one hand. 'I'm not trying to be critical. If you like it, I like it.'

'Now, that's what I call loyalty.'

Brian lowered his cup to the table and gave her a grin. 'On the other hand, it is a bit small for two.'

'Two what?'

He slid his arm around her. 'The two of us.'

He kissed her then, their lips and tongues meeting. They had kissed before, and Rebecca had enjoyed the sensation of warmth, the strong feel of Brian's arm, the delight in once again being in a man's embrace. She liked the way Brian approached lovemaking; he was gentle but sure, assertive and yet willing to stop when she called a halt.

This time, however, Rebecca wasn't sure that she wanted to stop. She had a desperate urge to erase Guy's image from her mind and to forget that he was in New York waiting for her phone call. She wanted to bury her fears somewhere, anywhere, and Brian was offering her the opportunity to seek a sweet oblivion in physical release. For the first time since she had gone out with Brian, Rebecca eagerly sought his caresses, and he responded to her with a fervour that proved how firmly he had held his passion in check.

His tongue licked the corner of her mouth, one hand descended to caress the fullness of her breast. All the desires, conscious and subconscious, that had driven Rebecca to go out with Brian in the first place and to accept the unspoken meaning of his courtship surfaced and pushed her to transform their platonic affair into a sexual one. Making love to Brian would move her in the direction of marriage to him, a home, a family. With him, she was assured of a future that held a maximum of security and a minimum of emotional upset. And by committing the very act that she had resisted for months, Rebecca was rejecting the man who had, brashly and without warning, thought he could come to New York and pick up the broken strands of their affair. Yes, Rebecca thought angrily as she wound her arms around Brian's neck, Guy would want to sleep with her again. Tamara had been right about that; no matter what other motives had prompted him to seek her out, she knew that sex was predominant. And she was not easy pickings, not for a man who had ignored her existence for nine months and who had, assuredly, slept with half a dozen women in the interim.

Fury made her press herself against Brian, her tongue seeking his in a frenzy that he mistook for passion. His fingers released the zipper at the back of her dress, slid the shoulders down so that the nape of her neck was exposed to his mouth, and unhooked the clasp of her bra so that the swell of her flesh was visible when she sat back, her nipple a dark pink in the lamp's illumination.

His voice was husky; his eyes dark with desire. 'I'm not going to want to stop,' he said.

'Don't then,' she said fiercely. 'And don't talk.'

He switched the light off then and, by a mutual and silent consent, they joined together on the carpeted floor where Rebecca had thrown several large pillows. Light from a thousand skyscrapers glittered in through the window, the large vista of Manhattan witnessing the mouths that met, the hands that tugged away at clothes, the white gleam of two bodies entangled in the shadows. Rebecca tried hard, desperately hard, to respond to Brian's touch, to be ready for him, to achieve the arousal that Guy had brought her to within moments of entering her, but there was an emptiness at the centre of her that his body couldn't fill. She knew it instantly; she knew her failure at the very moment he consummated their lovemaking, and she hated herself for it, her body suddenly rigid, her misery bringing tears to her eyes.

There was a long silence as Brian lay on top of her, his face against her neck. Then something of her unhappiness must have been communicated to him, because he rolled off her and whispered her name. 'Rebecca? Are you all right?'

No, nothing was right, and her throat ached with the pain of knowing that what she had done was wrong, *wrong*. But all she said to Brian was, 'Yes.'

'I had no idea you wanted to . . .'

'Brian, could you please go. I . . . need to be alone.' She lay still with her forearm over her eyes.

Tentatively, he touched her on the shoulder. 'Hey, don't worry about it. The first time together isn't always the greatest. What we need is a little bit of practice and . . .'

It took an enormous effort to be polite. 'Please go home.'

She moved her arm down, sat up and saw the bewilderment on his face in the dim glow of the outside lights. 'Did I do something wrong?'

'It's not you. It's me.' She was on her knees now and pulling on her dress, her fingers shaking.

'But I'm not the first m . . .'

'No,' the word was forced out of her and the tears began to trickle down her cheeks, 'there's someone else.'

For a moment, Brian was silent and then he picked up his pants. 'Is? There *is* someone else?'

'Yes.'

'You've been dating someone else?'

Rebecca shook her head. 'He doesn't live here. I haven't seen him in months.'

Brian's voice was flat as he dressed. 'But you'd like to.'

Guilt assailed her, guilt at using Brian and putting him through this highly emotional aftermath. 'I'm sorry,' she said. 'I didn't think he meant anything to me any more.'

She was crying in earnest now, and her tears confused him. Whatever anger had filled him seemed to drain away. 'Look, maybe you'll feel differently about it in the morning. You know my number.'

'Oh, Brian,' she wailed, 'please don't say that.'

'Why not?'

'Because I don't deserve it.'

He was dressed now and heading towards the door. He looked down at Rebecca who was still huddled on the floor, half-dressed, her head bent, her hair covering her damp cheeks. 'You don't,' he said a bit grimly, 'but I'm a nice guy.'

'Brian . . .'

'Call me if you change your mind.' And with that he was gone.

Despite her exhaustion, both mental and physical, Rebecca was unable to sleep that night. As the sky lightened and the grey light of dawn filtered in through the windows, she lay on the bed, staring sightlessly at the shadowed skyline of New York. The tears had dried on her face, but inside she cried for what she had done, for her dishonesty and her desire for revenge. The only reason she had slept with Brian was to injure an imaginary Guy and, in doing so, she had deeply hurt a man who had been kind and affectionate to her. Underneath, she had known full well that she didn't love Brian, but she had concealed this knowledge with rationalisations: she was fond of him, they were compatible, Brian would make a good husband. She had never bothered to worry about the fact that she would not make him a good wife. But the moment that they had made love, she had realised that truth: that she had chosen the wrong man. She could not marry Brian, knowing that every time he took her in his arms she would wish he were someone else.

Guy. Why couldn't she get rid of Guy? What was there about him that kept his face before her, his touch still on her skin, his voice in her head? He had ignored her for nine full months. Had he expected that she would be waiting for him like a faithful Penelope, so focused on the past that she refused to take part in the present? She wasn't like that. In fact, she had buttressed herself against the memories, taking on a job and a boy-friend. She had tried desperately to survive in the only way she knew how, by keeping her life in tight control, by not shaking the boat, by narrowing her world, but all her efforts had failed. The past, she had discovered, had an unbreakable hold on her. She could not love another man; she could not make love to another man. Until she exorcised Guy from this possession of her psyche, Rebecca knew that she would never be free.

As the sky lightened and the hour hand of the clock neared six, Rebecca came to understand that she had run as far as she could. There were no more refuges to be found, no more places that she could hide. Guy's arrival in Manhattan and sleeping with Brian had brought her face-to-face with a reality that she had been desperately avoiding for nine months. She loved Guy, had loved him and still did. Everything that she had done since the rescue had been attempts to stifle that emotion. Working for the Downes had provided her with a quasi-family; Brian was meant to replace Guy in her heart. Neither was capable of giving her what she truly wanted.

She had to find out what Guy had come for, and she had to face the possibility that it wasn't her. Rebecca's hand was steadier than she would have ever thought possible as she dialled the number of the New York Hilton, but her heart was beating against her ribs, shaking the confines of her chest.

'Room 1228,' she said.

The phone rang for a while and then the operator came back on, her voice tinny and nasal. 'I'm sorry, but no one is answering.'

Perhaps he had gone to breakfast. 'Can I leave a message?'

'I'll connect you to the front desk.'

Another operator, equally nasal. 'Yes?'

'I'd like to leave a message for Mr McLaren, Room 1228.'

There was a brief pause and then, 'Mr McLaren checked out.'

'Checked out!'

'Last night, miss.'

'Didn't he . . . ? Did he leave any messages?'

'No, miss. I'm sorry, but he didn't.'

CHAPTER ELEVEN

MARTINE's brunch began auspiciously with an assortment of guests arriving all at once, initiating a hustle and bustle at the door where coats were taken off and welcomes were made. Martine had hired a waiter to pass around drinks and pick up used plates, but Celia and Rebecca had been organised to make the canapés. They were still in the kitchen, rolling slices of roast beef, ham and prosciutto when the doorbell began to ring.

'I feel like Cinderella,' Rebecca moaned, 'but that isn't really fair because that would make you one of the ugly stepsisters.'

Her comment brought a faint smile to Celia's face, but nothing more. She was the prettiest of the three sisters, although the promise of her looks had not really been evident until now when she was growing into womanhood. She was slender and tall and had the same blue eyes as Tamara and Rebecca, their father's eyes, but her hair was her crowning glory, a coppery-red that glowed as if it held its own fire, its straight thickness cascading down her back. She had the highest cheekbones in the family, a lovely straight nose and a face that tapered to a small cleft chin. But she was pale, almost too pale, and Rebecca couldn't help worrying about her.

Being away from Fairfax had given Rebecca a perspective on her younger sister that was unnerving and upsetting. Celia had always been quiet and withdrawn, but she had at least laughed occasionally or talked. Now she was silent, closed in, her face shuttered with secrets and shadows. Nothing Rebecca could say or do elicited any particular spark or response. Celia kept her thoughts, judgement and feelings to herself, hidden behind lowered lids and an expressionless face.

Rebecca glanced at her sister's bent head and repressed a sigh. It wasn't as if she hadn't tried, but Celia had rebuffed every overture and every appeal. She hadn't wanted to go to the movies, the Lincoln Center or the museums. She went to school, came home and stayed in her room, the door shut, silence reigning behind its panels. Martine called her shy, a bookworm and an introvert and had given up trying to make Celia come out of her shell. Tamara was convinced that living with Martine had warped her personality. But Rebecca had a more intuitive understanding of her sister's behaviour. She sensed that silence was Celia's only defence against Martine's intrusions and that, behind the closed expression, was a mind that was adult, clever and amused. On a number of occasions, she had caught a gleam in Celia's eye that could only be interpreted as knowing and not adolescent at all.

'Well,' Rebecca sighed as the platter of hors d'oeuvres was finished, 'we can always find jobs as caterers if . . .'

'Rebecca! Celia! Come out and meet Mrs MacMullen. She hasn't seen you in years.'

Celia patiently removed her apron, saying as she

did so, 'We're all ugly stepsisters. It's Mother who wants to be Cinderella.' And walked out of the kitchen smoothing down the front of her blue jumper.

Rebecca stared after her and shook her head in bewilderment. When Celia did speak, her words were riddles. Whatever had she meant by that? Martine didn't want to be Cinderella; she was not young, she had no interest in men, she didn't believe in Prince Charming. Rebecca finally shrugged as she took off her apron and, lifting the swathe of her long hair, put it behind her shoulders. She had dressed carefully that morning, making a supreme attempt to conceal the effects of fatigue and misery, of a sleepless night and a desire to yield to self-pitying tears. Her make-up was smooth and she had worn a grey linen dress with a pleated bodice, flowing skirt and matching strapless sandals. Her hair was down, parted in the middle and held back with tortoise-shell combs, its length brushed until the waves gleamed mahogany.

She had left her apartment early that morning, walking the twenty blocks to Martine's apartment and trying to see if the repetitive motions of placing one foot before the other could obliterate the constant refrain of self-castigation and shame in her head. But it had not worked. She had barely noticed the loveliness of a spring morning, the way the sun tinted the streets and buildings a pale clear yellow, or the flock of sparrows that swooped over the pavement, their wings glinting silver and then grey as they changed direction in mid-flight.

Rebecca blamed herself for everything; for leading Brian on, for using him heartlessly, for being too cowardly to call Guy, for waiting so long that she was a failure. She had thought she was controlling her life, but instead it was in a shambles. And, her own headlong rush into self-destruction had its repercussions. She had destroyed Brian's faith in himself; she had seen the bleak look in his eyes, and quite possibly she had hurt Guy more than she would ever know. He had spent time, energy and money trying to find her, and she had turned her back on him, only thinking of herself and not the fact that he might be suffering from his own fears and uncertainties.

'And you remember Rebecca,' her mother was saying to a grey-haired woman who had gone to school with Martine thirty years earlier.

'As only this high,' Mrs MacMullen said, waving her hand at waist height as Rebecca smiled politely. 'Imagine, Martine, all these years.'

'I never liked it in Fairfax,' Martine said. 'I couldn't wait to get back to New York.'

It struck Rebecca as she watched Martine talk that her mother had been and still was more beautiful than all her daughters. She had Celia's coppery-red hair highlighted with gleams of gold. She wore it in a smooth chignon at the nape of her neck, its elegance enhancing high cheekbones, delicate features, dark eyes and a flawless complexion. Her figure was still slim and, dressed in black with diamonds glistening at her throat, ears and fingers, she was a commanding figure. *I wonder why she never remarried*, Sarah had said and her words now echoed in Rebecca's inner ear. She glanced curiously at Martine and wondered, for the first time, what her mother had done for male companionship during the long years since the divorce. She had said she wasn't interested in men, but surely men had been interested in her. Martine had always had a career, and she was far too beautiful to be ignored. Rebecca could never remember a time when Martine had not looked well turned out and impeccably dressed.

'. . . and you must try the stuffed mushrooms,' Martine was saying.

'I'm on a diet,' Mrs MacMullen sighed.

'Regina, you've always been on a diet.'

'God, you're right. Boring, isn't it?'

Both women laughed, and Martine leaned forward and kissed her old friend on the cheek. 'Enjoy yourself,' she encouraged her, 'and later we can get together for a real chat.'

The other woman wandered over to the canapé table while Martine turned to Rebecca, a frown pulling the perfect arches of her eyebrows together. 'Where is Tamara?'

'I don't know.'

'Always late. She's always late.'

'Maybe she had a rehearsal.'

'On a Sunday morning?'

Rebecca knew better than to apologise for Tamara. 'She'll come.'

'In some outrageous outfit and a sleazy man on her arm. Where does she find them? In the gutter?'

'Mom! She has better taste than . . .'

'She brought one of them up to Fairfax a couple of years ago,' Martine said coldly. 'He was quote, an artist, unquote.'

'Maybe he was.'

'Don't be so argumentative, Rebecca. It's un-appealing.'

The attacks never came directly; they always arrived from an obscure angle, one that Rebecca couldn't foresee. She had forgotten that Martine could be utterly gracious one minute and vicious the next. She was making the rounds of the guests now, smiling and laughing, but Rebecca knew that she was seething inside, furious over Tamara's absence and waiting for any opportunity to vent her anger. She would lash out in any direction; any of her daughters serving as vulnerable targets. Rebecca felt the first pangs of an unaccustomed hunger and forced herself to ignore it. She told herself that she wasn't responsible for Tamara, that Martine's rift with her sister was too deep to be healed and that nothing she or anyone could do would end years of bitter fighting.

Tamara was the most rebellious of the sisters, and she had battled with Martine over clothes, hair-styles, timetables and boys. Martine had called her immoderate, disobedient, stupid and gauche, and Tamara had reacted with behaviour that grew more outrageous and defiant with every passing year. The war between them had escalated to a frightening level by the time Tamara was seventeen. Rebecca had never known what final explosion had forced her sister to leave home, but she could remember the day she had left, a slender girl with no money and no skills, but a burning desire to get away. She had cried for days after Tamara had gone, but Martine had washed her hands of her middle daughter. 'She's made her own bed,' she had stated with an angry satisfaction. 'Let her lie in it.'

The brunch took on a nightmarish aspect for Rebecca after that. She was ultra-sensitive to Martine's moods, and the anger that lay beneath her mother's elegant and gracious behaviour was so apparent to her that she found herself trying to keep a distance from Martine, easing out of a group when her mother joined it, avoiding a one-to-one encounter. She once saw Celia's eyes on her and saw that she too had recognised the gathering storm. They both knew it would break, but neither knew when or where.

Martine had caught up with Rebecca. 'We need more ice and olives and . . .' Her head turned as the front door opened, and a small smile curved that cold mouth. 'At last.'

'Is it Tam?'

'Late, ostentatious and she didn't tell me she was bringing a man. Well, he's decent at least. Remind me to compliment her on such unusually good taste.'

Tamara stood at the door, making a highly visible and dramatic entrance. If any of Martine's guests had any doubts as to her identity, Tamara had done her best not to leave them wondering. She looked every inch the New York actress. She wore a white felt fedora tilted at a rakish angle over her carrot-coloured hair which was pulled back into a black velvet net. Her long white coat was open to reveal silky black evening pants and a beaded black jacket that plunged to her waistline and glistened with jet in an intricately stitched yoke. Her eyes were made up with dark mascara, her mouth was a vivid red. The guests had all turned by this time, some of them openly gaping at the vision at the door.

Rebecca was staring as well, but she wasn't even looking at Tamara. Instead her eyes were riveted on the man at her sister's side, her heart taking up the beat of her pulse with an incessant, heavy drumming. He was tall and lean, dressed in a business suit of dark blue with a white shirt and silvery tie. She found that she had forgotten nothing about him, not the way his dark hair dipped in the front, the deep set of his eyes, the strong line of his jaw. If she reached out and touched him, she would know just how he would feel, the line of musculature, the coarse hair, the hard edge of bone beneath skin. The nine months of separation might never have existed at all; a barrier that had dissolved as if it were a shadow, insubstantial and spectral.

Only Guy felt Tamara tremble as they stood in the doorway.

'Where is she?' he hissed.

'For God's sake, give me a break. She's here; I know she's here.'

Guy looked towards the large living room with its vast white carpet and pale blue curtains. There were, in clumps and small gatherings, a crowd of well-dressed New Yorkers holding goblets of wine and small plates of canapés. For a second he could discern no particular face in the group. Just eyes turned their way and taking in the appearance of the woman at his side.

He had been on Tamara's doorstep at seven o'clock that morning, sitting hunched over and angry with his suitcase beside him, when she came walking along the pavement at eight, feeling and looking like hell with her head pounding, her hair hanging uncombed down her back and her make-up smudged.

She had gaped at him. 'What do you want?'

Guy had taken her elbow in a cruel grip. 'I want to talk to Rebecca.'

'Don't raise your voice,' she pleaded. 'I've got a horrible hangover. I spent the night with some friends and we . . .'

'You'll have worse,' he promised with a growl, 'if I don't get to see your sister.'

Tamara futilely pressed a hand against her aching head. 'All right,' she had said. 'All right.'

But Rebecca's phone had rung without being answered.

'Where is she?' Guy demanded.

'Hell, how should I know!' Tamara sank down wearily on to her couch and wished desperately that someone would remove this angry madman from her living room. All she wanted to do was crawl into bed and die.

'Is she with someone? Another man?'

'I doubt it.'

He was quick. 'She has someone then?'

'God.' Tamara said with a moan. 'All right, she has a boy-friend.'

'A lover?'

'I . . .'

Guy shook her then. 'God damn it, tell me the truth.'

Tamara closed her eyes and forcibly willed her

queasy stomach into quiet submission. 'I don't think they're lovers.'

Guy was all for sitting out in front of Rebecca's apartment building and waiting for her ultimate return, but Tamara remembered Martine's brunch.

'We'll go there then,' Guy said.

Tamara shook her head and then winced. 'Not me. I was planning to skip it. I'll give you the address.'

'You're coming with me. Let's just say I'm holding you hostage.' And he had given her an ominous smile which let her know, in no uncertain terms, that she had little choice but to obey.

Guy hadn't let Tamara out of his sight. She had been forced to use the bathroom with the door open while he sat in the next room, and she had to dress in the closet. By the time they arrived at Martine's, her head felt like it was splitting in two, her stomach was rolling in nausea, her knees could barely support her weight, and she thought that she would fall over with exhaustion.

'If she isn't here . . .' Guy began.

Tamara finally and with great relief shook off his arm. 'She is—over there. By the piano.'

Guy saw Rebecca then, a tall slender woman with flowing dark hair in a pale grey dress that rested smoothly on curves he discovered that he had memorised. He knew every solid inch of her beneath that prim linen, the softness of skin at her wrist, the round fullness of her breasts, the indentations at her waist and thigh. Their eyes locked over the distance of chairs and carpet in a silent arc that carried a smouldering intensity, a sudden leap of tension.

They both took a step forward when Guy's way was blocked by a woman, an elegant woman in black with hair the colour of gleaming pennies and diamonds glittering at her ears. She smiled up at him and held out her hand, forcing him to reciprocate, to look away from Rebecca, to take that smooth hand in his.

'And who is this, Tamara?'

'Mother, this is Guy McLaren. Guy, this is my mother, Martine Clark.'

Guy had been impatient but now he looked down with interest into a pair of dark eyes, a smiling red mouth. 'Rebecca's mother,' he said.

'Mr McLaren from Calgary. Are you visiting New York?'

'Actually, I've come to find your daughter.'

'You've come to the right place then.'

'Why didn't you tell her that I'd phoned?'

If Guy had thought he could make Martine lose her poise, he was wrong. She laughed and patted his hand. 'I do remember your phoning, Mr—may I call you, Guy?—but Rebecca had given me instructions not to let anyone through and, being the obedient mother that I am, I always do as I'm told.' She turned slightly. 'Don't I, dear?'

Rebecca was standing beside Martine, her eyes wide and shocked. 'You phoned?'

Guy looked at her over Martine's head. 'Last October.'

He watched her close her eyes briefly and then open them again as if she were in pain. 'I . . . wish I had known.'

'But she didn't,' Martine smiled smoothly and tucked her hand under Guy's elbow, 'and she really wasn't ready to know. Rebecca's gone through a difficult time. It's been hard on all of us, but she's landed on her feet. I'm really quite proud of her.' She was moving Guy away from Rebecca and into the crowd in the living room. He glanced backwards and saw Rebecca standing there, her hands knotting together. For a moment, he was desperate to throw off Martine's grasp of his arm, to rid himself of that cool, aloof voice, but she was a woman of his mother's generation and he had been brought up only too well. There was no polite way he could extricate himself from a welcome that was too warm, too clinging and altogether too possessive.

'Becks?'

'What's she doing?'

'Martine? She's taking over as usual.'

Guy was being introduced to various guests; Martine was offering him a glass of wine. Rebecca watched his broad shoulders dip as he acknowledged someone's greeting, the dark head bend as he listened to someone's voice. How could she have thought that she didn't love him? The moment she had seen him again, she had felt the world change, grow larger, more vivid, more intense. The very light in the room had brightened, and she was aware of a sudden warmth in the air that suffused her body, making the blood race through her veins and rapidly beating heart.

'Becks?'

Guy was smiling now at something Martine had said. 'What?'

'He was at my house this morning. I couldn't get rid of him.'

'It's all right. I'd decided that I did want to . . . see him.'

Tamara slumped a bit with relief. 'There was no stopping him,' she continued. 'He wouldn't even let me out of his sight. He was afraid I'd phone you and scare you off. I had to leave the bathroom door open. I had to dress in the closet, for God's sake.' And added dramatically, 'I was a prisoner in my own apartment.'

But Rebecca wasn't listening. She was frowning, her eyes intent on the crowd in the living room. 'What's Martine doing?'

Tamara looked in the direction of Rebecca's glance and then said drily, 'Haven't you ever noticed the way our mother covets beautiful things?'

'Beautiful things?'

'Jewellery, furniture, paintings, men.'

'Men?'

Tamara shrugged. 'Attractive, beautiful men like Guy. She loves masculine attention. Funny you never noticed.'

'I never noticed,' Rebecca replied slowly, but she was noticing now. Watching her mother flirt with Guy, look up into his eyes, touch his hand with that proprietary tap of hers. Feeling the old hunger come back in vast waves and fighting the emptiness that clawed at her, demanding to be filled, satisfied, satiated.

'Martine seeks mirrors,' Tamara said bitterly.

'Reflections of her glamorous image in men's eyes.'

'But our father . . .'

'Ignored her, slept with other women, never gave her the strokes she wanted. I'll bet she's frigid. Oh, I know all the psychological reasons,' Tamara said, 'but that doesn't mean I have to like her.' Her face was white and strained as Martine's laugh came over the sounds of the other guests. 'The fact is—I hate her damned guts.'

'. . . of course, they said the weather up there was bad, but we had a week of wonderful sunshine and . . .'

The round face in front of him was earnest and smiling and Guy was doing his damnedest to be gracious, polite, a good guest, but his glance kept slipping away to the corner where Rebecca stood motionless, her auburn hair catching the spring light in its depth.

'And you must meet the Davidsons. They're so interested in Canadian art, aren't you, Marc?'

Martine at his elbow, walking him through a bunch of strangers. Guy felt as if he were in the midst of a nightmare, obstacle after obstacle leaping up into his path, blocking his way from the goal that he sought. Mouths smiled at him, lips moved, voices droned. His responses were automatic, but he didn't think he could stand it much longer. Then, he caught sight of Rebecca walking away, the grey linen dress disappearing behind a swinging door.

'Excuse me,' he said.

'. . . and the National Gallery in Ottawa had a good showing of . . .'

'Excuse me.' He inched his way past Martine who put her hand out.

'Have you met . . . ?'

He smiled at her, but his voice was firm and dismissive. 'Excuse me.'

He found Rebecca in the kitchen, breaking ice-cubes out of a tray and into an ice-bucket. Her profile was concealed from him, the wings of auburn hair falling forward and concealing her face.

'Rebecca.' The door behind him swung closed, the noise of the party receding into the distance.

She turned slowly to face him. 'How are you, Guy?' She was solemn, reserved, aloof. He couldn't read the expression in her blue eyes.

'Fine.'

'No more limp?'

'I had extra surgery.'

Rebecca winced. 'I'd hoped you wouldn't have to go through that.'

'So did I.'

'And your business?'

'Thriving.'

'Your parents? They must have been thrilled to have you back.'

'My father is recovering from a heart attack he had before we were rescued.'

'I'm . . . sorry,' she said lamely. 'How is he?'

'He's doing well.'

Why were they talking like this? Like two polite strangers who had nothing better to do than exchange gratuitous inanities. Why were they standing four feet apart when all he wanted to do was pull her into his arms, bury his face in the fragrance of her hair, feel the length and breadth of her body against his? She was even more beautiful than he remembered, but then his memories were of a woman whose skin was raw from sun and wind, whose hair hadn't been trimmed and brushed, whose face had grown gaunt and thin.

Rebecca cleared her throat. 'And Maureen? How is she?'

Guy frowned in bewilderment. 'Maureen? I suppose she's all right.'

Rebecca slowly digested this. 'I saw you together in the hospital,' she said. 'She seemed very . . . friendly.'

'You saw us together in the . . . God, Rebecca, that wasn't why you took off, was it?' Guy took a step towards her, intending to breach the distance between them, but Rebecca suddenly flung the words between them.

'Did you stay with her afterwards?'

Guy stopped, halted by the meaning of her question. He cursed to himself, knowing what it would sound like, knowing the misinterpretation that could be placed on the four months he had spent with Maureen. 'She nursed me,' he answered carefully, 'until I was well enough to live on my own again.'

'I see,' Rebecca said in a flat voice.

'You don't see,' he declared forcibly. 'We're friends, that's all. Just friends.'

'You told me she didn't want the marriage to end.'

'She didn't, but I did. And being with her again was the proof. There was nothing left between us, and she recognised it, too. If what you really want to know is—did I sleep with her?—then the answer is no, I didn't.'

A dull flush had come into Rebecca's cheeks. 'I didn't ask you that.'

'You wanted to.'

'I . . .'

'Rebecca! Since when do we entertain in the kitchen?' The door had swung open, the chattering and clinking of glasses once more invading his senses. Martine had entered with another guest, a tall thin man with greying hair. 'Here he is,' she went on, the dark eyes flashing at both men. 'Stephan is a political analyst on Canadian-American affairs. He's been asking me where you were.'

Good manners made Guy acknowledge the other man with a smile and forced him to be led out into the living room again. The other man was talking earnestly about the next elections and what did Guy think about the Parti Québecois and the Western Conservatives? He missed the look that Martine threw at Rebecca and the words that were hissed at her.

'I've never liked grey on you,' she said. 'It makes you look so sallow.'

Hunger clawed at her, raked the sides of her stomach and made her want to double over in pain. Rebecca gripped on to the edge of the counter and fought the sensation as it came over her in heavy crashing waves. She bent her head and squeezed her eyes shut, trying to force away the images that swept before her. Guy's face angry and defensive. *Did I sleep with her?—the answer is no, I didn't.* Martine, beautiful and malicious. *You look so sallow . . . so sallow . . . so sallow.* Echoes of previous words from other times came back to haunt her. *Stripes make you look fat. You're so big-boned; it must be from your father's side of the family. You used to be such a pretty little girl.*

Events of the past few days jumbled together, mixed and separated in a violent clash of noises and colour: Brian's sandy hair bent over his coffee, Sarah kissing baby Ellenor, Tamara's vivid red lipstick, Martine's cold voice, Guy standing in the foyer, his hair black against the pure white wall. Rebecca felt herself pulled in a thousand and one directions, the fragile entity of her mind battered on all sides by the emotions, wants and passions of others. They all seemed gargantuan, greater than life-size, huge actors marching across the stage of her life and trampling her with their pity, cynicism, jealousy and anger. The old feeling came back—that she was shrinking in size, disappearing, that there would be nothing left of her when the others had finished but a shell, drained and empty.

Rebecca didn't feel the tears that coursed down her cheeks; she had lost all sense of time and place. She only knew that she had to get out of Martine's apartment and away from all of them. She felt the void growing within her, its blackness threatening to engulf her. She only knew one way to ease the hurt, the fear and that horrifying sensation that she was hollow inside. She ached for substance to fill her, for taste that would let her know that she was alive. The hunger invaded every crevice of her, its demands coursing through her bloodstream, besieging the nerve endings, obscuring every other thought. Guy was forgotten, his presence fading as the hunger took over, its commands dominant and overwhelming. Rebecca lost every vestige of choice and control that she had exercised for the past nine months. Her actions were automatic, almost robotlike. She straightened up, brushed back her hair and wiped the tears off her cheeks with the back of one hand. Then, without a glance towards the living room, she left the kitchen through the service door.

'Where is she?' Guy demanded.

Tamara looked weary as she lifted a glass of wine from the tray that the waiter was presenting to her. 'The tail of the dog that bites you,' she said, lifting the glass as if in a toast.

'Where is she?' he repeated.

'I thought you found Rebecca.'

'She's gone.'

Tamara gave him a slow smile. 'You keep on losing her, Guy. Is this a habit of yours?'

Guy went into the kitchen again and then passed through it to the hallway. He threw open every door, the wood-panelled den, the pink and white girl's bedroom, the mauve bathroom that smelled of rose scent, the pale blue guest-room. Where had Rebecca gone? He had extricated himself from Stephan and the dry conversation of politics as fast as he could. He hadn't seen her leave; in fact, he had been watching the door to the kitchen as the other man had droned on. Guy opened the door to the master bedroom and

almost missed Celia who was half-hidden by the green
and gold drapes. She was so motionless and silent that
it was only the glint of sun on her coppery-red hair that
caught his eye.

Guy had not been introduced to her, but he immediately recognised who she was. 'Have you
seen . . . .?'

'Here,' she replied calmly, pointing out of the
window.

Guy stood next to her and, following the angle of
her finger, watched as a woman in a pale grey linen
dress climbed into a Checkers taxi. 'Damn!' he cried in
exasperation and ran his fingers angrily through his
dark hair. 'How did she get out?'

'This apartment has a servants' entrance.'

The taxi drove off, its tyres squealing against the
pavement, and Guy cursed again, forgetting the girl
standing next to him as it disappeared out of sight.

Celia glanced up at him. 'She's not running away
from you,' she told him.

Guy looked down at her in surprise, because this
was precisely what he had thought—that he had said
or done something that had made Rebecca bolt once
again. The sky-blue eyes, so like Rebecca's, tilted up at
him, enigmatic yet knowing. 'Who is she running
away from?' he asked.

'My mother.'

Martine's smile, her hand on his arm, the subtle
pressure she had imposed on him to conform to the
party came back now in full relief. He had been trying
so hard to break free and get to Rebecca that he had
only noticed Martine's efforts as distracting and

annoying. He had seen no particular underlying motive, no malicious intent. But she had been the one who had stopped his message from getting through to Rebecca months ago, and now she had been successful at keeping them apart once again. He stared once more at the window and the unfeeling landscape beyond it. He had an intense desire to smash his fist through the pane of glass and shatter the static and stolid angles of brick and pavement as if, in breaking, they too would feel his anger, frustration and despair.

Celia followed his gaze. 'Rebecca probably went back to her apartment. I'll give you the address, and I have a spare key.'

'Do you?' Guy stared at her, suddenly nonplussed by Celia's air of knowledge and confidence. She had the calm reassurance of someone who has foreseen all complications and made the necessary arrangements. 'Where did you get it?'

'From her dresser drawer once when I was visiting.'

'And you'd give it to me?'

'Of course.'

'You know who I am then?'

Celia's smile had a Mona Lisa quality to it. 'Oh yes,' she said. 'I know exactly who you are.'

When Guy went back, Martine was in the foyer saying goodbye to some departing guests. She smiled up at Guy as he reached for his raincoat in the closet. 'I've been waiting to have a good, long chat with you,' she said.

'I have to go now.'

'So soon?' Her smile was gay, forced and glittery.

'Yes.' His hand went to the doorknob.

Martine's hand closed over his, her touch cool and dry. 'We really haven't had a chance to get acquainted.'

Guy glanced down at her hand lying over his, and it all became very clear; the carefully applied façade of sophistication, the air of possession, the subtle flirtation. He had been utterly naïve where Martine was concerned, equating her with Cordelia because she was a woman of his mother's generation and because she had children. He had expected from her all the qualities of his own mother; candour, honesty, the ability to age graciously and a maternal instinct. He had never quite believed Rebecca's stories about Martine; they had seemed far too fantastic. But now the incredible was real, the horror of it coming home to him.

Their eyes locked for a long period of time. In hers, Guy read a malicious amusement and a sly understanding at the same time as he saw a desperate pleading. It suddenly struck him as pathetic that a woman close to fifty should be competing with her twenty-six-year-old daughter for the attention of a man who was almost twenty years younger than she was. Beneath the glamour, the diamonds and the make-up was the real Martine; lonely, insecure and unhappy. The hatred he had begun to feel towards her dissipated into pity.

'I'm sorry,' he said gently and, in a low voice so that no one else could hear, added, 'I don't want you. I want Rebecca.'

The hand dropped from his and, for a second, he

saw the naked hurt before the mask was pulled down, the façade firmly re-established. Martine gave a small brittle laugh. 'Good luck,' she said. 'She's probably stuffing her face.'

'I won't let her.'

'Really, Mr McLaren? Nobody could stop her before.'

He pulled open the door and gave her a smile that was far more confident than he felt. 'I can,' he said.

The shelves glittered at her; the candies in their foil wrappers, cookies wrapped in see-through plastic, the peaks of frosting on cakes rising at her like waves through the portholes of white boxes. Rebecca could smell the sweet, rich aromas as she picked out the cream-filled cookies, the mocha cake, the bars of chocolate. Hunger drove her down the aisle, forcing her to fill the cart, one box after another, piled high into a confectionary mountain. Although her eyes were now dry, her mouth watered continually and she had to keep swallowing even though there was a lump in her throat, an aching, painful lump. Other shoppers stared at her as she went past, her face pale and strained, her mouth stretched into a grimace. When she got to the check-out, the clerk stared first at her, then at the fully-laden cart, and then back at Rebecca's unhappy face.

'Quite a party,' she commented.

Rebecca nodded.

'Lots of kids?'

The lie came so easily, but then dishonesty had

always played a part in the way she had eaten. 'A hundred,' she said.

The clerk's eyes widened. 'A hundred kids. Wow.'

Guy never thought a taxi would appear and, when it did, the cabbie took a route that caught them in an unusual Sunday traffic jam. 'Must be having some kind of street fair,' the driver muttered as horns blared around them and Guy drummed his fingers on the door handle, his tension and impatience obvious. Forty frustrating minutes elapsed before they finally reached Rebecca's apartment building and, when Guy entered, he was in far too great a hurry to take the elevator. He ran up the five flights of stairs to arrive at her floor with his breath coming hard and quick, his chest straining with the effort. The door to 5D was closed and there was silence behind it. Guy knocked hard, but, when there was no answer, he cursed out loud and wondered if he had guessed wrong. Rebecca might not have come back to her apartment; perhaps she had gone to the man she had been dating, the one that Tamara had mentioned. He had quizzed Tamara about him, browbeating her until she finally admitted that Rebecca had dated him for four months and that they jogged together. She had given Guy the impression that Rebecca didn't much care for this other man, but then it was possible that Tamara had not known the truth. Perhaps . . .

You're fighting shadows, Cordelia had said, and she had been right. Guy gritted his teeth and put the key that Celia had given him in the lock. The reality might be far worse than anything his imagination could conceive about a possible rival. Rebecca might be behind that door, committing an act so damaging to her psyche that even all the love he had to offer might not be able to repair it. The lock clicked and the door gave way before his arm. Guy burst into the apartment and the woman on the floor looked up at him. She was on her knees with the remains of her terrible feast strewn around her; torn packages, box tops, crumpled bits of foil, broken pieces of cake, chocolate smeared on the carpet. One of her hands clutched a cookie, and there were crumbs on her lips. Tears streamed down her face, the sky-blue eyes wet, their look of misery piercing him right to the heart.

He filled the doorway of her apartment, his dark hair almost touching the lintel, his wide shoulders rubbing against the frame. His face was white, his mouth grim as he looked down at her. Rebecca shrank back and inadvertently crushed the cookie she was holding. She looked down at it and, with a movement like that of an automaton, she lifted the hand to her mouth and stuffed the crumbs into it. Tears had fallen into the crumbled cookie and softened it into a sugary mush. She hated the taste and texture of it, but she couldn't help herself. She couldn't stop the hand that kept feeding her without surcease. She was sick, nauseous, close to vomiting but she hadn't been able to stop eating.

'Go away,' she breathed softly.

Then he was down on the floor beside her, sweeping away the boxes and the crumbs, taking the pack of cookies out of her hand. The rapacious hunger

swept through her in another tidal spasm, and she
frantically began to pull the boxes back towards her.

'Rebecca, you're hurting yourself.'

She pushed a package of cookies out of his reach.
'It's my life.'

She could hear his voice straining to be calm. 'You
don't want to get heavy again.'

He hadn't reached all the candies and she pushed a
Mars bar under her leg where he wouldn't see it.
'Leave me alone!'

He grabbed her wrist. 'I won't.'

'Let . . . go of me!'

Rebecca tried to yank her wrist out of his grasp, but
when that didn't work, she tried to claw his face with
her other hand instead. Guy grabbed that wrist as
well, and the two of them were locked into an intense
struggle, their bodies straining against one another
and trapped in a space defined by four walls and the
coffee table.

'I don't . . . want you here,' she screamed at him as
her hair tumbled around her face in a wild halo and
tears streaked down mascara-marked paths.

'I don't care,' he returned grimly.

She bent her head, determined to bite the hands that
held her so firmly in their grip that she couldn't move,
couldn't attack him, couldn't get any more food. Guy
saw her intent and, swiftly letting go of her wrists,
grabbed her by the shoulders and held her back from
him.

Rebecca was panting with her exertions. 'I don't.
Want your. Help.'

'You need me.'

'No!'

Dark hair had fallen across his forehead, and a sheen of sweat gleamed on his skin. Rebecca was only dimly aware of who he was; she didn't see him as the man she loved but as the ultimate enemy, standing between her and the ravenous demands of her cravings. She lunged for him, breaking his hold on her, and began to hit him wherever she could, her fists drumming against his shoulders, chest and arms.

'Go away!'

'Never!' Guy pulled her up to him so that her arms were trapped and she was unable to hit him. Their faces were inches apart, their eyes meeting in combat. Rebecca could feel his chest moving rapidly against hers, his breath on her cheek. Once she had been able to wrestle him to the ground, but this time, she didn't have the advantage of superior strength. Try though she might, she couldn't break out of the iron circle of his arms.

'I hate you,' she snarled.

'No, you don't,' he replied, his teeth clenched together.

'Yes, I do. You come here and think you can take control of my life and . . .' She tried to twist out of his hold.

Guy's arms tightened. 'I love you.'

The words penetrated slowly like light coming through a very thick fog, and somehow they brought to Rebecca a vision of Sarah, swollen and pregnant, wrapped in Dave's embrace. Her brain seemed to clear and the thought of love entered it; love that was comprised of acceptance and understanding, of human frailties and weaknesses. 'If you love me,' she challenged, her voice bitter, 'you'll take me any way I come.'

'Rebecca . . .'

'You'd love me obese! Fat!' Guy's arms loosened and then fell to his side. 'You only want me on your terms, but maybe I can't be that way. Maybe I was meant to be fat.'

Guy stared into her face, seeing it as lovely despite the wildness of her hair and the darkened trails of tears. He loved her as she was now, not fat and shapeless, and the knowledge of the inadequacy of such love had haunted him for nine months.

'You're right,' he said slowly.

Rebecca flung her head back and picked up the Mars bar under her leg. 'You see,' she jeered triumphantly. But her trembling fingers belied her sense of victory. She could barely remove the candy's wrapper.

His voice was low. 'I could love your voice and the gentleness of your hands and the way your hair gleams a dark-red in the sunlight. I could love the colour of your eyes that reflect the sky and the sound of your laughter and all the memories we share, but, no, I couldn't *love* you that way. You wouldn't be the woman that I fell in love with any longer. You'd be the old Rebecca, frightened of men and hating her body. There would be nothing left of your confidence, the happiness you felt in being attractive, the sexual spark that existed between us because you gloried in our differences as a man and a woman. I'm afraid,' he went on, his voice even lower, 'that there would be nothing left of the passion that bound us together.

Perhaps, if you were fat again, I could love you as the sister I never had, but I . . . I couldn't make love to you. That sort of love isn't unconditional, it's physical, it's sexual, part of the way my body reacts towards yours. A man can't make love when his body refuses, and I'm afraid that's what would happen to me if you were obese again.'

He had slumped backwards on to his heels and there was a look on his face then, a tightening of the muscles around his mouth, an unhappy tension in the dark eyes, his skin lined and drawn, that transported Rebecca out of her surroundings and back into the Arctic. Her fingers ceased their frantic motions, and she was suddenly still. She had seen that look a thousand times; when he had been in pain, when a plane had flown overhead and not seen them, when he had thought she had cut her hand with the axe, when he had said, *Will you sleep with me before we die in this godforsaken place?*

She had been about to cram the candy in her mouth, but his look had reached the core of her, the small part of her that had held its sanity throughout the frenzied madness of her eating. It was as if a spell had been broken, allowing Rebecca to return to reality, to the fact that she was in her apartment with Guy before her, to the knowledge of the sun slanting through the windows, its light turning the bits of coloured foil on the white carpet to crinkled jewels. Slowly she put her hand down until the candy fell from her fingers, making a soft thud as it hit the carpet.

'But people change,' she said slowly.

'Yes,' Guy answered, instinctively understanding

what she was saying. 'You'll grow old and so will I. We'll both be grey and have wrinkles. Love can weather changes like that; it has in my parents' marriage. But, Rebecca, this is different.' And his hand indicated the broken remains of cookies, cake and candy. 'You know it is.'

Yes, she did know, but now other questions were crowding in on her, waiting to be asked. 'If you love me,' she queried, 'then why didn't you come sooner?'

His gaze was level. 'Because I was afraid of myself and you. Because I thought you might have got heavy again or had another man. Because I didn't know if my memories of the Arctic were real or fantasies I had created out of dreams.'

'And why did you choose to come now?'

The dark level glance wavered and then rested on her. 'I went out with another woman and couldn't make love to her because she wasn't you.'

Rebecca sat back as if she had been slapped across the face. She had known Guy would resume a sexual life after the rescue, but she hadn't pictured it in any concrete way, knowing that the images evoked would be far too painful for her to contemplate. Now, with the words put so baldly to her, she felt the shock of them reverberate inside. 'Oh, Guy,' she said in a low voice. 'I wish . . .'

'And what about you?'

Rebecca felt her throat grow dry and constrict. 'I've been dating someone.'

She had demanded honesty from him and now he demanded it of her. 'And . . . ?'

'And I . . . slept with him.' She saw Guy flinch as

she spoke, the pain of it crossing his face in a spasm that made her heart feel as if it had been wrenched. 'Only once,' she whispered.

'So much for the vaunted male prowess,' Guy said wryly.

'I wasn't successful either,' Rebecca confessed. 'He wasn't you. It . . . wasn't a very good experience.' The room was silent for a moment as they sat there looking at one another and then she went on, 'I'm sorry about running away from the hospital, and I should have called you afterwards. But I was afraid, too, scared that you wouldn't want me any more. I didn't think I could bear that sort of rejection.'

'I love you, Rebecca; you're the only woman I've ever felt that way about.'

Rebecca looked down at her hands, the hands that now seemed as if they had belonged to someone else, tearing at packages, ripping away box covers, bringing food to her mouth. 'I'm not hungry any more,' she said in a wondering voice, and it was true. With Guy's words the inside of her had come to a quiet peace, the beast of her appetite satiated and appeased.

Guy reached forward and took her hand in his warm one. 'I want to marry you,' he declared. 'That's why I came to New York.'

She looked into his face, that beautiful face of angles and planes and deep-set eyes. 'Oh, Guy,' she murmured, her voice trembling, 'after all this?'

'After all this,' he confirmed and then pulled her into his arms. Rebecca felt the hardness of his chest against her cheek and a warmth flowed into her, the warmth of love and happiness, of being in the arms of the man you loved and knowing yourself safe there. She didn't think that she ever wanted to come out from that embrace and even resisted a bit when he pushed her away and looked down at her. 'I'll make sure that you'll never want to eat like that again.'

Rebecca shook her head. 'I can't seem to handle certain situations. It's stress or . . .'

'It's your mother.'

'Well, she adds to it.'

'She's the cause. Don't you understand what she's been doing to you? She kept you fat all those years.'

'She hated it when I was fat.'

'Darling, that was the message on the surface. Underneath, she was making sure that you weren't attractive enough to compete for male attention.'

'Me? I was only thirteen.'

'But growing up, becoming a woman. I know what you've told me about her and I can guess at the pattern. Her marriage was coming apart, your father was chasing other women and she was threatened by any female near her who was pretty and feminine. I don't think she knew she was doing it. I suspect it was a subconscious thing, but she wanted to keep you fat.'

It seemed too incredible to Rebecca and she protested, 'But I was her *daughter*.'

'And what does an adolescent daughter signify? That her mother is getting older, past her prime, no longer young and capable of attracting men the way she used to. Your mother is a very competitive woman. She didn't want us to get together. She was threatened by my feelings for you.'

Rebecca looked back into the darkness of her adolescence and Guy's words began to make sense. She had never been able to please Martine, no matter what she had done, and each disapproval spelled another intake of calories. They had both been aware of this connection, but her mother had not stopped the incessant criticisms, the sniping, the harsh judgments. It must have been much easier for Martine to think of herself as youthful and attractive when Rebecca remained obese.

'I never understood,' Rebecca said slowly.

'Your mother was giving off very sexual vibes this morning,' Guy confirmed. 'I don't know how far it would have gone if I were receptive, but they were there.'

Rebecca gave him a strange glance. 'Did you think she was beautiful?'

'Yes.' He gently kissed her mouth. 'But nowhere near as beautiful as you are. Marry me, darling, and come with me to Calgary. My mother is dying to meet you. Frankly, she can't wait for grandchildren, but we can put her off for a time.'

'You want children?'

'Do I want children? Rebecca, I want a house, a mortgage, evenings before the fire, a baby crying in the morning, a wife in bed next to me . . . Darling, there's only one thing I don't want.'

'What's that?'

'Fish dinners. Honey, I'm sorry, but . . .'

Rebecca was laughing now, her smile shining through her tears like a rainbow arcing in the sky, its colours sparkling in the rain. 'Oh, Guy,' she giggled, slumping against him, the laughter making her weak, 'I can't stand fish either.'

He grinned down at her. 'Not fried, sautéed, roasted, boiled, grilled, broiled or in chowders.'

Rebecca's mouth turned down at the corners. 'We've wasted all these months.'

Guy gently touched her mouth with his. 'Maybe we had to. Maybe each of us had to find our own personal way before we could find the path back to one another. I thought I could survive without you, but I couldn't.'

'I thought I could love another man, but I couldn't.'

His voice was soft. 'Marry me?'

Her eyes were clear as the sky. 'Tomorrow if I can.'

'Sleep with me?'

'Oh, yes.'

'Love me?'

Rebecca wrapped her arms around his neck and pulled him to her. 'For ever,' she whispered. 'Now and for ever.'

EPILOGUE

Dear Tam,

Are blushing brides allowed to gush? Is it permissible? Do you mind if I go on and on about Guy and our house and Calgary and being married and discovering that I'm pregnant? The baby is due next summer, and we are ecstatic about the news. Actually, Guy's parents are even more enthusiastic than we are although that seems almost impossible. I've never been so happy.

I hadn't ever thought, Tam, that such happiness existed, and I still wonder sometimes why it happened to me. Every once in a while, I have to pinch myself to see if it is real, that Guy and I are actually sitting opposite one another having dinner with the candles glowing or that this house with its gables and skylights really belongs to us. And I like the city and Guy's family and his friends. I'd even like to do a bit of matchmaking and pair you up with his partner, Jake. Somehow I think the two of you would find one another challenging.

Oh, remember Crazy Maude? Guy and I drove up to Edmonton about a week ago and looked her up. She was just as feisty as ever, but down in the dumps because she hadn't been able to keep up the payments on her television. It was clear to both of us that there was no changing her lifestyle, but we bought her a big television with remote control. She promised that she'd name us in her will! Imagine being the heirs to mix 'n' match china, rickety old furniture and rag-bag clothes. We thanked her as if it was one of the greatest honours ever bestowed on us.

I was sorry to hear that your play closed, but you did get great reviews so perhaps it will lead to bigger and better things. Or perhaps I can seduce you into coming west and setting Calgary on its ear. I just finished decorating the guest-bedroom, and Guy has got over his—well, unusual—meeting with you. In fact, he's decided that he has one of the most unique sisters-in-law in existence. Please say you'll come.

Give my love to Celia and please watch over her for me. I'd like to get her out here but I know Martine won't allow it yet. Still, I'm keeping my fingers crossed that she'll come eventually. I worry about her.

Good luck with the auditions and love for now . . .

Becks

Follow the turbulent life of Rebecca's flamboyant actress sister, Tamara, in this stirring sequel to ARCTIC ROSE

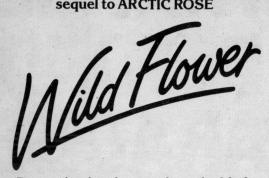

Determined and outspoken, the kind of girl who would stand out in a crowd, Tamara is the complete opposite of her home-loving sister. Rebecca would have her happily married and settled down, but men are given no permanent place in Tamara's hectic life-style.

Striving to make a success of her acting career, the gruelling pace has taken its toll of Tamara's health and she welcomes the opportunity to recharge her batteries by visiting Rebecca and her family.

But her visit turns out to be no holiday as she suffers a number of shocks — not least of these being the critical sniping from the maddening Jake DeBlais, cynic and womaniser *extraordinaire* ...

WHAT LIES BEYOND PARADISE

Catching the pulse of a
woman in the Twenties.

A woman with a dream.
A man with all his dreams
shattered. The search for a
long-lost father. And the
discovery of love.

Available from 14th
March 1986. Price £2.50.

W🌐RLDWIDE